the Case

~

"I'm crazy about Chekhov. I never knew anyone that wasn't."
Woody Allen

"Chekhov's stories are as wonderful (and necessary) now as
when they first appeared. It is not only the immense number
of stories he wrote – for few, if any, writers have ever done
more – it is the awesome frequency with which he produced
masterpieces, stories that shrive us as well as delight and
move us, that lay bare our emotions in ways
only true art can accomplish."
Raymond Carver

"As reader of imaginative literature, we are always seeking
clues, warnings: where in life to search more assiduously;
what not to overlook; what's the origin of this sort of
human calamity, that sort of joy and pleasure;
how we can live nearer to the latter, further off
from the former? And to such seekers as we are,
Chekhov is guide, perhaps *the* guide…"
Richard Ford

"Chekhov lived his whole life expending the capital of his
soul… He was always himself inwardly free."
Maxim Gorky

"What writers influenced me as a young man? Chekhov!
As a dramatist? Chekhov! As a story writer? Chekhov!"
Tennessee Williams

ONEWORLD CLASSICS

The Woman in the Case

and Other Stories

Anton Chekhov

Translated by April FitzLyon
and Kyril Zinovieff

Wife for Sale

Translated by David Tutaev

ONEWORLD
CLASSICS

ONEWORLD CLASSICS LTD
London House
243-253 Lower Mortlake Road
Richmond
Surrey TW9 2LL
United Kingdom
www.oneworldclassics.com

All stories in this volume, except for 'Wife for Sale', were first published,
under the title *The Woman in the Case*, in this translation in 1953 by Neville
Spearman Limited and John Calder Limited. 'Wife for Sale' first published in
this translation by David Tutaev in 1959 by John Calder (Publishers) Limited.
This edition first published by Oneworld Classics Limited in 2009

Translation of 'The Woman in the Case', 'A Visit to Friends', 'Appropriate
Measures', 'The Boa-Constrictor and the Rabbit', 'History of a Business
Enterprise', '75,000', 'The Mask', 'An Unpleasant Incident', 'The Eve of the
Trial', 'Sinister Night', 'The Lodger', 'The Dream', 'Out of Sheer Boredom',
'A Disagreeable Experience', 'His First Appearance', 'Holy Simplicity', 'The
Diplomat', 'Moral Superiority', 'Tædium Vitæ', 'Other People's Trouble', 'A
Reporter's Dream', 'One Man's Meat', 'The Guest' © April FitzLyon and Kyril
Zinovieff, 1953
Translation of 'Wife for Sale' © John Calder (Publishers), 1959

Printed in Great Britain by CPI Antony Rowe

ISBN: 978-1-84749-081-0

Contents

Apart from 'History of a Business Enterprise' and 'A Visit to Friends', which originally appeared in 1892 and 1898 respectively and are more representative of the later works of the mature Chekhov, the stories collected in this volume were all published between 1882 and 1888, when the author was just at the beginning of his literary career. In tone and content they range from amusing trifles and humorous stories to psychological and tragic pieces, providing a fascinating glimpse into the development of one of the world's most influential storytellers and playwrights.

Anton Chekhov (1860–1904)

Anton Chekhov with his
brother Nikolai

Maria Chekhova,
Anton's sister

Yevgenia and Pavel, Chekhov's parents

The birthplace of Anton Chekhov
in Taganrog

The out-building to Chekhov's residence in Melikhovo,
where he wrote *The Seagull*

Olga Knipper as Mme Ranevskaya
in *The Cherry Orchard*

Olga Knipper as Masha
in *Three Sisters*

The House-Museum in Sadovo-Kudrinskaya Street, Moscow,
where Chekhov lived between 1886 and 1890

The Woman in the Case

The Woman in the Case

S MYCHKOV, A MUSICIAN, was walking from town to Prince Bibulov's country villa, where, to celebrate an engagement, there was to be an evening of music and dancing. On his back lay an enormous double bass in a leather case. Smychkov was walking along the bank of a river, the cool water of which was running if not majestically, at least extremely romantically.

Shall I have a bathe? he thought.

Without further ado he undressed and plunged his body in the cool current. It was a gorgeous evening. Smychkov's romantic soul was beginning to harmonize with its surroundings. But what a blissful feeling seized his heart when, after swimming along about a hundred paces, he saw a beautiful girl sitting on the steep bank, fishing. He held his breath, overwhelmed by a welter of mixed feelings: reminiscences of childhood, nostalgia for the past, awakening love... Good Heavens, and he had thought that he could no longer love! After he had lost faith in humanity (his wife, whom he had loved passionately, had run away with his friend Sobakin, the bassoon-player), his heart had been filled with a feeling of emptiness, and he had become a misanthrope.

What is life? He had asked himself the question more than once. What do we live for? Life is a myth, a dream... ventriloquy...

But standing before the sleeping beauty (it was not difficult to observe that she was asleep), suddenly, regardless of his will, he felt in his breast something resembling love... He stood before her for a long time, devouring her with his eyes.

But that's enough... he thought, letting out a deep sigh. Farewell, lovely vision! It's time I went to His Highness's ball...

He looked once more at the beauty, and was just about to swim back, when an idea flashed through his mind.

I must leave her something to remember me by! he thought, I'll hitch something onto her line. It'll be a surprise from 'person unknown'.

Smychkov swam quietly to the bank, picked a large bunch of field and water flowers and, tying it up with a bit of pigweed, he hitched it onto the hook.

The bouquet fell to the bottom, and took the pretty float down with it.

Prudence, the laws of nature and my hero's social position demand that the romance should end at this precise point, but – alas! – an author's fate is inexorable: owing to circumstances beyond the author's control the romance did not end with a bouquet. In spite of common sense and the nature of things, the poor and humble double-bass player was to play an important part in the life of the rich and noble beauty.

When he swam to the bank, Smychkov was thunderstruck: he could not see his clothes. They had been stolen... While he had been admiring the beauty, some unknown rascals had carried off everything except the double bass and his top hat.

"Damnation," exclaimed Smychkov. "Oh men, you generation of vipers! I don't so much resent being deprived of my clothes – for clothes decay – as the thought that I shall have to go stark naked and thus violate social morality."

He sat down on the double-bass case and tried to find a way out of his awful predicament.

I can't go to Prince Bibulov's with nothing on! he thought. There'll be ladies there! And besides, with my trousers the thieves have taken the rosin which was in them!

He thought for a long time painfully, till his head ached.

Oh! he remembered at last. Not far from the bank, in the bushes, there's a little bridge... I can sit under the bridge until it gets dark, and when night falls I'll creep to the nearest cottage...

Dwelling on this thought, Smychkov put on his top hat, hoisted the double bass on his back, and trudged along to the bushes. Naked, with the musical instrument on his back, he was reminiscent of some ancient, mythical demi-god.

Now, reader, while my hero is sitting under the bridge and giving himself up to sorrow, let us leave him for a time and turn our attention to the girl who was fishing. What happened to her? When the beauty woke up and did not see the float on the water, she hastened to give her rod a jerk. The rod strained, but the hook and float did not appear from under the water. Evidently Smychkov's bouquet had become sodden in the water, had swollen and grown heavy.

Either there's a big fish caught on it, thought the girl, or else the hook has got entangled.

After jerking the rod a bit more, the girl decided that the hook had got entangled.

What a pity! she thought. And they bite so well in the evening. What shall I do?

And without further ado the eccentric girl threw off her diaphanous clothes and plunged her lovely body in the current right up to her marble shoulders. It was not easy to unhook the bouquet, which had become entangled with the line, but patience and labour won the day. After about a quarter of an hour the beauty came out of the water, radiant and happy, holding the hook in her hand.

But she was in the hands of cruel fortune. The scoundrels who had taken Smychkov's clothes had abducted her dress too, leaving her nothing but a jar full of worms.

What shall I do now? she wept. Must I really go about like this? No, never! Death would be better! I'll wait until it gets dark; then, in the darkness I'll get as far as Agafia's and send her home for a dress... And while I'm waiting I'll hide under the bridge.

Choosing a way where the grass was longest, and bending down, my heroine ran to the bridge. When she crawled under the bridge, she saw there a naked man with a musical mane and a hairy chest; she gave a cry and fainted.

Smychkov was frightened too. At first he took the girl for a naiad.

Is this a river siren, come to lure me? he thought, and he found this conjecture tempting, for he had always had a very high opinion of his personal appearance. And if she's not a siren, but a human being, how can this strange transformation be explained? Why is she here, under the bridge? And what is the matter with her?

While he was deciding these questions, the beauty came to.

"Don't kill me!" she whispered. "I am Princess Bibulova. I beseech you! You'll be given a lot of money! I was in the water just now disentangling my hook, and some thieves stole my new dress, shoes and everything!"

"Madam," said Smychkov in an imploring voice, "they stole my clothes too. And what's more, together with my trousers they carried off my rosin, which was in them!"

Usually no double-bass and trombone players have any presence of mind; Smychkov, however, was a pleasant exception.

"Madam," he said, after a moment. "I see that you are embarrassed by my appearance. But, you will agree, I cannot leave this place for the same reasons as yourself. I've got an idea: would you care to lie down in my double-bass case and cover yourself with the lid? That would hide me from you…"

Having said this, Smychkov pulled the double bass out of its case. For a moment it seemed to him that, in handing over the case, he was profaning Sacred Art, but he did not hesitate for long. The beauty lay down in the case and curled herself up in a ball, while he tightened the straps and began to rejoice that Nature had endowed him with such brains.

"Now, madam, you can't see me," he said. "Lie there, and don't worry. When it's dark I'll carry you to your parents' house. I can come back here for the double bass later."

When darkness fell, Smychkov hoisted the case with the beauty inside it onto his shoulders, and trudged off in the direction of the Bibulovs' villa. His plan was as follows: to begin with, he would go as far as the first cottage and acquire some clothes, and then go on…

Every cloud has a silver lining… he thought, scattering the dust with his bare feet and bending under his burden. Bibulov will probably reward me handsomely for the warm interest I have taken in the princess's fate.

"Are you comfortable, madam?" he asked, in the tone of a cavalier gallant inviting a lady to a quadrille. "Please don't stand on ceremony, and do make yourself absolutely at home in my case!"

Suddenly the gallant Smychkov thought he saw two human figures wrapped in darkness walking ahead of him. On looking more closely, he became convinced that this was not an optical illusion: two figures were, in fact, walking along, and were even carrying some sort of bundles in their hands…

I wonder if those are the thieves? the thought flashed through his mind. They're carrying something. It's probably our clothes!

Smychkov put the case down on the road, and started in pursuit of the figures.

"Stop!" he cried. "Stop! Stop thief!"

The figures looked round and, seeing that they were being pursued, took to their heels… For a long time the princess heard rapid footsteps and cries of "Stop!" At last all was silent.

Smychkov was carried away by the chase, and probably the beauty would have had to lie in the field by the road for a good while longer, if it had not been for a happy coincidence. It so happened that at that very time and along that very road Smychkov's friends, Zhuchkov, the flautist, and Razmakhaikin, the clarinettist, were walking to the Bibulovs' villa. They stumbled over the case, both looked at each other, and raised their hands in amazement.

"A double bass!" said Zhuchkov. "Why, it's our Smychkov's double bass! But how did it get here?"

"Probably something happened to Smychkov," decided Razmakhaikin. "Either he got drunk, or else he was robbed. In any case, it wouldn't be right to leave the double bass here. Let's take it with us."

Zhuchkov hoisted the case on his back, and the musicians continued on their way.

"It's the devil of a weight!" the flautist grumbled all the time. "I would not agree to play a monster like this for anything in the world… ugh!"

When they arrived at Prince Bibulov's villa, the musicians put the case down in the place reserved for the orchestra, and went to the bar.

The chandeliers and sconces were already lit in the villa. The fiancé, Lakeych, a handsome and attractive official of the Ministry of Transport, was standing in the middle of the ballroom and, with his hands in his pockets, was chatting with Count Shkalikov. They were talking about music.

"You know, Count," said Lakeych, "in Naples I was personally acquainted with a violinist who really performed miracles. You wouldn't believe it! On the double bass… on an ordinary double bass he produced such devilish trills that it was simply amazing! He played Strauss waltzes!"

"Come now, that's impossible," said the Count sceptically.

"I assure you! He even performed a Liszt rhapsody! I was living in the same hotel as he was and, as I had nothing better to do, he taught me how to play a Liszt rhapsody on the double bass."

"A Liszt rhapsody! Mmm – you're joking…"

"You don't believe me?" laughed Lakeych. "Then I'll prove it to you now! Let's go to the orchestra!"

The fiancé and the Count went off to the orchestra. They went up to the double bass, and began quickly to undo the straps... and – oh, horror!

But there, while the reader, giving his imagination free rein, pictures the outcome of the musical argument, let us turn to Smychkov... The unfortunate musician did not catch up with the thieves, and when he returned to the place where he had left the case, he did not find his valuable burden. Lost in conjecture, he walked up and down the road several times and, not seeing the case, decided that he must be on the wrong road...

This is awful! he thought, tearing his hair, and his blood running cold. She'll suffocate in the case! I'm a murderer!

He walked the roads and searched for the case till midnight, but finally, deadbeat, he went back under the bridge.

I'll have another look at dawn, he decided.

His search at dawn yielded the same result, and Smychkov decided to wait for night under the bridge...

"I'll find her!" he muttered, taking off his top hat and tearing his hair. "I'll find her, if I have to search for a year!"

And still, so the peasants living in those parts say, at night near the bridge a nude man may be seen, overgrown with hair and wearing a top hat. Now and again, from under the bridge, can be heard the rumble of a double bass.

A Visit to Friends

A LETTER CAME ONE MORNING:

Dear Misha,
You have quite forgotten us, do come as soon as you can, we want to
see you. We both implore you on bended knee, come today, show us
the light of your countenance. Awaiting you with impatience.

Ta and Va
Kuzminki, 7th June

The letter was from Tatyana Alexeyevna Losev, who, some ten or
twelve years ago when Podgorin had been living in Kuzminki, had been
known as Ta for short. But who was Va? Podgorin recalled long talks,
happy laughter, youthful crushes, walks in the evening, and a whole
flower bed of young girls who used to live in and near Kuzminki, and he
recalled a simple, lively, intelligent face with freckles that went so well
with the dark copper of the hair – that was Varya or Varvara Pavlovna,
Tatyana's friend. She had taken a degree in medicine and was working
in a factory somewhere near Tula, and now apparently had gone to
Kuzminki on a visit.

Dear Va! thought Podgorin, giving himself up to memories. How
nice she is!

Tatyana, Varya and he were almost of the same age; but at that time
he had been a student, while they were grown-up, marriageable young
girls, and regarded him as a boy. And though by now he was a lawyer
and his hair was going grey, they still called him Misha and considered
him young, and said that he had not yet experienced anything in life.

He loved them dearly, but probably loved them more in retrospect
than in actual fact. He knew little of their present life, had no
understanding for it, and felt it to be alien to him. Alien, too, was
this short, skittish letter, which had probably cost them a great deal
of time and strain to compose, and while Tatyana was writing, her

9

husband, Sergei Sergeych, was probably standing behind her... She had received Kuzminki as her dowry only six years before, but it was already ruined by this same Sergei Sergeych, and now, every time they had to pay the bank or pay interest on the mortgage, they turned to Podgorin for advice because he was a lawyer; indeed, they had twice already asked him for a loan. Now, too, they obviously wanted either his advice or his money.

He no longer had any desire to go to Kuzminki, as he used to in the old days. It was sad there. Gone were the laughter and the noise and the happy, carefree faces, and trysts on calm moonlit nights, and gone, above all, was youth; and anyway, it was all probably charming in retrospect only... Apart from Ta and Va there was also Na, Tatyana's sister Nadezhda, whom in fun and in earnest they used to call his betrothed; he had seen her grow up, they had counted on him marrying her, and at one time he had been in love with her and was going to propose to her – but she was twenty-four by now, and he was still unmarried...

Strange, the way it all turned out, he mused now, rereading the letter in some perplexity. But I couldn't not go, they'd be hurt...

The fact that he had not visited the Losevs for a long time weighed on his conscience. And after walking up and down his room and giving some thought to it, he made an effort and decided to go and spend about three days with them, perform that service and then be free and have a clean conscience, at least till summer. And making ready after lunch to go to Brest station, he told the servant that he would be back in three days' time.

It was a two hours' railway journey from Moscow to Kuzminki, and then a ride of some twenty minutes in a horse-carriage from the station. There was a view from the station of Tatyana's wood and of the three narrow villas begun – but never finished – by Losev, who, during the first few years of marriage, had ventured into all sorts of speculative deals. His ruin was caused by these villas and by all kinds of business enterprises, and by frequent visits to Moscow, where he lunched at the Slavyansky Bazaar, dined at the Hermitage and finished his day in the Malaya Bronnaya Street or the Zhivoderka with the gypsy singers (he called this "shaking himself up"). Podgorin, too, used to drink, sometimes a great deal, and used to visit women without being too particular about it, but he did it lazily and coldly, experiencing no pleasure; and he had a feeling of repulsion when others in his presence gave themselves up to it with passion, he did not understand people who felt themselves freer in Zhivoderka than they did at home with decent women, and he did not like such people; he had the impression that every kind of uncleanliness stuck to them like a thistle. And he did not like Losev, and considered him uninteresting, no good at anything, lazy, and often had a feeling of repulsion in his company…

Just after he had passed the wood, he was met by Sergei Sergeych and Nadezhda.

"My dear fellow, why have you forgotten us?" said Sergei Sergeych, kissing him three times and then holding him by the waist with both hands. "You don't love us any more, old friend!"

He had large features, a fat nose and a sparse beard; he brushed his hair sideways, merchant-fashion, in order to appear simple and purely Russian. When he talked, he breathed straight in the face of the person he was speaking to, and when silent breathed heavily through his nose. His body, well-fed and full to bursting, constrained his movements, and in order to ease his breathing he constantly puffed out his chest, and this gave him a haughty air. By his side his sister-in-law, Nadezhda, appeared ethereal. She was a light blonde, pale, slender, with kind, affectionate eyes; Podgorin could not make out whether she was pretty or not, for he had known her from childhood and was used to her appearance. Now she was wearing a white dress with an open neck, and this impression of a long, bare, white neck was new to him and not quite pleasant.

"My sister and the rest of us have been expecting you ever since this morning," she said. "Varya is staying with us and is also expecting you."

She took his arm and suddenly laughed for no reason and let out a light, joyful cry, as if suddenly charmed by some thought. The field, with its flowering rye motionless in the still air, and the wood lit up by the sun, were beautiful; and it looked as if Nadezhda had noticed it only now, as she was walking by Podgorin's side.

"I have come to spend three days with you," he said. "You must forgive me, I couldn't get away from Moscow any earlier."

"Bad, bad, you have forgotten us," Sergei Sergeych reproached him good-naturedly. "*Jamais de ma vie!*"* he said suddenly, and snapped his fingers.

He had a habit, when the person he was speaking to was not expecting it, of saying a phrase by way of exclamation which bore no relation to

11

the conversation, and of snapping his fingers as he said it. And he was always imitating somebody; if he rolled his eyes, or carelessly tossed his hair back, or spoke with pathos, it meant that the day before he had been to the theatre or to a dinner at which speeches were made. Now he was walking as if suffering from gout, taking small steps and not bending his knees – probably imitating someone again.

"You know, Tanya did not believe you'd come," said Nadezhda. "But Varya and I had a premonition; I knew somehow that you'd arrive by just this train."

"*Jamais de ma vie*!" repeated Sergei Sergeych.

The ladies were waiting for them on the terrace in the garden. Ten years ago Podgorin – he was a poor university student then – used to teach Nadezhda mathematics and history in exchange for board and lodging; and Varya, then a girl student, had profited by this opportunity to take Latin lessons from him. But Tanya, already then a beautiful grown-up girl, thought of nothing but love, and wanted only love and happiness, wanted them passionately, and waited for a husband and dreamt about him day and night. And now, when she was already over thirty, just as beautiful and striking as ever, dressed in a wide gown, her arms full and white, she thought only of her husband and of her two little girls, and her expression seemed to signify that though she now was talking and smiling, she was keeping her thoughts to herself all the same, that she was mounting guard over her love and her rights to that love, and was ready at any moment to attack any foe who might wish to deprive her of her husband and children. Her love was strong and, she thought, mutual, but jealousy and fear for the children were constantly tormenting her and prevented her from being happy.

After the noisy greetings on the terrace, everyone except Sergei Sergeych went to Tatyana's room. The rays of the sun did not penetrate there through the drawn blinds, and the room was plunged into semi-darkness, so that all the roses gathered in a large bunch appeared to have the same colour. Podgorin was made to sit in an old armchair next to the window. Nadezhda sat down at his feet on a low stool. He knew that besides the affectionate reproaches, fun and laughter which were heard now and which reminded him so much of the past, there would also be an unpleasant conversation about bills and mortgages – that was unavoidable – and he thought that it might perhaps be better to have the business talk at once, without putting it off till later, get it over quickly, and then – out into the garden and the fresh air...

"Shall we talk business first?" he said. "Anything new in Kuzminki? Is something rotten in the state of Denmark?"

"We are in trouble here in Kuzminki," replied Tatyana, and sighed sadly. "Oh, we are in such difficulties, in such difficulties that I don't think we could be in greater difficulties," she said, and paced up and down the room in her excitement. "Our estate is being sold, the auction is fixed for 7th August, it's been advertised everywhere, and buyers come here, walk about the rooms, look round... Everyone now has the right to enter my room and have a look round. Legally this is just, perhaps, but I feel deeply humiliated and offended. We have no money and we can no longer borrow. In short, it's terrible, terrible! I swear to you," she continued, her voice trembling and tears gushing out of her eyes, "I swear to you by everything that's sacred, by my children's happiness, I cannot live without Kuzminki! I was born here, this is my nest, and if it's taken away from me, I shall not survive it, I'll die from sheer despair."

"I think you take too gloomy a view," said Podgorin. "Everything will turn out all right. Your husband will find a job, you will start afresh, you'll begin a new life."

"How can you say that?" cried Tatyana; now she looked very beautiful and strong, and the fact that she was ready at any moment to pounce on the foe who would want to deprive her of husband, children and nest was expressed particularly bluntly on her face and her whole body. "New life, indeed! Sergei is trying to get a job, he has been promised the job of an Inland Revenue inspector somewhere in the Ufa or Perm Province, and I am ready to go anywhere – to Siberia, if necessary – I'm ready to live there ten, twenty years, but I must know that sooner or later I shall finish up by returning to Kuzminki. I can't live without Kuzminki. I can't, and I won't. I won't!" she cried and stamped her foot.

"You are a lawyer, Misha," said Varya, "you're a bit of a wrangler and it is your job to give advice as to what to do next."

There was only one fair and reasonable answer: nothing can be done, but Podgorin did not have the heart to say so frankly, and mumbled haltingly:

"It'll have to be considered... I will think."

There were two men inside him. As a lawyer he had occasionally to deal with coarse subjects, in court rooms and with clients his behaviour was haughty, and he was always forthright and trenchant when expressing an opinion, and when he went on the razzle with other men he did it crudely. But with close friends and people he had known for a long time he was extraordinarily considerate, was shy and sensitive, and did not know how to be forthright. One tear, an unfriendly glance, a lie or even an ugly gesture was enough to make him shrink and lose his will-power. Now Nadezhda was sitting at his feet, and he did not like her bare neck; this embarrassed him, and he even wanted to go home. Once, a year ago, he had met Sergei Sergeych in a lady's flat in Bronnaya Street, and he now felt ill at ease with Tatyana, as if he had himself been party to this infidelity. And this conversation about Kuzminki put him in a very awkward situation. He was used to the fact that all ticklish and unpleasant problems were solved by judges or the jury, or simply by some legal clause; but whenever a problem was put up to him for his own personal solution he became confused.

"Misha, you are a friend, we all love you as one of the family," Tatyana continued, "and I tell you frankly: we are putting all our hopes on you. For God's sake tell us what to do. Should we send in an application somewhere, perhaps? Perhaps it isn't too late to transfer the estate legally to Nadya or Varya?... What should we do?"

"Come to the rescue, Misha, do," said Varya, lighting a cigarette. "You have always been intelligent. You haven't lived much, haven't had any experience of life, but you have a good head on your shoulders... you'll help Tanya, I know..."

"I'll have to think... perhaps I'll think of something." They went for a walk in the garden and in the fields. Sergei Sergeych went out for a walk with them too. He took Podgorin's arm and was all the time dragging him on to walk in front, apparently wanting to talk to him about something, probably about the unsatisfactory money matters. But to walk next to Sergei Sergeych and talk to him was sheer torment. He constantly kissed you, and did it three times on each occasion, took you by the arm, put his arm round your waist, breathed in your face, and gave the impression of being covered with a sweet glue and just about to stick to you; and the expression in his eyes which meant that he needed something from Podgorin, and that he was at any moment

14

going to ask for something, was most distressing – just as if he were aiming a revolver at you.

The sun set, it was getting dark. Here and there along the railway line lights were lit, green, red... Varya stopped and, looking at the lights, began reciting:

> "Straight lies the railway, with narrow slopes banking it,
> Bridges, and fence posts, and rails,
> And all along, there are Russian bones flanking it...
> Many, how many!..."*

"How does it go on? Good Heavens! I've forgotten it all!"

> "There were we straining in winter-time, summertime,
> Bent were our backs, ever bent..."

She recited with feeling in a beautiful, rich voice; her cheeks glowed and tears stood in her eyes. This was the old Varya, Varya the student, and listening to her, Podgorin thought of the past and remembered that when he was a student he too used to know a lot of good poetry by heart and had liked reciting it.

> "No more unbending his back hunched so crookedly,
> Now he keeps silence, is dumb evermore..."

But Varya could remember no further... She was silent, and smiled wanly a weak smile, and now she had finished reciting, the green and red lights looked sad...

"Oh, I've forgotten!"

But then Podgorin suddenly remembered – it had somehow stuck in his memory from his student days – and recited quietly, in a half-whisper:

> "People of Russia have lived through enough,
> Lived through this railway, too, while they were making it,
> Will live through all – and at long last, victorious,
> Hew out a road, broad and clear, coming through...
> Only it's sad..."

"Only it's sad," Varya interrupted him as she remembered, "Only it's sad that this epoch, so glorious, will not be lived in by me, or by you!"

And she laughed and clapped him on the shoulder.

They went home and sat down to supper. Sergei Sergeych negligently tucked a corner of his napkin behind his collar, in imitation of someone.

"Let's have a drink," he said, pouring out a vodka for himself and Podgorin. "We old students, we could drink and act and wax eloquent. I drink to your health, old friend, and you, you must drink to the health of an old fool of an idealist, and wish him to remain an idealist till his death. In cases like mine, the grave is the only physician."

Throughout dinner Tatyana threw tender glances at her husband, felt jealous and worried that he might eat or drink something that was bad for him. She was under the impression that he was spoilt by women, and tired – she found this attractive in him, but at the same time she suffered. Varya and Nadya also dealt with him tenderly and looked at him with a worried expression, as if afraid that he would suddenly leave them. When he wanted to pour himself out another glass, Varya frowned and said:

"You are poisoning yourself, Sergei Sergeych. You are a nervous, impressionable man and can easily become a dipsomaniac. Tanya, have the vodka taken away."

In general, Sergei Sergeych had a great success with women. They liked his tall figure, his well-built frame, his large features, his idleness and his misfortunes. They said he was very kind and therefore a spendthrift; that he was an idealist and therefore impractical; that he was honest, pure-hearted, unable to adapt himself to men and circumstances, and that therefore he had nothing and had never found a steady job. They had a deep faith in him, adored him and spoilt him with their worship, so that he now himself believed that he was an idealist, impractical, honest, pure-hearted, and that he was head and shoulders above, and better than, these women.

"Don't you think they are lovely, my little girls?" Tatyana said, looking lovingly at her two girls – healthy, well-fed, for all the world like a couple of buns – and giving them platefuls of rice. "You have a good look at them! They say all mothers praise their children, but I assure you I am being objective, my girls are quite extraordinary – especially the elder."

Podgorin was smiling at her and at the girls, but he found it strange that that healthy, young and intelligent woman, a big complex organism really, should be spending all her energies, all her vitality on such a simple and trivial task as the building-up of a nest which anyway had already been built up.

Perhaps this is how it should be, he thought, but it is neither interesting nor intelligent.

"He had the bear on top of him before he could say 'Knife'," said Sergei Sergeych, and snapped his fingers.

They finished supper. Tatyana and Varya made Podgorin sit on the sofa in the drawing room and spoke to him in a low voice, again about business matters.

"We must come to Sergei Sergeych's rescue," said Varya, "it's our moral duty. He has his weaknesses, he is not thrifty, doesn't think of the rainy day, but that's because he is kind and generous. He has the heart of a child. If you give him a million he will have nothing left in a month; he'll have given it all away."

"That's right, that's right," said Tatyana, and tears flowed down her cheeks. "He has made me suffer a lot, but I must say he is a wonderful man."

And both of them, Tatyana and Varya, could not restrain themselves from reproaching Podgorin a little cruelly:

"But your generation, Misha, is no longer the same!"

What has my generation got to do with it? thought Podgorin. After all, Losev is about six years older than I am, no more…

"Life is no easy matter," said Varya and sighed. "Man is always threatened with some loss or other. Either they want to take your estate away from you, or else a member of your family falls ill and you are afraid he might die – and so it is, day in, day out. And there's nothing we can do about it, my friends. We must submit uncomplainingly to the Supreme Will, we must remember that nothing in this world is fortuitous; everything has its distant aims. You, Misha, you haven't lived much yet and haven't suffered much, and you'll laugh at me; do, by all means, but I'll still say: at the time of my bitterest worries, I experienced several cases of clairvoyance, and this has stirred me to the innermost depths of my being, and now I know that nothing is fortuitous, and that all that happens in our life is essential."

How unlike Varya the student, the red-haired, carefree, noisy, daring Varya, was this Varya, grey-haired by now, tightly laced into her corset, wearing a fashionable dress with high sleeves, Varya, rolling a cigarette in her long, bony fingers, which trembled for some reason, Varya, so readily lapsing into mysticism and speaking in such a lifeless and monotonous way…

And where is it all gone now! thought Podgorin, feeling bored as he listened to her.

"Sing something, Va," he said to her, so as to stop this conversation about clairvoyance. "You used to sing well in the old days."

"Oh, Misha, that's all gone and finished now."

"Well then, recite something from Nekrasov."

"I've forgotten everything. I did it quite spontaneously just now."

In spite of the corset and the high sleeves, it was obvious that she was living in want and was leading a starveling existence in her factory near Tula. And it was very obvious that she had overworked herself; hard, monotonous toil, constant interference in other people's affairs and care for others had tired her out and aged her, and Podgorin, looking now at her sad, already faded face, thought that it was not Kuzminki or Sergei Sergeych, on whose behalf she took so much trouble, that should really be helped, but she herself.

University education and the fact that she had become a doctor, seemed not to have touched the woman in her. She liked weddings, confinements, christenings, long conversations about children, quite as much as Tatyana did; she liked thrillers with a happy ending, and in newspapers read only about fires, floods and grand ceremonies; she very much wanted Podgorin to propose to Nadezhda, and had that happened, she would have cried from sheer emotion.

He did not know whether it happened by chance or whether Varya had prearranged it – he remained alone with Nadezhda; but the mere suspicion that he was being watched and that something was expected of him embarrassed and disconcerted him, and in Nadezhda's company he felt as if they had been put together in the same cage.

"Let's go out into the garden," she said.

They went out into the garden: he – moody and annoyed, not knowing what to talk to her about, and she – beaming with joy, proud that he was near her, obviously pleased that he was staying for another three days and full, perhaps, of sweet dreams and hopes. He did not know

18

whether she loved him, but he knew that she had long ago grown used and attached to him, and still regarded him as her tutor, and that the emotions that now filled her heart were the same as her sister Tatyana's had once been, that, in other words, she thought of nothing but love, of how to get married as quickly as possible, have a husband, children and her own home.

"It's getting dark," he said.

"Yes. The moon rises very late."

They kept on walking along the same drive, near the house. Podgorin did not want to go deeper into the garden: it was dark there, he would have to take Nadezhda's arm, be very near to her. Some shadows were moving on the terrace, and he had the feeling it was Tatyana and Varya watching him.

"I must ask your advice," said Nadezhda, standing still. "If Kuzminki is sold, Sergei Sergeych will work in an office, and then our life must change completely. I'll not go with my sister, we shall part because I don't want to be a burden to her family. I must work. I'll find some job in Moscow, will earn something and will help my sister and her husband. You'll help me with your advice, won't you?"

Quite ignorant of toil, she was now inspired by the thought of an independent, toiling life, and was building plans for the future – so much was written on her face; and a life during which she would be working and helping others seemed to her beautiful and romantic. He saw near him her pale face and black eyebrows, and remembered what an intelligent and clever pupil she had been, what great gifts she had and how pleasant it had been to give her lessons. And probably even now she was not just a young lady looking for a husband, but an intelligent, noble-minded girl, uncommonly kind, with a meek and gentle soul which could be moulded like wax into any shape, and in a suitable environment she would make an excellent woman.

Why shouldn't I marry her, really? thought Podgorin, but for some reason the thought frightened him and he went back to the house.

Tatyana was sitting at the piano in the drawing room, and her playing reminded him vividly of the past, when in that very drawing room people had played, sung and danced till late at night, with the windows open, and the birds in the garden and near the river had sung too. Podgorin cheered up, began romping about, danced with both Nadezhda and Varya, and then sang. A corn on his foot worried him and he asked for permission to put on Sergei Sergeych's slippers, and oddly enough in those slippers he felt himself to be a member of the household, a relative (Just like a brother-in-law – the thought flashed through his mind), and he cheered up even more. At the sight of him they all revived, brightened up and became almost younger. Their faces all shone with hope: Kuzminki was saved! It was so easy, after all: all that had to be done was to think of something, to search through the laws a bit, or for Nadya to marry Podgorin... And obviously things were already beginning to point that way. Nadya, pink and happy, her eyes full of tears, in expectation of something unusual, was whirling round as she danced and her white dress billowed about her and revealed her small, pretty feet in flesh-coloured stockings... Varya, very pleased, took Podgorin's arm and, wearing a significant expression, said to him in a half-whisper:

"Misha, don't run away from your own happiness. Take it while it offers itself of its own accord; later on you will be running after it, but it'll be too late, you won't catch it."

Podgorin wanted to make promises and encourage hopes, and he was himself ready to believe that Kuzminki was saved and that it was so simple to do.

"'And of this earth you'll be the queen',"* he began to sing, striking an attitude, but he suddenly remembered that he could do nothing for those people, nothing at all, and fell silent, feeling guilty.

And afterwards he sat silently in a corner with his feet in borrowed slippers tucked up under him.

At the sight of him the others, too, understood that nothing more could be done, and became silent and quiet. Someone closed the piano. And they all noticed that it was late, time to go to bed, and Tatyana put out the big lamp in the drawing room.

Podgorin's bed had been made ready for him in the annexe he had formerly lived in. Sergei Sergeych took him there, holding a candle high above his head, although the moon was already rising and it was light. They were going along a drive with lilac bushes on either side, and the gravel was scrunching under their feet.

"He had the bear on top of him before he could say 'knife'," said Sergei Sergeych.

And Podgorin had the impression of having heard this phrase a thousand times before. How tired he was of it! When they had reached the annexe, Sergei Sergeych got a bottle and two glasses out of his ample jacket and stood them on the table.

"That's brandy," he said. "Number 0 0. In the house there's Varya; you can't drink when she's there, she launches forth about dipsomania right away, but here we can do what we please. The brandy is superb."

They sat down. The brandy turned out to be really good.

"Let's drink thoroughly tonight," continued Sergei Sergeych, sucking a lemon. "I was a student in my day, and like to shake myself up sometimes. It's essential."

But in his eyes there was the same expression as before, that he needed something from Podgorin and that he was about to ask for something.

"Let's drink, my friend," he continued with a sigh. "Life has become intolerable without it. It's all over for cranks like me – finished. Idealism is not the fashion nowadays. The rouble is king now, and if you don't want to be shoved out of the way, fall down on your face and worship the rouble. But I can't. It just makes me sick."

"When's the date of the auction?" asked Podgorin to change the subject.

"The seventh of August. But I haven't the slightest intention of saving Kuzminki, my dear fellow. We are very badly in arrears on the mortgage and the estate brings in no income at all, nothing but a loss every year. It isn't worth it... Tanya is sorry of course, it's her ancestral home, but I am even pleased to a certain extent, to tell you the truth. I'm not a country dweller. A big, noisy city is my field, struggle is my element!"

He said other things too, but never what he wanted to say, and watched Podgorin closely, as if waiting for a suitable moment. And suddenly Podgorin saw his eyes close to him, felt his breath on his face...

"My dear fellow, save me!" said Sergei Sergeych, breathing heavily. "Give me two hundred roubles! I implore you!"

Podgorin wanted to say that he was himself hard up, and thought that it would be better to give these two hundred roubles to a pauper or even merely to lose them at cards, but he felt terribly shy; he felt himself trapped in that little room with its one candle, wanted to get rid as quickly as possible of that breath, of those soft hands which were holding his waist and seemed to have already stuck to him, and he quickly began to search his pockets for the diary in which he kept his money.

"There you are…" he mumbled, taking out a hundred roubles. "I'll let you have the rest afterwards. I have no more with me. You see, I don't know how to refuse," he went on irritably, his anger mounting. "I have an execrable feminine nature. Only please let me have this money back. I am short of cash too."

"Thank you, thank you, friend!"

"And for God's sake stop imagining that you are an idealist. You are as much of an idealist as I am a turkeycock. You are just a thoughtless idler and no more."

Sergei Sergeych heaved a deep sigh and sat down on the sofa.

"You are annoyed, my dear fellow," he said, "but if you knew how hard it is for me! I am living through a dreadful time now. My dear fellow, I swear it's not myself I'm sorry for, oh no! I'm sorry for my wife and children. If it wasn't for the children and my wife I'd have done away with myself long ago."

And suddenly his head and shoulders shook and he began to sob.

"That's the last straw!" said Podgorin, walking about the room in his agitation and feeling very annoyed. "What can be done with a man who has done a lot of evil and then sobs? These tears of yours disarm one, I haven't got it in me to say anything to you. You sob, therefore you are right."

"I have done a lot of evil?" asked Sergei Sergeych, getting up and looking at Podgorin in surprise. "My dear fellow, is that you saying it? I have done a lot of evil? Oh, how little you know me! How little you understand me!"

"All right, let's assume I don't understand you, only please don't sob. It's disgusting."

"Oh, how little you know me!" Losev was repeating, in all sincerity. "How little you know me!"

"Look at yourself in the glass," continued Podgorin. "You are not a young man any more, you'll be old soon, it's about time you gave some thought to your behaviour, time you realized a little who you are and what you are. Doing nothing all your life, all your life this idle, childish prattle, poses and affectation – I'm surprised your head's not spinning and you aren't tired of living so. You're a depressing man to be with! One gets into a mental torpor in your company out of sheer boredom!"

Having said this, Podgorin left the annexe and slammed the door.

Probably for the first time in his life he had been sincere and had said what he wanted.

But only a little later he was sorry for having been so stern. What was the use of speaking seriously or arguing with a man who constantly lied, ate a lot, drank a lot, spent a lot of other people's money, and at the same time was convinced that he was an idealist and a martyr? This case was one of stupidity or bad habits which had gone on for a long time, had bitten deep into the man's organism like a disease and was by now incurable. Anyway, indignation and stern reproaches were of no use here – laughter would be more in place; one good jibe would do a great deal more than a dozen sermons!

Even simpler would be to pay no attention at all, thought Podgorin, and above all not to give money.

And then in a little while he no longer thought either about Sergei Sergeych or his hundred roubles. The night was quiet and still and very light. Whenever on moonlit nights Podgorin looked at the sky, it always seemed to him that nothing was awake except the moon and himself, and that all else was either asleep or dozing; and his thoughts refused to busy themselves with either men or money, and his mood gradually became quiet and peaceful; he felt alone in the world, and in the stillness of the night the sound of his own footsteps seemed to him so sad.

The garden was surrounded by a white stone wall. In the right-hand corner of the side facing a field stood a tower built a long time ago at the time of the serfs. The lower part was made of stone and the upper part of timber, with a platform, a conical roof and a tall spire on which could be seen the black shape of the weathervane. There were two doors at the bottom, which made it possible to go straight from the garden into the field, and a staircase which creaked under one's footsteps, leading up to the platform. Broken old armchairs were thrown together in a heap under the staircase, and the moonlight which now penetrated through the doorway lit up these armchairs, and they, with their little curved legs sticking up in the air, seemed to have come to life and to be lying in wait for someone in the stillness of the night.

Podgorin went up the stairs to the platform and sat down. Immediately on the other side of the wall there was a dividing ditch with a bank, and beyond was the field, wide and floodlit by the rays of the moon. Podgorin knew that there was a wood directly in front of him, about two miles away from the park, and now he imagined he saw a dark streak in the distance. Corncrakes and quails were crying; and coming from the direction of the wood he could hear a cuckoo, which was awake too.

He heard footsteps. Somebody was walking in the garden and was approaching the tower.

A dog began to bark.

"Beetle!" a woman's voice called quietly. "Beetle, come back!"

He heard someone entering the tower, and a minute later a black dog – an old friend of Podgorin's – appeared on the bank of the ditch. It stopped, looked up in the direction where Podgorin was sitting, and began wagging its tail in friendly gesture. And then a little later a white figure rose up from the ditch like a shadow and also stopped on the bank. It was Nadezhda.

"What do you see there?" she asked the dog, and peered up.

She did not see Podgorin, but probably felt his near presence, for she was smiling and her pale face, lit up by the moon, seemed happy. The tower's black shadow stretching along the earth far into the field, the motionless white figure with a blissful smile on a pale face, the black dog, the shadows of both, and the whole thing together something like a dream.

"There's no one there," said Nadezhda quietly.

She stood and waited for him to come down and call her and tell her all that was on his mind, for them both to be happy in this still and beautiful night. White, pale, slender, very beautiful in the moonlight, she was waiting for affection; her constant dreams of happiness and love had worn her out, and she was no longer capable of concealing her feelings, and the whole of her figure and the brightness of her eyes and the happy smile congealed on her lips betrayed her innermost thoughts; but he felt embarrassed, shrank within himself, and sat quietly, not knowing whether he should speak up in order to treat it all as a joke afterwards, or whether he should keep silent, and he was annoyed and thought only of the fact that there in the park, on a moonlit night, by the side of a beautiful, lovelorn, dreamy girl, he was just as indifferent as he was in the Malaya Bronnaya Street – obviously because both the poetry and the coarse prose of life were equally dead for him. Dead, too, were trysts and moonlit nights, and white figures with slender waists, and mysterious shadows, and towers and parks, and such "types" as Sergei Sergeych and such as himself, Podgorin, with his cold boredom, constant annoyance, inability to adapt himself to real life, inability to take from it what it was capable of giving, the exhausting, aching thirst for what did not and could not exist on earth. And now, sitting there in that tower, he would have preferred a good firework display, or some procession in the moonlight, or Varya, who would have recited 'The Railway', or another woman who, standing on the bank where Nadezhda was now standing, would be telling him something interesting and new, bearing no relation to either love or happiness, and even if she had been talking of love, it would be a call to new forms of life, lofty and rational, on the eve of which we are now living, and of whose existence we sometimes have a premonition...

"There's no one there," said Nadezhda.

And after standing and waiting for another minute, she went quietly, with bowed head, in the direction of the wood. The dog ran on in front. And for a long time Podgorin could see a white spot.

"Strange, the way it has all turned out, really..." he repeated to himself on his way back to the annexe.

He could not imagine what he would talk about with Sergei Sergeych and Tatyana and how he would behave towards Nadezhda the following day, or the day after either – and in anticipation of it he felt embarrassment, fear and boredom. How could he fill in the three long days he had promised to stay there? He recalled the conversation about clairvoyance and Sergei Sergeych's phrase: "He had the bear on top of him before he could say 'knife'", he remembered that tomorrow, in order to please Tatyana, he would have to smile to her replete, podgy little girls – and he decided to leave.

At half-past five Sergei Sergeych, in a bukhara dressing gown and a tasselled fez, appeared on the terrace of the big house. Without wasting a minute, Podgorin came up to him and began saying goodbye.

"I must be in Moscow by ten o'clock," he said, without looking at him. "I quite forgot that I was expected at the solicitor's. Please let me go. As soon as your people are up, make my excuses to them. I am terribly sorry..."

He did not hear what Sergei Sergeych was saying to him and did not look back at the windows of the big house for fear that the ladies might wake up and detain him. He was ashamed of being so nervous. He felt that that was the last time he would ever be in Kuzminki, and that he would never go there again, and as he was driving off, he looked back several times at the annexe, where in the past he had spent so many happy days – but within him he felt cold and felt no sadness.

On his table at home the first thing he saw was the note which he had received the previous day. "Dear Misha," he read. "You have quite forgotten us, do come as soon as you can…" And for some reason he remembered how Nadezhda had whirled round as she danced, how her dress had billowed about her and revealed her feet in flesh-coloured stockings…

But in another ten minutes he was sitting at his table, working, and no longer thought about Kuzminki.

Appropriate Measures

THE SMALL PROVINCIAL TOWN, which, as the local prison superintendent had once put it, could not be distinguished on any map even under a telescope, is lit up by the midday sun. Peace and quiet everywhere. A sanitary commission consisting of the town doctor, the police inspector, two representatives of the town council and one trade deputy is slowly proceeding from the town hall towards the shopping quarter. Constables follow respectfully behind... The way of the commission, like the way to hell, is paved with good intentions. As they walk along gesticulating, the sanitary inspectors discuss uncleanliness, stink, appropriate measures and other unsavoury subjects. The discussions are so clever that the police inspector walking in front of the group is suddenly seized with delight, turns round and declares:

"We really should try to meet as often as we can and discuss matters! It's a pleasure and an entertainment. As it is, all we do is quarrel. We do, really."

"Whom shall we begin with, Anikita Nikolaych?" asks the trade deputy, addressing himself to the doctor in the tone of an executioner selecting a victim.

"What about starting off with Osheynikov's shop? Firstly, the man's a scoundrel, and... secondly, it's time he was got at. I had some buckwheat from him the other day, and I found rat droppings in it, if you'll pardon the expression... My wife couldn't eat it."

"Well then, we might as well start off with Osheynikov as with anyone else," says the doctor with complete indifference.

The inspectors walk into a shop labelled "Tea, Sugar, Coffee and other Groceries, A. M. Osheynikov", and immediately, without further ado, begin their inspection.

"Er... yes..." says the doctor, looking at attractively piled-up pyramids of laundry soap. "Regular Towers of Babel you've built here! Very ingenuous, I must say! Oh, eh, eh! What's all this? Just look at him! Look at Demyan Gavrilych cutting soap and bread with the same knife!"

27

"That won't give people cholera, Anikita Nikolaych!" says the shop-keeper reasonably.

"That's true enough, but it's disgusting all the same! After all, I buy bread here, too."

"We have a special knife for the better sort of customer. Don't you worry, sir..."

The police inspector peers short-sightedly at a ham, scratches it for a long time with his nail, smells it loudly, then taps it with his finger and asks:

"You never have these with strichines in, have you?"

"What a thing to say, sir... Come, come now... as if I could!"

The police inspector is overcome with embarrassment, leaves the ham and peers at the price list of Asmolov & Co. The trade deputy puts his hand into a barrel containing buckwheat and feels something soft and velvety... He has a look, and tenderness spreads over his face.

"Pussies... pussies! My little darlings!" he murmurs. "Lying in the buckwheat with their little faces up... all cuddly... Now, Demyan Gavrilych, you might send me just one little kitten!"

"Of course, sir... Well, and here you have the delicatessen counter, in case you want to inspect it... Herrings here... cheese... cured sturgeon this is... The sturgeon I got on Thursday, the best kind... Mishka, give me a knife!"

The sanitary inspectors cut themselves a piece of cured sturgeon each, smell it and taste it.

"I might as well have a snack too, while we're about it..." says the grocer, Demyan Gavrilych, as if to himself. "I had a little bottle lying about somewhere. Ought to have a drink before eating the sturgeon... Gives it a different taste then... Let's have the bottle, Mishka."

Mishka, his cheeks blown out and eyes popping out of his head, uncorks the bottle and puts it on the counter with a resounding bang.

"Drink on an empty stomach..." says the police inspector scratching his head, unable to make up his mind. "However, if we just have one each... Only you be quick, Demyan Gavrilych, you and your vodka; we're busy!"

A quarter of an hour later the sanitary inspectors, wiping their lips and picking their teeth with matchsticks, make their way to Golorybenko's shop. As if to spite them, the way here is blocked...

Half a dozen young stalwarts, their faces red and sweaty, are rolling a keg of butter out of the shop.

"Keep to the right!... Pull it by the rim... Go on. Pull, pull! Put a bit of wood underneath... Oh, damn! Get out of the way, sir, we might crush your toes!"

The barrel sticks in the doorway and stops... The young stalwarts strain away at it and push it and pull it with all their might, puffing and snorting noisily and swearing at the top of their voices. After such efforts, in the course of which the air becomes considerably polluted by the puffing and the snorting, the barrel at last rolls out, but for some unknown reason, rolls back again in defiance of all natural laws, and once more sticks in the doorway. The puffing and snorting begins anew.

"Oh, blast!" exclaims the police inspector. "Let's got to Shibukin. These devils will be puffing away at it all day."

The sanitary inspectors find Shibukin's shop locked.

"But it was open!" say the sanitary inspectors, looking at each other in astonishment. "As we were going into Osheinikov's shop, Shibukin was standing on the threshold and was washing out a copper teapot. Where is he?" they ask a beggar standing near the locked shop.

"Spare a copper for a poor cripple, in the name of God," wheezes the beggar. "Many thanks to you, guv'nors... bless you and your parents."

The sanitary inspectors wave him away, and continue on their way, all except the town council representative Plyunin. He gives the beggar a copeck, crosses himself hastily as if afraid of something, and runs off in pursuit of the rest of the company.

About two hours later the commission is wending its way back. The sanitary inspectors look tired and worn out. They have not laboured in vain; a constable strides solemnly along carrying a large tray full of rotten apples.

"Well now, after our righteous labours, a bit of a snifter might not be a bad idea," says the police inspector, glancing at a signboard: "Wine and vodka cellar". "We need something to give us back our strength. Er – yes, might do us some good. Let's go in if you like!"

The sanitary inspectors go down into the cellar and sit down round a table with bent legs. The police inspector nods to the bar-keeper, and a bottle appears on the table.

"Pity one can't have a snack with it," says the trade deputy, making a wry face as he empties a glass. "Haven't you got a little cucumber, or something. However..."

The deputy turns to the constable with the tray, chooses the least spoilt of all the apples and eats it.

"Oh... some of them aren't all that rotten!" says the police inspector in a seemingly surprised tone of voice. "Let's have them here. I'll choose some too! Just put the tray here... The better ones we'll take out and peel, and you can destroy the others. Anikita Nikolaych, let's have another drink! We really ought to get together a bit more often and discuss things. As it is, we just live on in these backwoods – no education in these parts, no club, no decent company – might as well be Australia! Come on now, pour out some more! Doctor, have some apples! I've peeled them for you with my own fair hands!"

"Where would you like me to put the tray, sir?" the constable asks the police inspector, who is leaving the cellar with the rest of the company.

"Tr-tray? What tray? Oh, I see! Destroy it together with the apples... Because it's contagious."

"You have eaten the apples, sir."

"Oh... excellent! Look... you go over to my house and tell my wife not to be angry... I'll only go off for an hour or so... to Plyunin's, to get some sleep... Do you understand? Sleep... in the arms of Morpheus. Tra-la-la."

And raising his eyes to heaven, the police inspector shakes his head bitterly, spreads out his hands and says:

"And that's the way our life goes!"

The Boa-Constrictor and the Rabbit

PYOTR SEMYONYCH, A BEDRAGGLED, bald-headed individual in a velvet dressing gown with crimson tassels, stroked his fluffy whiskers and continued:

"Well, *mon cher*, if you like, there is one other method. This is the subtlest, cleverest, most cunning method – and the most dangerous one for husbands. It can only be understood by psychologists and connoisseurs of the female heart. It has a *conditio sine qua non*: patience, patience and patience. If a man doesn't know how to wait and be patient, then this method is not for him. According to it, in order to seduce somebody else's wife you keep as far away from her as possible. When you feel madly attracted to her, you cease visiting her, you meet her as rarely as possible, and then only for a moment, while at the same time denying yourself the pleasure of talking to her. When using this method, you operate at a distance. The whole thing is a kind of hypnotism. She must not see, but must feel you, like a rabbit feels the gaze of the boa-constrictor. You hypnotize her not by your gaze, but by the poison of your tongue, and the husband can serve as the best transmission wire for this.

"For example, I'm in love with a certain N.N. and want to seduce her. Somewhere in the club or at the theatre I meet her husband.

"'And how's your wife?' I ask him in passing. 'A most charming woman, I must say. I like her awfully! In fact, I like her a hell of a lot.'

"'Mm... What is it you like so much about her?' asks the husband, very pleased.

"'She's a most delightful, romantic creature, who could even move a stone and make it fall in love with her! Incidentally, you husbands are prosaic people, and you only understand your wives during the first month of marriage... Take it from me, your wife is an absolutely ideal woman! Take it from me, and rejoice that Fate has sent you such a wife! Women like that are precisely what we need in these times... just like that!'

"'Why, what is there so very special about her?' says the husband, surprised.

31

"'Good Heavens! Why, she's a beauty, full of grace, life and truth, romantic, sincere and yet mysterious! Once women like that fall in love, they love violently, passionately...'

"And more in the same strain. That very same day, when he is going to bed, the husband can't refrain from telling his wife:

"'I saw Pyotr Semyonych today. He praised you up to the skies! Was in ecstasies... You're a beauty, and graceful, and mysterious... and apparently you're capable of loving in some special way. He really let himself go... Ha-ha!'

"After that, without having seen her, I try to meet the husband again.

"'By the by, old boy...' I say to him. 'A painter dropped in to see me yesterday. He's had a commission for two thousand roubles from some prince or other to paint the portrait of a typical Russian beauty. Asked me to look for a model for him. I'd have liked to send him to your wife, but felt shy about doing so. But your wife would be just right for it! She has a charming little head! I think it's a damned shame that no artist will ever see such a marvellous model. A damned shame!'

"One would have to be a terribly unkind husband not to pass that on to one's wife. Next morning his wife looks at the mirror for a long time and thinks:

"'What makes him think that I've got a typically Russian face?'

"After that she thinks of me every time she looks in the mirror. Meanwhile my chance meetings with her husband continue. After one such meeting the husband comes home and begins peering at his wife's face.

"'What are you looking at me like that for?' she asks.

"'Why, that queer chap Pyotr Semyonych says you have one eye darker than the other. For the life of me, I can't see it!'

"His wife goes to the mirror again. She looks at herself for a long time, and thinks:

"'Yes, I think the left eye is a little darker than the right one... No, I think the right one is darker than the left... but then it may just have seemed like that to him!'

"After the eighth or ninth meeting the husband says to his wife:

"'I saw Pyotr Semyonych at the theatre. He apologized for never coming to see you: he has no time! He says he's very busy. I don't think he's been to see us for about four months... I began to haul him over the coals for it, but he apologized and said that he wouldn't come to see us until he'd finished some work or other.'

"'Well, and when will he finish it?' asks his wife.

"'Not for a year or two, he says. But what kind of work that beggar can be doing, I'm damned if I know. He is a queer chap, honestly! Kept on at me for hours; why doesn't your wife go on the stage? With such an attractive appearance, he says, with such intelligence and ability to feel, it's a sin to stay at home. She should give up everything, he says, and go where her inner voice tells her. Worldly limitations were not made for the likes of her. Natures like hers, he says, must stand outside time and space.'

"His wife, of course, only dimly understands this harangue, but melts and is transported with delight all the same.

"'What nonsense!' she says, trying to appear indifferent. 'And what else did he say?'

"'If I wasn't so busy, he says, I'd take her away from you. Well, go on, I says, take her – I shan't fight you for her. You don't understand her, he shouts! She must be understood! She has an exceptional nature, he says, a powerful one, searching for an outlet! I'm sorry that I'm not Turgenev,* he says, or I'd have written about her long ago! Ha-ha!... You've certainly made an impression on him! Well, old fellow, I thought, you should live with her for a year or two, then you'd change your tune... He is a queer chap!'

"And his poor wife is gradually overwhelmed by a passionate desire to meet me. I am the only man who has understood her, and there is so much she could say only to me! But I persevere in not going to see her or running into her. She has not seen me for a long time, but my excruciatingly sweet poison has already infected her. Her husband transmits my words to her with a yawn, but she feels that she hears my voice and sees my shining eyes.

"The time has come to seize my chance. One evening her husband comes home and says:

"'I've just seen Pyotr Semyonych. He seemed dull and sad – crestfallen.'

"'Why? What's the matter with him?'

"'Can't make it out. He complains that he's sunk in melancholy. I'm lonely, he says; I haven't anyone close to me, no friends, no kindred spirit who would understand me and blend with my spirit. No one understands me, he says, and now there's only one thing I want: death…'

"'What nonsense!' his wife says, but she thinks to herself: 'Poor thing! I understand him perfectly! I'm lonely too, no one understands me except him, so who could understand his state of mind better than I?'

"'Yes, he really is a queer chap…' the husband continues. 'I feel so sad, he says, I don't even go home; I just walk up and down the N*** Boulevard all night.

"His wife is all in a fever. She passionately wants to go to the N*** Boulevard and have a look – if only out of the corner of her eye – at the man who has contrived to understand her and who is now sunk in melancholy. Who knows? If she were to talk to him now, say a few words of consolation to him, perhaps he would stop suffering. If she were to tell him that he has a friend who understands and values him, he might rise again spiritually.

"'But it's impossible… mad,' she thinks. 'I shouldn't even think of it. I might fall in love with him if I'm not careful, but this is fantastic… stupid…'

"When her husband finally falls asleep, she raises her feverish head, puts her finger to her lips, and thinks: what if she takes the risk of leaving the house now? Afterwards she can always concoct some story or other, say that she ran round to the chemist or the dentist.

"'I'll go!' she decides.

"She already has a plan prepared: she will leave the house by the back stairs, go to the boulevard in a cab, once there she will walk past him, have a look at him, and then go home. In that way she will compromise neither her husband nor herself.

"And she gets dressed, quietly leaves the house, and hurries to the boulevard. The boulevard is dark and deserted. The bare trees are sleeping. There is no one there. But then she sees someone's silhouette. That must be him. Trembling all over, oblivious of everything, she approaches me slowly… and I approach her. For a minute we stand in silence, looking into each other's eyes. Another minute passes in silence and… the rabbit falls defencelessly into the jaws of the boa-constrictor."

History of a Business Enterprise

ANDREI ANDREYCH SIDOROV INHERITED four thousand roubles from his mother, and decided to open a bookshop with the money. Now there was a great need for such a shop. The town was stagnating in ignorance and prejudice; old men did nothing but go to the public baths, civil servants played cards and swilled vodka, ladies gossiped, young men lived without any ideals, young girls dreamt of marriage all day long and ate buckwheat porridge, husbands beat their wives and pigs wandered about the streets.

We need ideas, more ideas! thought Andrei Andreych. Ideas! When he had rented the necessary premises, he went to Moscow, from which he returned with a great many books, both classical and the most modern authors, and a great many text books, and he arranged all that stuff on the shelves. Not a single customer came in the course of the first three weeks. Andrei Andreych sat behind the counter reading Mikhailovsky* and trying to think honestly. For example, when it would suddenly occur to him that it would not be a bad idea to have some bream with gruel to eat, he would immediately catch himself out: "Oh, how trivial!" he would say to himself.

Every morning a servant girl chilled with cold, wearing a kerchief and with leather galoshes on her bare feet, would rush headlong into the shop and say:

"Give us two copecks' worth of vinegar!'

And Andrei Andreych would answer her disdainfully:

"You've mistaken the door, madam! You've come to the wrong place, madam!"

When one of his friends came to see him, he would put on an important and mysterious expression, reach for the third volume of Pisarev* from the highest shelf, blow the dust off it and, with a look as if he had something else as well in the shop but was afraid to show it, he would say:

"Yes, sir, this little piece is so to speak… well, I mean in fact… You read it, it would make you sit up all right… m-m-m…"

"Look out you don't get it in the neck for reading it, old man!"

Three weeks passed before the first customer came. He was a fat, grey-haired gentleman with side whiskers, and wearing a cap with a red band round it – by all appearances, a landowner. He demanded the second part of *Our Native Tongue*.

"You haven't any slate pencils?" he asked.

"I don't keep them."

"Pity… It's a bore to have to go to the bazaar for a little thing like that."

It really is a pity that I don't keep slate pencils, thought Andrei Andreych when the customer had left. It's no use specializing too narrowly here in the provinces, one should sell everything that has anything to do with education and which promotes it in one way or another.

He wrote to Moscow, and before a month was out pens, pencils, pen-holders, school exercise books, slates and other school materials were displayed in his window. Boys and girls began dropping in from time to time, and there even came a day when his takings were one rouble, forty copecks. One day the servant girl in leather galoshes rushed headlong into the shop; he had already opened his mouth to tell her disdainfully that she had come to the wrong place, when she shouted:

"Give us a copeck's worth of paper and a seven copeck stamp!"

After that Andrei Andreych began keeping stamps, as well as application forms. About eight months after the opening of the shop a lady came in to buy pens.

"You don't happen to have any school satchels?" she asked.

"Alas, madam, I don't keep them!"

"Oh, what a pity! In that case, show me what dolls you have, only they mustn't be expensive…"

"I haven't any dolls either, madam!" said Andrei Andreych sadly.

Without further ado he wrote to Moscow, and soon satchels, dolls, drums, swords, accordions, balls and all sorts of toys appeared in his shop.

"Those are all trifles!" he said to his friends. "But just you wait, I'll introduce educational toys and instructive games! You see, in my shop the educational section will be founded, as the saying goes, on the subtlest deductions of science, in short…"

He ordered dumb-bells, croquet, backgammon, bagatelle, gardening tools for children and about two dozen very clever instructional games. Then, to their great delight, the inhabitants of the town saw, as they passed his shop, two bicycles, one large and the other slightly smaller. And business went with a swing. Business was especially good before Christmas, when Andrei Andreych hung a notice in the window that he had Christmas tree decorations for sale.

"You'll see, I'll get hygiene across to them yet," he said to his friends, rubbing his hands. "Just you let me get to Moscow! I'll have such filters and all kinds of scientific improvements as in fact you've never dreamt of! Science can't be ignored, my friends, no-o-o!"

Having made a lot of money, he went to Moscow and bought – for cash and on credit – about five thousand roubles' worth of goods. There were filters, and excellent lamps for writing tables, and guitars, and hygienic underpants for children, and feeding bottles, and purses, and zoological collections. While he was about it, he bought five hundred roubles' worth of best-quality china, and was glad that he had done so, as beautiful things develop refined taste and make for gentler manners. On his return from Moscow he set about arranging the new goods on the shelves and bookcases. Somehow it so happened that, as he climbed up to tidy the top shelf, something shook, and one after another the ten volumes of Mikhailovsky fell off the shelf; one volume hit him on the head, the others fell down right on the lamps, and broke two lamp globes.

"How... heavily they do write!" muttered Andrei Andreych, rubbing himself.

He collected all the books together, tied them up firmly with string, and hid them under the counter. About two days later he was told that his neighbour the grocer had been sentenced to hard labour for assaulting his nephew, and therefore the shop was to let. Andrei Andreych was very pleased, and asked if he could have the first refusal for it. A door was soon made in the wall, and both shops, joined into one, were filled up with goods; as the customers who went into the second half of the shop all asked for tea, sugar and kerosene from habit, Andrei Andreych without more ado introduced groceries as well.

He is now one of the most prominent shop-keepers in our town. He sells china, tobacco, tar, soap, bread rolls, red wine, haberdashery and chandlery, rifles, skins and ham. He has taken over a wine cellar in the market and, it is rumoured, is going to open public baths and a hotel. As to the books which once lay on his shelves, they – including the third volume of Pisarev – have long ago been sold for one rouble, five copecks the hundredweight.

At name-day parties and weddings his former friends, whom Andrei Andreych now calls "Americans" in derision, sometimes bring the conversation round to progress, literature and other elevated subjects.

"Andrei Andreych, have you read the last number of the *European Herald*?" they ask him.

"No, I haven't read it…" he replies, screwing up his eyes and playing with his thick watch chain. "That doesn't concern us. We are occupied with more constructive business."

75,000

ONE NIGHT, AT ABOUT MIDNIGHT, two friends were walking along the Tverskoi Boulevard. One was tall, dark and handsome, dressed in a shabby bear-skin coat and a top hat, the other a small, red-haired man wearing a rust-coloured coat with white bone buttons. They both walked in silence. The man with the dark hair was faintly whistling a mazurka, the red-haired man was looking at his feet and frequently spitting to the side.

"Shall we sit down?" proposed the dark-haired man at last, when both friends saw the sombre silhouette of Pushkin's monument and the little light over the gates of the Strastnoi monastery.

The red-haired man silently agreed, and the friends sat down.

"I've got a little request to make of you, Nikolai Borisych," said the man with dark hair after a short silence. "Could you lend me ten or fifteen roubles, old man? I'll pay you back in a week's time..."

The red-haired man was silent.

"I wouldn't have bothered you if it wasn't a dire necessity. Fate played a rotten trick on me today... This morning my wife gave me her bracelet to pawn... She has to pay for her little sister at school. Well, I pawned it and then... I lost the money at cards quite accidentally, when you were with me today..."

The red-haired man stirred and grunted.

"You're a poor fish, Vasili Ivanovich!" he said, and a malicious sneer spread over his mouth. "A poor fish! What right had you to sit and play cards with ladies if you knew that it was not your money, but someone else's? Well, aren't you a poor fish, aren't you a fop? Wait, don't interrupt... Let me give you a piece of my mind, once and for all... What are all these eternal new suits for, that tiepin there? Is fashion for paupers like you? What's that idiotic top hat for? You, living on your wife, pay fifteen roubles for a top hat when, without doing any harm to fashion or taste, you could very well go about in a three-rouble cap! Why all this boasting about non-existent friendships? You know Khokhlov and Plevako and all the editors! When you were lying about

39

your friends today, my eyes and ears were burning for you! You lie and don't even blush! And when you play with those women, lose your wife's money to them, you smile in such a trite and stupid way that… you make one feel that you aren't even worth a slap in the face!"

"Oh, drop it, drop it… You're out of sorts today…"

"Well, let's say that your foppishness is all due to youth, that you're merely behaving like a schoolboy… I'm ready to admit that, Vasili Ivanovich… you're still young… But I won't admit… there's one thing I don't understand… How could you cheat when you were playing with those dolls?… When you were dealing, I saw you give yourself the ace of spades from underneath!"

Vasili Ivanovich blushed like a schoolboy and began to justify himself. The red-haired man stood his ground. They quarrelled loud and long. At last they both became silent, plunged in thought.

"It's true, I have got into an awful mess," said the man with dark hair after a long silence. "It's true… I've spent everything, run into debt, used a bit of other people's money, and now I don't know how to extricate myself. Do you know that unbearable, awful feeling when your whole body itches, and you can't do anything about it? That's rather like the feeling I'm experiencing now… I'm entangled up to my ears… I'm ashamed of myself, and ashamed of other people's opinion… I do masses of stupid and disgusting things. for the pettiest of reasons, and at the same time I simply can't stop myself… It's awful! If I was to inherit or win some money, I'd give up everything in the world, I believe, and be born anew… But don't pass judgement on me, Nikolai Borisych… don't throw the first stone… Remember Palmov's Neklyuzhev."

"I do remember your Neklyuzhev," said the red-haired man. "I remember… He gobbled up other people's money, gorged himself, and then wanted to have some after-dinner relaxation: he went and snivelled to a flapper. He was careful not to snivel before dinner… Authors should be ashamed of idealizing rotters like that. If Neklyuzhev hadn't had an attractive appearance and a gallant way with him, a rich man's daughter wouldn't have fallen in love with him and there wouldn't have been any regrets… In general, Fate gives rotters an attractive appearance… Why, you're all cupids! They love you, they fall in love with you… You're frightfully lucky so far as women are concerned!"

The red-haired man stood up and walked round the bench.

"Now, take your wife, for example... an honest, noble-minded woman... what could have made her fall in love with you? What? And today, the whole evening while you were lying and putting on airs, a pretty blonde couldn't take her eyes off you... They love you, you Neklyuzhevs, offer themselves to you – whereas one works all one's life, struggles like mad... as honest as honesty itself, and – if only one had one moment of happiness! What's more... do you remember? I was engaged to your wife Olga Alexeyevna before she met you, I was happy for a little, but you turned up and... I was done for."

"Jealousy!" laughed the man with dark hair. "Why, I didn't know you were so jealous!"

A look of annoyance and repulsion passed over Nikolai Borisych's face... He stretched his hand out mechanically, without realizing what he was doing... and made a gesture. The sound of a slap broke the silence of the night... The top hat flew off the dark-haired man's head and rolled on the trodden snow. All this happened in a second, unexpectedly, and was stupid and ridiculous. The red-haired man immediately felt ashamed of his slap. He buried his face in the collar of his coat and strode off along the boulevard. When he reached Pushkin, he looked round at the man with dark hair, stood motionless for a minute, and then, just as if he was frightened of something, he ran in the direction of Tverskaya Street...

Vasili Ivanovich sat on for a long time in silence. He never moved. Some woman walked past him and, with a laugh, handed him his top hat. He thanked her mechanically, stood up, and walked away.

Now for the nagging, he thought, half an hour later, as he climbed the long staircase to his flat... I'll catch it from my spouse for losing! She'll preach at me all night! To hell with her! I'll say that I mislaid the money...

He reached his door, and rang timidly. The cook let him in.

"Congratulations!" the cook said to him, grinning all over her face.

"Why?"

"You'll see, sir. God has been good to you!"

Vasili Ivanovich shrugged his shoulders and went into the bedroom. There at the writing table sat his wife, Olga Alexeyevna, a small blonde with her hair in curlers. She was writing. Before her lay several letters, already written and sealed. When she saw her husband, she jumped up and threw her arms around his neck.

"You've come!" she said. "What luck! You can't imagine what luck! It was such a surprise that I had hysterics, Vasya... Here, read this!"

She jumped up, picked up the newspaper from the table, and thrust it in her husband's face.

"Read it! My lottery ticket has won 75,000 roubles! I have got a ticket, you know! Honestly I have! I hid it from you because... because... you would have pawned it. Nikolai Borisych gave me this ticket when I was engaged to him, and then afterwards he didn't want to take it back. What a good man Nikolai Borisych is! Now we're frightfully rich! Now you'll turn over a new leaf, you won't lead a dissolute life. Why, you went out on the spree and deceived me because you were in need, you were poor. I understand that. You're intelligent, decent..."

She paced up and down the room and laughed.

"It was a surprise! I was walking up and down the room and cursing you for your dissoluteness, hating you, and then I sat down to read the paper out of sheer boredom... And suddenly I saw it!... I've written letters to everyone... to my sisters, to my mother... How pleased they'll be, poor things! But where are you going to?"

Vasili Ivanovich had a look at the paper... Stunned, pale, not listening to his wife, he stood for some time in silence, thinking something out, then put on his top hat and left the house.

"To Number **, Bolshaya Dmitrovka!" he shouted to the cabby.

He did not find the person he wanted in the hotel. The room which he knew was locked.

She must be at the theatre, he thought: and after the theatre she went to have supper somewhere... I'll wait a little.

And he remained there, waiting... Half an hour passed, an hour... He walked down the corridor and chatted to a sleepy servant... Downstairs the clock in the hotel hall struck three... Finally he lost patience and began slowly to go down the stairs to the exit... But Fate took pity on him...

At the very entrance he met a tall, brown-haired, emaciated woman wrapped up in a long boa. Close on her heels followed a gentleman wearing dark glasses and an astrakhan cap.

"Excuse me," Vasili Ivanovich addressed the lady. "Could I trouble you for a moment?"

The lady and gentleman frowned.

"I won't be a moment," the lady said to the man, and went with Vasili Ivanovich towards the gas bracket… "What do you want?"

"I've come to see you… on business, Nadine," began Vasili Ivanovich, stuttering… "It's a pity you've got that gentleman with you, or I'd tell you all about it…"

"Well, what is it? I'm in a hurry!"

"You've got yourself some new admirers, so you're in a hurry! You're a fine one, I must say! Why did you send me packing at Christmas time? You didn't want to live with me because… because I didn't supply you with sufficient means of existence… Well, it turns out that you were wrong… Yes… Do you remember that ticket I gave you on your name-day? Well, read this! It's won 75,000 roubles!"

The lady took the newspaper in her hands, and with greedy, almost frightened eyes she began to search for the telegram from Petersburg… And she found it…

At that very same time, other eyes, red with tears and dulled by grief, almost crazy, were looking for the ticket in a casket… Those eyes searched for it all night, and did not find it. The ticket had been stolen, and Olga Alexeyevna knew who had stolen it.

That same night red-haired Nikolai Borisych was tossing from side to side and trying to fall asleep, but he did not do so before morning. He was ashamed of that slap.

The Mask

Aᴀɴᴄʏ-ᴅʀᴇss ʙᴀʟʟ ᴏʀ – as the local ladies called it – a *bal paré*, was being given in aid of charity in the Social Club at X***.

It was midnight. The non-dancing intelligentsia – there were five of them – who were not wearing masks, were sitting round a big table in the reading room and, with their noses and beards buried in newspapers, were reading, snoozing and, as the local correspondent of the metropolitan papers – a gentleman of very advanced ideas – expressed it, cogitating.

Strains of the quadrille 'Vyushka' reached them from the main ballroom. Waiters kept on running past the door, stamping their feet loudly and clattering crockery. In the reading room itself deep silence reigned.

"I think it'll be more comfortable in here!" a low, slightly smothered voice, which seemed to be coming from the stove, was suddenly heard to say. "Hop in here! This way, you lot!"

The door opened, and into the reading room came a broad, thickset man dressed in a coachman's costume and a hat with a peacock's feather in it, and wearing a mask. Behind him came two ladies in masks and a waiter with a tray. On the tray was a fat bottle containing liqueur, about three bottles of red wine and some glasses.

"This way! It'll be cooler in here," the man said. "Put the tray on the table… Sit down, *mardemoselles*! *Je vous prie à la trimonrin.** And you move up, gentlemen… and look sharp!"

The man swayed and swept some magazines from the table with his hand.

"Put it here! And you, you readers, move up; this isn't the time for newspapers and politics… Drop it!"

"Would you mind being a little quieter, please," said one of the intellectuals, looking at the mask through his glasses. "This is the reading room, not the bar… You can't drink here."

"Why can't I drink here? Does the table rock, or is the ceiling likely to fall in? Odd! But… I've no time for conversation! Drop those

44

newspapers... You've read a bit, and that's enough; you're very clever as it is anyway, and what's more you'll spoil your eyes, but most important of all – I don't want it, and that's that."

The waiter had put the tray on the table, and stood at the door with a table napkin over his arm. The ladies at once set to work on the red wine.

"How clever these people must be to like their newspapers better than these drinks..." the man with the peacock feathers began to say, pouring himself out a liqueur. "But in my opinion you, my dear sirs, like your newspapers because you haven't anything to buy drinks with. Am I right? Ha-ha! Reading! Well, what do they write about? You, gentleman in the glasses! What are you reading about? Ha-ha! Go on, drop it! Go on, don't be difficult! Better have a drink!"

The man with the peacock feathers got up and snatched the newspaper out of the hands of the gentleman in glasses. The latter grew pale, then blushed and looked in amazement at the other intellectuals – and they at him.

"You're forgetting yourself, sir!" he spluttered. "You are turning the reading room into a public house, you make so bold as to behave rowdily, snatch newspapers out of people's hands! I won't allow it! You don't know who you're dealing with, my dear sir. I'm Zhestyakov, the bank manager!"

"I don't care a damn whether you're Zhestyakov or not! And as to your newspaper – that's what it's good for..."

The man picked up the newspaper and tore it into scraps.

"Gentlemen, what is this?" stammered Zhestyakov in stupefaction. "It's odd, it... it's almost supernatural..."

"They're getting waxy..." laughed the man. "Fie, fie! You're in a funk! You're shaking in your shoes! That's how it is, my dear sirs! But jokes apart, I'm not keen on chatting with you... Because I want to be alone with *mardemoselles*, and because I want to have some fun and games here, I would ask you not to counterdict, but to go away... If you please, gentlemen! Mr Belebukhin, go to the devil! Why are you wrinkling your snout like that? I said get out, so get out! You'd better look sharp, or you'll get a kick in the pants if you're unlucky!"

"What is this?" asked Belebukhin, treasurer to the orphans' trust, blushing and shrugging his shoulders. "I can't even understand it...

Some cad or other bursts in here and... suddenly starts saying things like that!"

"What was that word – cad?" shouted the man with the peacock feathers, getting angry, and he hit the table with his fist so that the glasses jumped on the tray. "Who are you speaking to? Do you think that because I am wearing a mask you can call me names? You spitfire, you! Get out when I tell you. Bank manager, get out while the going's good! Get out, all of you, I don't want any of you swine here! Get along, go to hell!"

"We'll just see!" said Zhestyakov, whose very glasses were sweating from agitation. "I'll show you! Hey, tell the club steward on duty to come here!"

A moment later a small, red-haired steward wearing a blue ribbon in his lapel came into the room, out of breath from dancing.

"Would you please go out of here!" he began. "This isn't the place to drink. Please go to the bar!"

"Where did you spring from?" asked the man in the mask. "Did I send for you?"

"Please don't be familiar, and leave the room!"

"Look here, my good man: I'll give you one more minute... As you're the steward, and the chief person here, just you take these chaps by the arm and lead them out. My *mesdemoiselles* don't like it if there are strangers here... They're shy, and I want them in a natural state so as to get my money's worth."

"This preposterous autocrat obviously doesn't realize that this isn't a pigsty," shouted Zhestyakov. "Ask Evstrat Spiridonych to come here!"

"Evstrat Spiridonych!" resounded through the club. "Where is Evstrat Spiridonych?"

Evstrat Spiridonych, an old man in a police officer's uniform, was not slow in appearing.

"Would you please leave!" he croaked, his awe-inspiring eyes protruding and his moustache bristling.

"Why, he really frightened me!" said the man, and roared with laughter from sheer delight. "Honest to God, he did! What terrifying things one does see, strike me pink! Whiskers like a cat, eyes popping out... Ha, ha, ha!"

"I'd ask you not to argue!" Evstrat Spiridonych shouted with all his strength, trembling. "Get out! I'll have you thrown out!"

An inconceivable noise arose in the reading room. Evstrat Spiridonych, as red as a lobster, shouted and stamped his feet. Zhestyakov shouted. Belebukhin shouted. All the intellectuals shouted, but all their voices were drowned by the low, thick, slightly smothered bass of the man in the mask. Owing to the general confusion the dancing had stopped, and the public poured from the ballroom into the reading room.

Evstrat Spiridonych, so as to look imposing, summoned all the police officers who were in the club, and sat down to write a report.

"Go on, write, write," said the masked man, prodding at the pen with his finger. "What will become of me now, poor thing? Poor little hothead! What are you ruining me for – and me a poor little orphan! Ha-ha! Well? Is the report ready? You've all signed? Well, now have a look! One… two… three!…"

The man stood up, stretched to his full height, and tore off his mask. Having uncovered his drunken face and looked at everyone, admiring the effect he had produced, he fell into an armchair and guffawed joyfully. And he had indeed made an extraordinary impression. All the intellectuals looked at each other in embarrassment and turned pale, some of them scratched the backs of their heads. Evstrat Spiridonych groaned like a man who had unexpectedly done something extremely foolish.

They had all recognized that the ruffian was the local millionaire, a manufacturer called Pyatigorov, a "Honorary Citizen" who was well-known for his scandalous behaviour, for his philanthropy and, as the local paper had more than once remarked, for his love of enlightenment.

"Well, will you go away or won't you?" asked Pyatigorov after a moment's silence.

The intellectuals went out of the room on tiptoe, without saying a word. Pyatigorov closed the door behind them.

"But you knew it was Pyatigorov!" croaked Evstrat Spiridonych in an undertone a moment later, shaking the shoulder of the waiter who had taken the wine into the reading room. "Why didn't you say so?"

"He told me not to, sir."

"Told me not to! I'll put you in jug for a month, damn you. I'll give you 'told me not to'. Get out!! And you're fine ones, gentlemen," he turned to the intellectuals. "You started a riot! You couldn't even go out of the reading room for five minutes! You've made your bed, now you must lie on it. Oh, gentlemen, gentlemen! I don't like the look of it, I really don't!"

The intellectuals went about the club despondent, lost, guilty, whispering to each other, behaving as if they had a premonition of something unpleasant. Their wives and daughters, when they learnt that Pyatigorov was "offended" and cross, fell silent and began going home. The dancing stopped.

At two o'clock Pyatigorov came out of the reading room; he was drunk and walked unsteadily. He went into the ballroom, sat down near the orchestra and dozed off, lulled by the music; then his head drooped sadly, and he gave a snore.

"Stop playing!" the stewards made signs at the musicians. "Sh! Yegor Nilych is asleep…"

"Wouldn't you like me to take you home, Yegor Nilych?" asked Belebukhin, bending down to the millionaire's ear.

Pyatigorov pursed his lips exactly as if he wanted to blow a fly off his cheek.

"Wouldn't you like me to take you home?" Belebukhin repeated. "Or order the carriage?"

"Eh? Who? You… what d'you want?"

"To take you home, sir. It's time for bye-byes…"

"I w-want to go home… T-take me!"

Belebukhin beamed with pleasure and began lifting Pyatigorov up. The other intellectuals jumped to help him and, smiling pleasantly, they lifted the "Honorary Citizen" up and carefully carried him to the carriage.

"Why, only an artist, someone with talent, can fool a whole party like that," said Zhestyakov gaily as he helped him into his seat. "I'm really amazed, Yegor Nilych! I'm still laughing about it… ha-ha! And there we were, getting worked up and making a fuss! Ha-ha! Would you believe it? I've never laughed so much even in the theatre… A wealth of humour! I shall remember this memorable evening all my life!"

When they had taken Pyatigorov home, the intellectuals cheered up and became calmer.

"He shook my hand when we said goodbye," said Zhestyakov, very pleased. "So it's all right, he's not angry…"

"Please God!" sighed Evstrat Spiridonych. "He's a scoundrel, a despicable fellow, but still – a benefactor!… One can't treat him like that!…"

An Unpleasant Incident

THE DISTRICT DOCTOR, Grigory Ivanovich Ovchinnikov, aged about thirty-five, a thin, highly-strung man known to his colleagues for his short treatises on medical statistics and his passionate interest in so-called "social problems", was going round the wards in his hospital one morning. He was, as usual, followed by the male nurse, Mikhail Zakharovich, a middle-aged man with an oily face, lanky, greasy hair and an earring in one ear.

The doctor had only just started on his rounds, when a trifling matter aroused his suspicions. It was the following: the male nurse's waistcoat kept wrinkling itself into creases and stubbornly rucking itself up in spite of the fact that the nurse was constantly smoothing it down and adjusting it. The male nurse's shirt was also all crumpled and rucked up. White down was sticking here and there to his long, black frock coat, to his trousers and even to his tie. Obviously the nurse had slept all night without undressing and to judge by the expression with which he was now smoothing down his waistcoat and adjusting his tie, he felt uncomfortable in his clothes.

The doctor had a close look at him and saw what the matter was. The male nurse did not sway and he answered questions coherently, but his dull and sullen face, his bleary eyes, the gooseflesh on his neck and shaking hands, the disorder in his dress, and above all the strenuous efforts he was making to master himself, and his desire to camouflage his real condition, were witnesses to the fact that he had only just got up from bed, that he had not had enough sleep and that he was drunk, very drunk still from the night before.

He was in the throes of the painful after-effects of drink and was suffering and very dissatisfied with himself.

The doctor, who did not like his male nurse for reasons of his own, felt a strong desire to say to him: "I see you are drunk!" The waistcoat, the long-skirted frock coat, the earring in the fleshy ear suddenly filled him with disgust, but he restrained this unkind feeling and said softly and politely, as always:

"Have you given Gerasim his milk?"

"I have, sir," answered Mikhail Zakharovich also softly.

As he was talking to the patient, Gerasim, the doctor glanced at the temperature chart and, feeling a new wave of loathing mounting up, held his breath so as not to speak, but could not restrain himself and asked gruffly, in a choking voice:

"Why isn't the temperature entered on the chart?"

"Oh, yes it is, sir!" said Mikhail Zakharovich softly, but, having looked at the chart and convinced himself that the temperature had not, in fact, been entered on it, he shrugged his shoulders in embarrassment and muttered, "I don't know, it's probably Nadezhda Osipovna's fault."

"Last night's is not entered either!" continued the doctor. "All you care about is getting drunk, damn you! Even now you are as drunk as a coot! Where is Nadezhda Osipovna?"

Nadezhda Osipovna, the maternity nurse, was not in the wards, though she had to be present every morning when the dressings were changed. The doctor looked round and it seemed to him that the ward had not been cleaned, that it was untidy, that none of the things that ought to have been done had in fact been done and that everything was as rucked up, crumpled and covered with down as his male nurse's disgusting waistcoat – and he wanted to tear off his own white coat, swear, throw everything up, leave it and go. But he made an effort and continued on his rounds.

Gerasim was followed by a surgical case with inflammation of the cellular tissues in the right arm. He had to have a new dressing. The doctor sat down on a stool in front of him and busied himself with the arm.

That's all because they were celebrating someone's name day... he thought, slowly taking off the dressing. You just wait, I'll show you name days! But actually, what can I do? Nothing at all.

He felt the abscess on the swollen, purple arm and said, "A scalpel!"

Mikhail Zakharovich, in an attempt to show that he was firm on his legs and fit for work, rushed off and quickly brought a scalpel.

"Not that one! Give me a new one," said the doctor.

The male nurse trotted off to a chair on which was placed a box with the dressing material and began hurriedly rummaging in it. There was a lot of whispering between him and the maids, he kept shuffling the box on its chair, rustled something, dropped something twice, while the doctor sat, waited and felt his back itching with irritation as a result of the whispering and the rustling.

"Well, how long are you going to be?" he asked. "You probably forgot them downstairs…"

The male nurse came running up with two scalpels, but inadvertently breathed in the doctor's direction.

"They're the wrong ones!" said the doctor irritably. "I'm telling you in plain Russian, give me the new ones. And anyway, go and have a sleep, you reek like a pub! You're not in your right mind!"

"What other knives do you want?" asked the male nurse irritably, and slowly shrugged his shoulders.

He was annoyed with himself and ashamed because the patients and the nurses were looking straight at him, and to show that he was not ashamed he gave a forced smile and repeated:

"What other knives do you want?"

The doctor felt tears in his eyes and his fingers shook. He made an effort and said in a trembling voice:

"Go and get yourself some sleep! I don't want to speak to a drunk."

"You can only reprimand me on account of my work," continued the male nurse, "and if, say, I'm a bit drunk, no one has the right to tell me how to behave. I'm doing my work, aren't I? What else do you want? Aren't I doing my work?"

The doctor jumped up and, without realizing what he was doing, he lifted his hand and slapped the male nurse's face with all his might. He did not understand what he was doing it for, but had a great feeling of satisfaction at the fact that his fist got the male nurse right in the face and that a respectable, sedate and pious family man, well aware of his own worth, had swayed, bounced like a ball and sat down on a stool. He had a passionate desire to strike once more, but on seeing the pale, worried faces of the maids near the hated face, the feeling of satisfaction left him, he made a gesture of annoyance and ran out of the ward.

In the courtyard he met Nadezhda Osipovna, a girl of twenty-seven, with a pale-yellow face and loose hair, who was going to the hospital. Her pink cotton dress had a very tight skirt which made her take very many and very small steps. Her dress rustled and she shrugged her shoulders with every step she took and shook her head as if she was mentally singing a gay little tune.

Ah, the mermaid! thought the doctor, remembering that in the hospital the maternity nurse had been given the nickname of mermaid, and he was pleased at the thought that he would now tear a strip off that mincing, over-dressed woman, who was so much in love with herself.

"Where have you been?" he shouted as he came up to her. "Why aren't you in the hospital? The temperatures aren't charted, chaos everywhere, the male nurse is drunk, you sleep till twelve o'clock!... Please look for another job! You're not working here any more!"

When he reached his flat, the doctor tore off his white coat and the towel he had tied round his waist, threw them both angrily into a corner and began pacing up and down his study.

"God, what people, what people!" he muttered. "Enemies of all work, that's what they are – they're not assistants! I can't work any more – I'm at the end of my tether. I'll leave!"

His heart was beating fast, he was trembling all over and wanted to weep; and to get rid of these feelings he began to soothe himself with the thought of how right he was and how well he had done to have struck the male nurse. To begin with, it was wrong, thought the doctor, that the male nurse should have obtained the job in the hospital not in the ordinary way but because he enjoyed the protection of his aunt, who was nanny to the children of the Chairman of the Rural Council (it was disgusting to look at that influential aunt, behaving as if she was at home whenever she came to hospital for treatment and claiming to be received out of turn). The male nurse had but a slight idea of discipline, knew little and did not at all understand whatever he did know. He was never sober, he was impertinent and dirty, he took bribes from patients and sold the hospital drugs on the sly. Everyone knew, too, that he had his own practice, and treated the young men in town for secret ailments and, besides, used his own home-made remedies for the purpose. It wouldn't have been half so bad if he had merely been a quack of a kind of which there were many, but he was a convinced and an inwardly protesting quack. He cupped the out-patients and did blood-letting for them by stealth behind the doctor's back, was present at operations with his hands unwashed, always probed wounds with a dirty probe – this was enough to see how profound and sweeping was his contempt for medical science with all its learning and pedantry.

After waiting till his fingers no longer shook, the doctor sat down at a table and wrote a letter to the Chairman of the Rural Council:

Dear Lev Trofimovich. Unless, on receipt of this letter, your Council dismisses male nurse Smirnovsky and grants me the right to choose my own male nurse, I shall feel compelled (not, of course, without regret) to ask you to consider me as being no longer doctor of N. hospital and to look for someone to take my place. Remember me to Lyubov Fyodorovna and to Yus.

Yours sincerely,

G. Ovchinnikov

The doctor reread this letter and found it short and insufficiently cold. Besides, the request to remember him to Lyubov Fyodorovna and Yus (such was the nickname of the Chairman's youngest son) was worse than out of place in an official business letter.

To hell with Yus! thought the doctor. He tore up the letter and began composing another:

Dear sir... he thought, sitting down at the open window and looking at the ducks and ducklings which tottered and stumbled as they hurried along the road, probably towards the pond; one duckling picked up on the road a length of pipe, choked and set up an anxious cheep; another ran up to it, seized the pipe out of its beak and also choked... Some distance away, near the fence, where young lime trees were casting the lacework of their shadows on the grass, Darya, the cook, was wandering round picking sorrel for green soup... He could hear voices... Zot, the coachman, with a bridle in his hand, and Manouilò, the hospital orderly, in a dirty white coat, were standing near a barn, talking about something and laughing.

That must be about my striking the male nurse... thought the doctor. The whole county will know of this row by the evening... Well then: Dear Sir, Unless your Council dismisses...

The doctor knew perfectly well that the Rural Council would never choose his male nurse in preference to himself and would rather have no male nurse in the whole county than lose so excellent a man as Doctor Ovchinnikov. Probably, immediately on receipt of the letter, Lev Trofimovich would arrive in his troika and start off: "What's this ridiculous idea, old man? My dear fellow, what's all this about? Good

God! Why? Whatever for? Where is he? Bring the beggar here! Sack him! We must sack him! He mustn't stay here another day, the old rascal!" After that, he would dine with the doctor, and after dinner he would lie down on that red sofa, stomach upwards, cover his face with a newspaper and snore; then having had his sleep, he would drink tea and depart, taking the doctor with him for the night. And the whole affair would end with both the male nurse staying in the hospital and the doctor not tendering his resignation. But in his heart of hearts the doctor wanted quite a different denouement. He wanted the orderly's aunt to triumph and the Council to accept his resignation without further ado and even with pleasure, in spite of his eight years' conscientious service. He was dreaming of how he would leave the hospital to which he was used, of how he would write a letter to the magazine *The Doctor*, of how his colleagues would present him with an address to show their sympathy for him...

The mermaid appeared on the road. With her dress rustling and taking small steps, she came up to the window and asked:

"Grigory Ivanych, will you be receiving the patients yourself or do you want us to do it without you?"

But her eyes were saying: "You lost your temper, but now you've calmed down and you feel ashamed, but I am magnanimous and take no notice of it."

"All right, I'm coming in a minute," said the doctor.

He again put on his white coat, girded himself with the towel and went to the hospital.

It was a bad thing to have run away after striking him... he thought; as if I was embarrassed or frightened... Behaved like a schoolboy... Very bad!

He thought that when he entered the ward the patients would be too embarrassed to look at him and that he would also feel ill at ease, but when he came in the patients were calmly lying in their beds and paid scarcely any attention to him. The face of Gerasim, the consumptive, expressed complete indifference and seemed to say: "He did something to annoy you, you gave him a bit of a lesson... Can't avoid that, old man."

The doctor lanced two abscesses on the purple arm and put on a dressing, then went to the Women's Ward, where he operated on a woman's eye, and all the time he was being followed by the mermaid, who helped him with an air as if nothing had happened and everything was fine. When he finished his round, he began the reception of out-patients. The window of the doctor's small consulting room was wide open. By merely sitting on the window sill and stooping down a little, one could see young grass about a yard away. The previous evening there had been a thunderstorm accompanied by a heavy shower and the grass therefore looked a bit trampled and glossy. The path running past the window and towards the ravine appeared washed, and the surgery's broken china, also washed and strewn on either side of it, gleamed in the sun and gave out rays of dazzling brilliance. And further away, on the other side of the path, young fir trees, clad in rich, green dresses, pressed close to one another, and behind them stood the birches with their trunks as white as paper, and through the birches' green leaves, lightly quivering in the wind, could be seen the bottomless blue sky. If one looked out of the window, the starlings hopping on the path would turn their stupid beaks towards the window and try to make up their minds whether to take fright or not. And having decided to do so, they would all, one after the other, rush off to the tops of the birches with a glad cry, as if making fun of the doctor who was unable to fly.

The freshness and the fragrance of the spring day came through the heavy smell of iodine. It was good to breathe!

"Anna Spiridonova," called the doctor.

A young peasant woman in a red dress entered the consulting room and made a short prayer to the holy image in the corner.

"Where's your pain?" asked the doctor.

The woman squinted mistrustfully at the door by which she had entered and at the door leading into the surgery, edged up to the doctor and whispered:

"No children!"

"Who else hasn't registered?" shouted the mermaid in the surgery. "Come in and register!"

The very fact, thought the doctor as he was examining the woman, that he has made me use force for the first time in my life marks him out as a brute. Never in all my born days have I used force before.

Anna Spiridonova went. She was followed by an old man with a venereal disease, then a woman with three children who had a rash, and work came in with a rush. The male nurse failed to put in an appearance. Behind the surgery door the mermaid's dress was rustling, she was making a clanking noise with the various utensils and keeping up a cheerful twitter; she constantly came into the consulting room to help give treatment or take prescriptions, and did it all with an air to show that everything was all right.

She is pleased I struck the male nurse, thought the doctor, listening to the maternity nurse's voice. After all, they get on no better than a cat and dog, and it'll be a red-letter day for her if he is sacked. The nurses are pleased too, I think… How awful it all is!

At the very height of the reception it began to seem to him that the maternity nurse and the other nurses and even the patients were deliberately trying to assume indifferent and cheerful expressions. It was as if they understood that he was feeling ashamed and hurt, but were too considerate to show it. And he, wanting to prove to them that he was not at all ashamed, shouted angrily:

"Hullo, you there! Shut the door, there's a draught."

But in truth he felt ashamed and had a heavy heart. He saw forty-five patients and left the hospital with slow and deliberate steps. The maternity nurse, who had had time to go to her flat and put on a bright-red shawl over her shoulders, was now hurrying away somewhere, probably to a case or on a visit to friends; she had a cigarette between her lips and a flower in her hair, which she wore loose. The patients were sitting on the threshold of the hospital and were silently warming themselves in the sun. The starlings were still making their noise and chasing the beetles. The doctor looked around him and thought that among all those even and quiet lives only two – the male nurse's and his own – stood out in sharp contrast and were as useless as broken keys in a piano. The male nurse was probably in bed trying to sleep off the effects of drink, but the thought that he had been in the wrong, had been insulted and had lost his job did not let him fall asleep. He was in a distressing situation. The doctor, on the other hand, never having struck anyone before, felt as if he had for ever lost his chastity. He was no longer accusing the male nurse or justifying himself; he was merely puzzled how it could have happened that he had struck someone – he, a decent man who had never even beaten a dog. When he had reached his flat, he lay down on the sofa in his study, turned his head to the wall and began to meditate thus:

He is a bad man and does harm to our work; in the course of his three years' service my resentment has been gradually increasing, but nevertheless, nothing can justify my action. I have taken advantage of the fact that I am in the stronger position. He is my subordinate, is in the wrong and, besides, he is drunk, while I am his chief, am in the right and am sober... In other words, I am in the stronger position.

Secondly, I struck him in the presence of people to whom I represent authority, and I have therefore given them a disgraceful example...

The doctor was called in to dinner... He ate a few spoonfuls of cabbage soup, got up from the table and lay down on the sofa again.

What shall I do now? he went on thinking. I must give him satisfaction as soon as possible... But how? As a practical man he considers duels to be foolish, or doesn't understand them. If I should apologize to him in that same ward and in the presence of nurses and patients, this apology would only satisfy me and not him; he is a bad man and would interpret my apology as cowardice or fear – fear that he will complain of me to the authorities. Besides, this apology of mine will completely ruin all hospital discipline. Should I offer him money? No, that is immoral and looks like bribery. If now, for the sake of argument, I should turn for the solution of the problem to our direct superiors, that is to the Rural Council... It could officially reprimand me or dismiss me... But it won't do that. Besides, it's a bit awkward, dragging the Council into the hospital's intimate internal concerns. And anyway, it has no right to meddle in those things...

About three hours after dinner the doctor, on his way to the pond for a bathe, was thinking:

Or should I do as everyone else does on these occasions? I mean, let him take legal action. I'm definitely the guilty party, I shall not try to defend myself and the magistrate will give me a prison sentence. In this way the offended party will be satisfied and those who take me to represent authority will see that I was in the wrong.

He liked that idea. He was pleased and began to think that the problem was solved satisfactorily and that there could not be a more just solution.

Well then, that's excellent! he thought, as he got into the water and watched shoals of small, golden carp scuttling away in all directions – let him take legal action... He can do it all the more easily as our official relationship is at an end and after this row one of us must leave the hospital anyway...

In the evening the doctor ordered the gig to be made ready as he wanted to go to the District Military Commander for a game of vint.

He was quite ready and was standing in the middle of the study in his hat and coat, putting on his gloves, when the outside door opened with a squeak and someone quietly entered the hall.

"Who is there?" asked the doctor.

"It's me, sir..." said the man who had come in, in a dull voice.

The doctor's heart suddenly began to beat violently and he grew cold from shame and a kind of incomprehensible fear. The male nurse Mikhail Zakharovich (for it was he) quietly cleared his throat and entered the study with some hesitation. He waited a little and then said in a dull, guilty voice:

"I'm sorry, Grigory Ivanych!"

The doctor felt embarrassed and did not know what to say. He saw that the male nurse had come to him in order to grovel and apologize, not out of Christian humility and not for the sake of annihilating the offender with his humility, but because he had figured it all out as follows: "I shall make an effort and will apologize, and perhaps I shan't be sacked and shan't be deprived of my daily bread..." What could be more offensive to human dignity?

"I'm sorry..." repeated the male nurse.

"Listen..." began the doctor, trying not to look at him and still at a loss as to what to say. "Listen... I have offended you and... and I must bear the consequences, that is I must give you satisfaction... You don't believe in duels... As a matter of fact, I don't believe in duels either. I have offended you and you... you can lodge an official complaint with the J.P. and I shall pay the penalty... But we cannot both of us remain here... One of us, you or I, must go." (Good Heavens! I'm not saying the right thing to him! thought the doctor with horror. How silly, how silly!) "In fact, you lodge an official complaint! But we can no longer work together! You or I... Lodge it tomorrow!"

The male nurse looked sullenly at the doctor, and his dark, lustreless eyes reflected the frankest possible contempt. He had always considered the doctor as an impractical and crotchety child, and now despised him for his shiver and for the incomprehensible fluster of his speech...

"And so I shall," he said with sullen spite.

"Go on then, lodge it!"

"I suppose you think I won't? I certainly shall... You have no right to fight. And you ought to be ashamed of yourself. Drunken peasants may fight, but you – you're an educated man..."

58

All the doctor's pent-up hatred suddenly flared up and he yelled at the top of his voice:

"Get out!"

The male nurse took himself off reluctantly (he gave the impression of wanting to say something else), went out into the hall and stopped there, deep in thought. Then he evidently made up his mind and resolutely left the house.

"How silly, how silly!" muttered the doctor when he had gone. "How silly and how trite it all is!"

He felt that his behaviour towards the male nurse just then had been childish, and saw now that all his thoughts about legal proceedings were not clever, and did not solve the problem but merely complicated it.

How silly! he thought when he was sitting in his gig and afterwards when playing vint with the Military Commander.

Have I really so little education and know life so little that I'm unable to solve this simple problem? But what should I do?

The next morning the doctor saw the male nurse's wife getting into a cart and driving off somewhere and thought: she must be going to his aunt. Let her!

The hospital was carrying on without a male nurse. An official statement had to be sent to the Rural Council, and the doctor could not think of the form the letter should take. The sense of the letter was now to be as follows: "I want you to dismiss the male nurse, though I am the guilty party, and he is not." But to express this thought without making it sound both stupid and disgraceful was, for a decent individual, almost impossible.

Some two or three days later, it was reported to the doctor that the male nurse had been to see Lev Trofimovich with an official complaint. The Chairman of the Rural Council did not let him say a single word, stamped his feet and sent him packing, screaming at him: "I know you! Out! I don't want to listen!" From Lev Trofimovich the male nurse went to the Rural Council and there served up a libellous statement in which he did not mention the slap in the face and asked for nothing for himself but reported to the Council that the doctor had several times in his presence passed unfavourable comment on the Council and its Chairman, that the doctor gave wrong treatment, was remiss in his visits to patients, etc. When he had heard this, the doctor laughed and thought: what a fool! And he felt ashamed and sorry that the male nurse should be behaving so stupidly; the more stupidly a man behaves in his own defence, the more defenceless and weak he obviously is.

Precisely a week after the morning described above, the doctor received a summons from the J.P.

Now that's really silly, he thought as he signed the receipt. Nothing could be sillier.

And on his way to the J.P. one dull and quiet morning he no longer felt ashamed, but annoyed and disgusted. He cursed himself, the male nurse and the circumstances…

"I'll just say in court: go to hell all of you!" he grumbled irritably. "You are all jackasses and you don't understand a thing!"

As he approached the J.P.'s office he saw on the threshold three of his nurses, who had been summoned as witnesses, and the mermaid. At the sight of the witnesses and the cheerful maternity nurse, who was showing her impatience by shuffling from one foot to the other and who blushed from sheer delight on seeing the chief character of the forthcoming case, the doctor wanted to fly at them like a hawk and stun them with the words: "Who has given you permission to leave the hospital? Please go back this minute", but he forbore and tried to look calm as he made his way through the crowd of peasants to the office. The office was empty and the J.P.'s chain of office was hanging on the back of an armchair. The doctor went into the secretary's room. There he saw a thin-faced young man in a linen coat with bulging pockets – that was the secretary – and the male nurse, who was sitting at a table and from nothing to do was turning over the pages of summons notices. When the doctor came in, the secretary got up; the male nurse was overcome with confusion and also got up.

"Alexander Arkhipovich has not been in yet?" asked the doctor, feeling shy.

"Not yet. He is at home…" answered the secretary.

The office was situated in a lodge within the grounds of the J.P.'s park, while the J.P. himself lived in the big house. The doctor left the office and made his way slowly to the house. He found Alexander Arkhipovich at his samovar in the dining room. The J.P., without coat or waistcoat and with his shirt unbuttoned on the chest, was standing at the table and, holding a teapot with both hands, was pouring coffee-coloured tea into his glass; on seeing his guest he quickly took another glass, filled it and asked without even greeting him:

"Sugar or no sugar?"

A long time ago the Justice had served in the cavalry; now, as a reward for his many years work as a J.P., he had been given an honorary Civil Service rank, but still kept his military uniform and his military habits. He had a long policeman's moustache and trousers with piping down the side, and all his words and actions were imbued with military elegance. When he spoke he held his head slightly thrown back, garnished his speech with juicy "E-er's" which made him sound like a general, shrugged his shoulders and rolled his eyes; whenever he greeted anyone or offered a light for a cigarette he clicked his heels, and when he walked he let his spurs ring so carefully and tenderly, as if each time they rang it caused him unbearable pain. Having made the doctor sit down to his tea, he patted himself on his broad chest and belly, heaved a deep sigh and said:

"Oh yes… Wouldn't you like some e-er… vodka and a snack perhaps? E-er?"

"No thanks, I'm not hungry."

Both felt that they could not avoid talking about the hospital row, and both felt embarrassed. The doctor was silent. The Justice with one elegant wave of his hand caught a mosquito that had just bitten him on the chest, examined it carefully from all sides and let it go, then sighed deeply, looked at the doctor and asked slowly and deliberately:

"Listen, why don't you sack him?"

The doctor caught a note of sympathy in his voice; he suddenly became sorry for himself and he felt tired and broken as a result of the mess-up he had lived through in the last week. He got up from the table with the air of a man whose patience was at last exhausted, frowned in irritation and said, shrugging his shoulders:

"Sack him! The way you all talk, really… Amazing, the way you all talk! How can I possibly sack him? You sit here and think that I'm boss in my hospital and that I can do whatever I want! Amazing, the way you all talk! How can I possibly sack a male nurse if his aunt is nanny to Lev Trofimovich's children and if Lev Trofimovich needs such intriguers and flunkeys as this Zakharovich? What can I do if the local authorities don't care a brass farthing for us doctors and throw every difficulty in our path? To hell with them. I don't want to work, and that's the end of it! I just don't want to!"

"Come, come now, old man… You attach far too much importance, so to speak, to…"

"The Marshal of Nobility tries as hard as he can to prove that we are nihilists, all of us, spies on us, and treats us as if we were his clerks. What right has he got to come to my hospital in my absence and question nurses and patients? Isn't that insulting behaviour? And that half-wit of yours, Semyon Alexeych, who walks behind his own plough and doesn't believe in medicine because he is as strong and healthy as a bull, calls us drones publicly and to our faces and grudges us a crust of bread. Damn him! I work here from morn till night, never take any rest, I'm more necessary here than all these half-wits, pious humbugs, reformers and other clowns taken together. I have sacrificed my health for the sake of my work, and all the thanks I get is to be grudged a crust of bread! Thank you very much! And everyone thinks he has the right to poke his nose into other people's business, teach, control! That Rural Councillor of yours, Kamchatsky, took the doctors to task at a local government meeting because we use a lot of potassium iodide and advised us to be careful in the use of cocaine! What does he know about it, I ask you? It's none of his business! Why doesn't he teach you how to judge?"

"But then, old man, he has no manners at all, he is a boor... You can't pay any attention to him."

"No manners at all and a boor, and yet you have elected that clown to the Council and you let him poke his nose into everything! You smile, I see. You think all this is trivial and trifling, but can't you see these trifles are so numerous that life is made up of them, like a mountain out of grains of sand! I can't any more! I'm at the end of my tether, Alexander Arkhipych! A little more and I can assure you I'll not only slap people's faces, I'll take to shooting them! Can't you understand my nerves aren't made of steel! I'm no less of a human being than you are..."

The doctor's eyes filled with tears and his voice shook; he turned away and looked out of the window. There was a silence.

"Ye-yes, my dear fellow..." muttered the Justice thoughtfully. "On the other hand, if you look at it dispassionately, there is..." (the Justice caught a mosquito, screwed up his eyes into very narrow slits, looked at it from every side, pressed it and threw it into a hand bowl) "...there is really no reason to sack him. Sack him and you'll get another in his place, just like him, and even perhaps a bit worse. You can change hundreds of times, but you won't find a good man... they're all rascals." (the Justice scratched himself under the armpits and slowly lit a cigarette) "You must reconcile yourself to this evil. I must admit tha-at nowadays you can find honest, sober and reliable workers only among the intelligentsia and the peasants, that is among these two extremes – that's all. You can, so to speak, find a very honest doctor, an excellent pedagogue, a very honest ploughman or smith, but the in-between classes, I mean, so to speak, men who have left the people but have not reached the intelligentsia, are an unreliable element. It's most difficult to find an honest and sober male nurse, clerk, bailiff and so on. Extremely difficult! Law has been my profession since the year dot, and in the whole course of that time I have never had one single honest and sober clerk, even though I've sacked masses of them in my day. They're people without any moral discipline, to say nothing of principles, so to speak…"

What's he saying it for? thought the doctor. We are not saying the things we should.

"Well now, only last Friday," continued the Justice, "my Dyazhinsky played the following trick. Just imagine: he invited some drunkards to spend the evening with him. I'm dashed if I know who they were, and they all drank themselves silly right through the night in the office. How do you like that? I have nothing against drink. Let people drink as much as they like, but why let strangers into the office? Just think, how long would it take to filch a document or a promissory note or something out of a file? No time at all! And do you know, after that orgy I had to spend about two days checking all the files to see if anything had disappeared… Well, what can you do with the rascal? Sack him? All right… And where's your guarantee that the next one won't be worse?"

"Besides, how can you sack him?" said the doctor. "It's easy enough to talk about sacking a man… But how can I sack him and deprive him of a crust of bread if I know that he has a family and will go hungry? Where will he go to with his family?"

Damn it all, I'm not saying the right things! he thought and it seemed odd to him that however hard he tried he could not fix his attention on a single definite thought or a single feeling. That's because I have a shallow mind and don't know how to exercise it, he thought.

"The in-between man, as you've called him, is unreliable," he continued. "We sack him, curse him, slap his face, but we should really try and see things from his point of view, too. He's neither peasant nor gentry, neither fish nor fowl; his past is bitter; his present is made up of a salary of twenty-five roubles a month, a hungry family and a dead-end job; in the future he will still have the same twenty-five roubles and a dead-end job, were he to stay there for a hundred years. He has no education and no property, no time to read and go to church, and he can't even hear what we have to say, because we don't let him come near us. And so he lives on from day to day till he dies, without a hope for a better future, on a starvation diet, terrified of being thrown out of his free flat at any moment, not knowing where his children's next home will be. And this being so, how can he possibly not take to drink or steal, you tell me that! And what principles can there be in these circumstances?"

We seem to have got on to social problems, he thought. And goodness, how incoherent we are about them, too. Good God! And what's it all for, anyway?

There was a sound of bells. Someone drove into the front yard and drove up first to the office and then to the steps of the big house.

"There he is himself," said the Justice, looking out of the window. "You'll get it hot and proper!"

"And you – you let me go as quickly as possible..." said the doctor. "Examine my case out of turn if you can. I have no time, really."

"All right, all right... Only I don't know yet if this case comes under my jurisdiction, old man. Your relations with the male nurse are, so to speak, official, you know, and besides you biffed him in the execution of his official duties. Anyway, I don't really know. Let's ask Lev Trofimovich now."

They heard hurried footsteps and heavy breathing and then Lev Trofimovich, the Chairman of the Rural Council, appeared in the doorway – a grey-haired old man with a bald patch, a long beard and red eyelids.

"Good morning..." he said, panting. "Ugh, my goodness! Well, Justice, get me some kvas! Oh, Lord..."

He lowered himself into an armchair, but jumped up at once, ran up to the doctor and, staring at him angrily, began to speak in a squeaky tenor:

"I'm very... I'm extremely grateful to you Grigory Ivanych! Much obliged, thank you! I'll never, never forget it! Friends don't act this way!

Think what you please, but you're really being unscrupulous even! Why didn't you let me know? Who do you think I am? Who? An enemy of yours or a stranger? Am I an enemy of yours? Have I ever refused you anything? Eh?"

Still staring and moving his fingers, the Chairman drank his kvas, quickly wiped his lips and continued:

"Thank you very, very much, indeed! Why didn't you tell me? If you had had any feelings at all towards me, you'd have come to me and said like any friend would: 'Lev Trofimovich, old man, that's how things are... This is what's happened, etc., etc...' I'd have fixed it for you in a trice and there would have been no need for all this scandalous business... That old fool's gone right off his head, peddling his slanders all round the county, gossiping with the women, and you, disgracefully enough, if you will allow me to say so, you have started up God knows what, you've forced that fool to take legal action against you! Disgraceful, absolutely disgraceful! Everyone's asking me what the matter is, what's it all about, and here I am, the Chairman of the Rural Council, and I know nothing of what is happening at your place. You couldn't care less about me! Thank you very, very much, Grigory Ivanych!"

The Chairman made such a deep bow that he flushed crimson, then he went up to the window and shouted:

"Zhigalov, tell Mikhail Zakharych to come here! Tell him to come this minute! You ought to be ashamed of yourself!" he said, as he left the window. "Even my wife felt hurt, and yet you couldn't be more of a favourite of hers. The trouble with you people is that you are all trying to be too clever! You're all eager to do things in oh! such a clever way and all according to principles and all with such cunning embellishments and all you succeed in doing is simply to cast aspersions on others."

"You are eager not to be too clever, and what do you succeed in doing?" asked the doctor.

"What do we succeed in doing? What we succeed in doing is that if I hadn't arrived here you would have disgraced both yourself and us... You should count yourself lucky that I have arrived!"

The male nurse came in and halted on the threshold. The Chairman stood sideways to him, put his hands in his pockets, cleared his throat and said:

"Apologize to the doctor at once!"

The doctor blushed and rushed out of the room.

"There, you see, the doctor doesn't want to accept your apologies!" continued the Chairman. "He wants you to prove that you are really sorry by the way you behave and not merely in words. Do you give me your word that from this day onwards you will obey and will lead a sober existence?"

"I do…" said the male nurse sullenly in a deep bass.

"Look out now! You better be careful! You'll lose your job in no time if I have anything to do with it! If anything happens, don't go about begging for mercy… Well, go home now…"

To the male nurse, who had by then become reconciled to his misfortune, such a turn of events was an unexpected surprise. He even turned pale from sheer joy. He wanted to say something and stretched out his hand, but said nothing, smiled sheepishly and went out.

"That's that!" said the Chairman. "And no need for a court case."

He heaved a sigh of relief and, with an air of having just accomplished something very difficult and important, examined the samovar and the glasses, rubbed his hands and said:

"Blessed are the peacemakers… Do pour me out a glass, Alexander. But perhaps you could let us have something to eat first… A drop of vodka, too, perhaps…"

"Look here, it's impossible!" said the doctor, coming back into the dining room, still red in the face, and wringing his hands. "It's – it's a comedy! It's wicked! I can't. I'd sooner have a hundred court cases than solve problems so farcically. No, I can't!"

"What do you want, then?" snapped back the Chairman. "Sack him? All right, I shall…"

"No, not sack him. I don't know what I want… but to have such an attitude to life… Oh, goodness me! It's torture!"

The doctor began to fuss about nervously and look for his hat, did not find it and sank exhausted into an armchair.

"Wicked!" he repeated.

"My dear fellow," whispered the Justice. "I don't quite understand you, so to speak… After all, you are the guilty party in this incident! Slapping people's faces at the end of the nineteenth century – in a way, you know, this is not quite the thing… He is a rascal, bu-u-t you must agree you behaved rashly, too…"

"Of course!" agreed the Chairman.

Vodka and snacks were brought in. Before saying goodbye the doctor ate a radish and washed it down with one glass of vodka. He did it quite mechanically. On his way back to the hospital, his thoughts were gradually being covered over with mist, like grass on an autumn morning.

Can it really be, he thought, that in the course of this last week people have suffered, thought and said so much only for everything to end in this trite and incongruous way! How silly! How silly!

He was ashamed of having implicated strangers in his personal problem, ashamed of the words he had said to these strangers, of the vodka he had drunk out of habit, of drinking and living to no set purpose, ashamed of his own shallow mind and its obtuseness. As soon as he was back in hospital he immediately began his round of the wards. The male nurse walked beside him, stepping softly like a cat, and softly answering questions... The male nurse and the mermaid and the other nurses pretended that nothing had happened and that everything was all right. And the doctor, too, did everything in his power to appear indifferent. He gave orders, lost his temper, joked with the patients, but one thought buzzed in his mind:

Silly, silly, silly...

The Eve of the Trial

The Defendant's Story

" SURE TO BE TROUBLE, SIR!" said the coachman, turning towards me, and pointing with his whip at a hare running across our road.

I had no need of a hare to tell me that my future was desperate. I was driving to the district assizes at X***, where I had to appear in the dock for bigamy. The weather was terrible. When, towards nightfall, I arrived at the post station, I was so chilled, soaked and stupefied by the monotonous jolting of the road that I looked like a man who had been covered with snow, drenched with water and badly whacked. I was met at the station by the station superintendent, a tall man in blue-striped underpants, bald, sleepy, and with a moustache which seemed to grow out of his nostrils and looked as if it would prevent him from smelling anything.

And it must be admitted that there was plenty to smell. When the supervisor, muttering something, breathing heavily through his nose and scratching his neck, opened the door of the station "rest room" and silently showed me my place of rest with his elbow, I was overwhelmed – almost to suffocation – by a strong smell of something sour, sealing wax and squashed bugs. The unpainted wooden walls were illuminated by a small tin lamp which stood on the table and was smoking like matchwood.

"Your place certainly stinks, signor!" I said, going in and putting my suitcase on the table.

The supervisor sniffed the air and shook his head incredulously.

"Smells as it always does," he said, and scratched himself. "That's just your impression, coming from outside. The coachmen sleep with their horses, and the gentlemen don't smell."

I dismissed the supervisor, and began inspecting my temporary abode. The sofa on which I would have to recline was as wide as a double bed, covered with oilcloth, and as cold as ice. Apart from the sofa, the room contained a large iron stove, the table with the above-mentioned lamp, someone's felt boots, someone's travelling handbag and a screen which barricaded one corner of the room. Behind the screen someone was peacefully sleeping. When I had made my inspection, I made the sofa ready for the night and began to undress. My nose soon became accustomed to the stench. I took off my frock coat, trousers and boots, stretched and scratched to my heart's content, smiled, hugged myself and began to skip round the iron stove, raising high my bare feet... This skipping warmed me up even more. After that it only remained to lie down on the sofa and go to sleep, but at that moment something odd happened. By chance my glance fell on the screen and... imagine my horror! A woman's head, with loose hair, black eyes, and teeth bared, was looking at me from behind the screen. Her black eyebrows were twitching, pretty little dimples were playing on her cheeks – so she must have been laughing. I was embarrassed. The head, noticing that I had seen it, also became embarrassed, and hid. With eyes cast down and a guilty look, I went meekly to the sofa, lay down and covered myself with my fur coat.

What a business! I thought. That means she saw me skipping! That's too bad...

And as I recalled the features of that pretty little face, I fell to dreaming. Pictures, each more beautiful and seductive than the last, thronged in my imagination and... and, as if to punish me for sinful thoughts, a sharp pain suddenly burned my right cheek. I clutched at it, caught nothing, but guessed what had happened: there was a smell of squashed bug.

At the same moment I heard a woman's voice. "It really is the very devil! These damned bugs obviously want to eat me up!"

Mm!... I remembered my good habit of always taking insect powder with me when I travelled. And I had not changed my habit this time. I took the tin of powder out of my suitcase in a matter of seconds. It only remained to offer the pretty head a remedy for bugs and – friendship would be struck up. But how could I offer it?

"This is awful!"

"Madam," I said in my most honeyed tones. "If I understand your last exclamation rightly, you are being bitten by bugs. Now, I have some insect powder. If you wish, then..."

"Oh yes, please!"

"In that case," I said, delighted, "I'll just... put on my fur coat and bring it to you..."

"No, no... give it me through the screen, but don't come here!"

"Of course I meant through the screen. Don't be afraid: I'm not a Bashi-Bazouk..."

"Who knows? You're just a passer-by, after all..."

"Mm… And even if I was to go behind the screen… there wouldn't be much harm in it… all the more so as I'm a doctor," I lied. "Doctors, policemen and ladies' hairdressers have the right to intrude in people's private lives."

"Is it true that you're a doctor? Seriously?"

"Word of honour. So may I bring you the insect powder?"

"Well, if you're a doctor, I suppose… But why should you have the trouble? I can send my husband to you… Fedya!" said the brunette, dropping her voice. "Fedya! Wake up, you mutt! Get up and go round the screen! The doctor's so kind, he's offering us some insect powder."

The presence of "Fedya" behind the screen was shattering news to me. I was thunderstruck… My heart was filled with the feeling which, in all probability, rifle cocks feel after a misfire: shame, vexation and sorrow… I felt so upset about it and, when he appeared from behind the screen, I felt that Fedya must be such a scoundrel that I almost shouted for help. Fedya turned out to be a tall, sinewy man of about fifty, with little grey whiskers, the set lips of a civil servant, and with blue veins running untidily over his nose and temples. He was in dressing gown and slippers.

"It's very kind of you, doctor…" he said, taking the insect powder from me and turning round to go back behind the screen. "*Merci…* You were caught by the snowstorm too?"

"Yes!" I snarled, lying down on the sofa and furiously pulling the fur coat over me. "Yes!"

"I see… Zinochka, there's a bug running down your little nose! Allow me to remove it!"

"All right!" laughed Zinochka. "You didn't get it! You're a senior civil servant, everyone's afraid of you, but you can't deal with a bug!"

"Zinochka, in front of strangers." A sigh. "You're always… Honestly…"

"The swine! They won't let me sleep!" I grumbled, getting angry without myself knowing why.

But soon husband and wife fell silent. I closed my eyes and, in order to fall asleep, began to think of nothing at all. But half an hour, an hour passed… and I was not asleep. Finally my neighbours, too, began to toss and turn and grumble in whispers.

"It's amazing, even insect powder doesn't do any good!" growled Fedya. "There's so many of them, these bugs! Doctor! Zinochka wants me to ask you why these bugs smell so loathsomely?"

We chatted. We talked about bugs, the weather, the Russian winter, medicine – of which I know about as much as I do of astronomy – we talked about Edison...

"Don't be shy, Zinochka... After all, he's a doctor!" I heard a whisper after the conversation about Edison. "Don't stand on ceremony, ask him... There's nothing to be afraid of. Shervetsov didn't do any good, perhaps this one will..."

"Ask yourself!" whispered Zinochka.

"Doctor," said Fedya, addressing himself to me. "Why does my wife get a congestion in her chest sometimes? A cough, you know... it feels congested, you know, a sort of clot..."

"That's a long story, it's impossible to say at once..." I replied, trying to dodge the question.

"Well, what if it is a long story? We've got plenty of time... we aren't sleeping anyway... Have a look at her, old fellow! I should tell you, Shervetsov is treating her... He's a good man, but... who can tell? I've no faith in him! No faith at all! I can see you don't want to, but do be so kind! You examine her, and while you're doing it I'll go to the superintendent and order a samovar to be put on."

Fedya shuffled off in his slippers and left the room. I went behind the screen. Zinochka was sitting on a wide sofa, surrounded by a quantity of pillows, and holding up her lace collar.

"Show me your tongue!" I began, sitting down beside her and frowning.

She put out her tongue and laughed. It was an ordinary red tongue. I tried to feel her pulse.

"Mm!..." I mooed, unable to find the pulse.

I cannot remember what other questions I put to her as I looked at her little laughing face – I only remember that by the time I had finished examining her I felt such a silly idiot that I definitely could not cope with any more questions.

It all ended with Fedya, Zinochka and myself sitting round the samovar; a prescription had to be written, and I composed it according to all the rules of medicine:

Rp. Sic transit   0.05
Gloria Mundi   1.0
Aquae destillatae   0.1
One tablespoonful every two hours
  Mrs Syelov
             Dr Zaitsev

In the morning I was on the point of leaving and, with suitcase in hand, was saying farewell for ever to my new friends, when Fedya buttonholed me and, holding a ten-rouble note, tried to make me take it:

"Oh, but it's your duty to take it! I always pay for all honest labour! You've studied and you've worked! You've sweated blood to acquire your knowledge! I understand that!"

There was nothing else to be done, I had to take the ten roubles!

That, in general outline, is how I spent the eve of my trial. I will not describe my feelings when the door opened in front of me and the bailiff showed me into the dock. I will only say that I grew pale and embarrassed when, looking round, I saw thousands of eyes fixed on me; and I felt my last hour had come when I looked at the serious, solemnly important faces of the jury...

But I cannot describe – and you cannot imagine – my horror when, raising my eyes to the table covered with red cloth, I saw in the public prosecutor's place – whom do you think? – Fedya! He was sitting there and writing something. As I looked at him I remembered the bugs, Zinochka, my examination of her – and it was not a mere shiver that ran down my spine, but the whole Arctic ocean... When he had finished writing, he looked at me. At first he did not recognize me, but then his pupils dilated and his jaw dropped weakly... his hands shook. He got up slowly and fixed a glassy stare on me. I too got up, not knowing myself why I did so, and stared at him...

"Will the defendant please tell the court his name and particulars?" the judge began.

The public prosecutor sat down and drank a glass of water. Cold sweat broke out on his forehead.

Well, now I'm for it! I thought.

Everything pointed to the fact that the public prosecutor was determined to cook my goose. He kept on losing his temper, went minutely into the witnesses' evidence, was crotchety, grumbled...

However, it's time I finished this. I am writing it in the courtroom during the luncheon interval... In a moment the prosecutor will make his speech.

I wonder what will happen?

Sinister Night

A Sketch

Dogs are barking – a short, snappy bark, followed by a nervous howl, like that of dogs that scent an enemy, but are unable to understand who or where it is. A variety of sounds float in the autumn air, disturbing the silence of the night: an indistinct murmur of human voices, a fussy, uneasy bustle, the squeak of a gate, the stamping of a horse.

Three dark figures are standing on an empty flower bed in the courtyard of Dyadin's farm, in front of the terrace of the manor house. Semyon, the nightwatchman, is easily recognizable by his bell-shaped sheepskin coat tied round with a string and with tufts of wool hanging down from it. Next to him stands a tall, spindly-legged man with sticking-out ears, dressed in a jacket – that is Gavrila, the footman. The third, wearing a waistcoat and shirt hanging outside his trousers, a rough-hewn man resembling one of those wooden toy men, is the coachman, and is also called Gavrila. All three are holding on to a wooden palisade and looking into the distance.

"Holy Virgin, have mercy on us," murmurs Semyon in a voice charged with emotion. "Terrible it is, terrible! The wrath of the Lord is upon us... Holy Virgin..."

"It's not far away, boys..." says Gavrila the footman in a bass voice. "About four miles, no more... I should say it's at the German farms..."

He is interrupted by Gavrila the coachman: "The German farms are more to the left. They are over there, the German farms, if you look at that there birch tree... At Kreshchenskoe, it is."

"It's at Kreshchenskoe," Semyon agrees.

Someone runs barefoot across the terrace, his heels striking the ground with a dull thud, and slams a door. The manor house is plunged in sleep. The pitch-black windows have a sullen, autumnal look about them, and only one of them shows a dim, weak light thrown by a small lamp protected by a pink shade. The young mistress, Marya Sergeyevna, is sleeping in the room with the lamp. Her husband, Nikolai Alexeyevich, has gone somewhere to play cards, and has not yet returned.

"Nastasya!" someone shouts.

"The mistress is awake," says Gavrila the footman. "Wait a bit, you two, I'll go and tell her what to do. She must let me take the horses and men, as many as there are, and I'll drive over to Kreshchenskoe and deal with that there in no time at all... Dull-witted people they are over there. Blockheads. I'll give them instructions what to do."

"You'll give them instructions all right! Look at him – wants to give people instructions and can't keep his own teeth from chattering! There are plenty of people there without you... Police officers and constables and gentry – they are all there, I dare say."

A glass door leading on to the terrace gives a clanking noise as it opens, and the mistress of the house makes her appearance.

"What's happening? What's all this noise?" she asks, coming up to the three silhouettes. "Is that you, Semyon?"

Before Semyon has time to answer, she recoils in horror and throws up her hands.

"My God, what a disaster!" she exclaims. "Has it been going on for long? Where is it? And why didn't you wake me?"

The whole southern half of the sky has flushed crimson. The sky looks inflamed and tense, and the sinister glow twinkles and shivers as if pulsating. Clouds, hillocks and bare trees stand out in high relief against the enormous crimson background. The hurried, fitful sounds of the tocsin can be heard.

"It's terrible, terrible," says the mistress. "Where's the fire?"

"Not far away, in Kreshchenskoe..."

"Oh, my God! Nikolai Alexeyevich is not at home, and I don't know what to do. Does the bailiff know?"

"He does, madam... He's gone over there with three barrels."

"Poor people!"

"And the worst of it is, madam, there's no river there. There's a rotten little pond, but even that's not in the village itself."

"As if water could put it out!" says Gavrila the footman. "The main thing is not to let the fire spread. They need people with some understanding who'd make them demolish cottages... May I have your permission to go there, madam?"

"There's no need for you to go," replies Marya Sergeyevna. "You'll only be in the way."

Gavrila coughs to indicate that he has taken offence, and walks away. Semyon and the other Gavrila, who cannot stand the cleverness and the haughty tone of the footman in the jacket, are very pleased with the mistress's rebuke.

"Of course he'd only be in the way!" says Semyon.

And both of them, nightwatchman and coachman, as if eager to show off the gravity of their outlook in front of their mistress, begin to pour out holy sentiments:

"The Lord has punished them for their sins... That's what it is! Man sins and takes no thought of it, but the Lord is there to sort of..."

The sight of the crimson sky affects them all in the same way. Mistress and servants alike suffer from an internal shiver and feel cold, so cold that they cannot keep their hands, heads and voices from shaking... They may be afraid, but they are even more impatient... They want to climb higher up, to see the actual fire, the smoke, the people. A thirst for strong sensations gets the better of fear and sympathy for other people's grief. Whenever the glow grows paler or seems to diminish, Gavrila the coachman declares joyfully:

"Well, it looks as if they're putting it out! May the Lord help them!"

But nevertheless a note of regret can be heard in his voice. And whenever the glow flares up and seems to expand, he sighs and throws up his hands in despair, but to judge by the panting and the puffing which accompany his efforts to stand up on tiptoes he must feel a certain pleasure. They all realize that they are witnessing a horrible disaster and they all shiver; but were the fire suddenly to stop they would have a feeling of dissatisfaction. Such a contradictory attitude is natural, and man – a selfish creature – should not be reproached with it. Beauty, however sinister, is beauty nonetheless, and human sentiment cannot refrain from paying tribute to it.

A faint sound of thunder can be heard: someone is treading heavily on the iron roof of the house.

"Is that you, Vanka?" shouts Semyon.

"It's me and Nastasya!"

"You'll fall, damn you! See anything?"

"Ye-es! It's at Kreshchenskoe, boys!"

"One could probably see from the dormer window," said Marya Sergeyevna. "Shall we go and look from there?"

The sight of disaster draws people together. The mistress – forgetting her pride – Semyon and the two Gavrilas enter the house. Pale, trembling from fear and craving for sensation, they go through all the rooms and climb the stairs to the attic. It is dark everywhere, and the candle held by Gavrila the footman does not make it any lighter, but only throws dim patches of light around. The mistress sees the attic for the first time in her life... The beams, dark corners, stove pipes, the smell of dust and spider webs, the strange, earthy ground under her feet – all this gives her an impression of a decor for a fairy tale.

So that's where the hobgoblins live? she thinks.

From the dormer window the glow appears wider and more crimson. The fire itself can be seen. A long, bright gold band stretches across the horizon. It moves and plays like quicksilver.

"It's certainly not just one cottage that's burning. Half the village's caught, I should say," says Gavrila the coachman.

"Listen! The bell's stopped ringing – the church must be on fire now."

"And it's a wooden church, too!" says the mistress, choking from the heavy smell given out by Semyon's sheepskin coat. "What a catastrophe!"

When they have had a good look, they go downstairs. Soon afterwards the master, Nikolai Alexeyevich, arrives. He has had a good deal to drink with his friends, and now, curled up in his carriage like a kitten, he snores loudly. They wake him up. He looks stupidly at the glow and mutters:

"Ahor... horse! Qu... quick!"

"Don't!" protests Marya Sergeyevna. "How can you possibly go anywhere in the condition you're in? Go to bed!"

"Ahor... horse!" he orders, swaying.

A horse is brought. He climbs into the saddle, shakes his head and disappears in the darkness. Meanwhile the dogs howl and strain, as if smelling a wolf. Women and boys collect around Semyon and the two Gavrilas. There is no end to the moans and the groans and the sighs and the signs of the cross they make. A man on horseback gallops into the yard.

"Six people burnt to death," he mumbles, panting. "Half the village – gone! Cattle lost too – goodness knows how many. The carpenter's – Stepan's – old woman – burnt to death."

The mistress's impatience reaches its bursting point. The movement and the talk egg her on. She orders the carriage and drives over to the fire herself. The night is dark and cold. The light, pre-dawn frost has slightly hardened the ground, and the horses' hooves make a dull thud on it, as if on a carpet. Gavrila the footman is sitting on the box beside the coachman and fidgets impatiently. He looks around, mutters to himself, continually gets up with an air which gives the impression that the fate of Kreshchenskoe depends on him...

"The main thing is not to let the fire spread..." he mumbles. "You must know how, whatever you do, and what do those country yokels know?"

After driving about three or four miles, the mistress sees something so extraordinary, so monstrous, that few people ever see it, and then only once in a lifetime, something not even the richest imagination could invent. The village is burning like an enormous bonfire. The entire field of vision is obscured by a sheet of moving, blinding flame, into which cottages, trees and church sink as into fog. Light almost as bright as sunlight blends with volumes of black smoke and lustreless steam, golden tongues slither up and down and lick the blackened shells of buildings with a greedy crackle, smiling and gaily winking as they do it. Clouds of red, golden dust drift swiftly to the sky and, as if to complete the picture, startled doves plunge into them. The air is filled with a strange medley of sounds: a monstrous crackle, the flapping of flames, resembling the flapping of thousands of birds' wings, human voices, bleating, mooing, the squeak of wheels. The church is awe-inspiring. Flames and clouds of thick smoke pour out of its windows. The steeple hangs down like a black giant in a mass of light and golden dust; it is completely charred, but the bells still hang, and it is difficult to see what is holding them...

There is a jostling crowd on either side of the road, reminiscent of a fair or the first ferry boat after the spring tides. People, horses, loaded carts, barrels, piles of personal possessions. All this moves, mixes, makes noises. The mistress contemplates this chaos, and hears her husband's shrill cry:

"Send him to the hospital! Pour water over him!"

Gavrila the footman stands on top of a loaded cart and waves his arms. Lit up by the fire he casts a long shadow, and he seems taller...

"Arson – that sticks out a mile," he shouts, whirling round like one possessed. "Hey, you there! You shouldn't let the fire spread! You mustn't let it spread!"

All around one sees pale, dull, seemingly wooden faces. Dogs howl, hens cluck...

"Look out!" cry the coachmen of neighbouring landowners who have driven over.

It is an extraordinary picture! Marya Sergeyevna cannot believe her eyes, and only the intense heat makes her realize that it is not a dream...

The Lodger

BRYKOVICH, A YOUNG BUT PREMATURELY BALD MAN rushed out of his flat onto the landing one midnight and slammed the door with all his might. He had formerly been a working lawyer, but was now doing nothing and living at the expense of his rich wife, the owner of an establishment called "Tunis" containing furnished rooms to let.

"Oh, the wicked, stupid, dull witch!" he muttered, clenching his fists. "Why has the Devil tied me to you!... Ugh!... I'd need to be a cannon to shout louder than that hellcat!"

Brykovich was choking with fury and indignation, and if at that moment, as he was pacing the long corridor of the "Tunis", he had come across some household utensil or a sleepy floor-waiter, he would have been only too delighted to give free play to his hands so as to work off his anger on something. He wanted to swear, scream, stamp his feet... And Fate, as if it understood his mood and wanted to gain his favour, brought him face to face with Khalyavkin, a musician who lived in Room No. 31 and was always late with his rent. Khalyavkin was standing in front of his own door, prodding the keyhole with his key and swaying visibly as he did so. He was breathing noisily and was sending someone to hell; but the key would not obey him and hit the wrong target every time. He was prodding convulsively with one hand and holding a violin case in the other. Brykovich swooped down on him like a hawk and shouted angrily: "Ah, it's you? Look here, my good man, when are you going to pay the rent? You haven't paid for a whole fortnight, my good man! I'll tell them not to heat your stove. I'll have you evicted, my dear sir. Damn you!"

"You are in my w... way..." answered the musician calmly. "Ore... rewar!"

"You ought to be ashamed of yourself, Mr Khalyavkin!" continued Brykovich. "You get one hundred and twenty roubles a month and could be punctual in your payments! It's unconscientious, my dear sir! It's mean to a degree."

At last the key clicked and the door opened.

"I mean, it's dishonest!" continued Brykovich, following the musician into the room. "I warn you, if you don't pay tomorrow, not later than tomorrow I'll take legal action. I'll show you! And please be good enough not to throw lit matches on the floor; you might set fire to my house! I will not have people of inebriate habits living in my rooms."

Khalyavkin looked at Brykovich with his drunken, laughing eyes and grinned.

"I really don't see why you are getting so worked up..." he muttered, lighting a cigarette and burning his fingers. "I don't see it! I don't pay my rent, agreed; I know I don't pay, but what's that got to do with you, can you tell me? What do you care? You don't pay any rent either, but I never pester you about it. You don't pay – all right then, don't."

"But how do you mean?"

"Just so... the la... landlord here is not you, but your most respected spouse... Here you... here you are just as much of a damned lodger as anyone else... The rooms aren't yours, so what are you worrying about? You take my example: I don't worry, do I? You don't pay a farthing's rent – and so what? Don't – if you don't want to. I am not worrying."

"I don't understand you, my dear sir!" muttered Brykovich and assumed the pose of a man who has been insulted and is ready at any moment to defend his honour.

"My fault, though! I quite forgot that you acquired the rooms as your wife's dowry... My fault! Though, as a matter of fact, if you look at it from the moral point of view," continued Khalyavkin, still swaying, "you mustn't get worked up, all the same... After all, you acquired them for no... nothing, for a pinch of snuff... They are, if you look at it broadly, just as much yours as mine... How did you app... appropriate them? By becoming the husband?... That's not much to boast of! It isn't a bit difficult to be a husband. You bring me twelve dozen wives here, my dear sir, and I'll be husband to all of them – free of charge! Do me the favour!"

The musician's drunken chatter apparently touched Brykovich on his sorest spot. He blushed and for a long time did not know what to answer, then came up to Khalyavkin and, giving him a furious look, struck the table with his fist with all his might.

"How dare you say this to me?" he hissed. "How dare you?"

"Now, now," muttered Khalyavkin, backing away. "That's playing it fortissimo. I don't see why you should take offence. I... I mean no offence, I mean it... as a compliment. If I were ever to come across a lady with such damn fine rooms, I'd snatch her up lock, stock and barrel... you just show her to me!"

"But... but how dare you insult me?" shouted Brykovich, and again struck the table with his fist.

"I don't understand!" said Khalyavkin, shrugging his shoulders and no longer smiling. "But as a matter of fact, I'm drunk... perhaps I have insulted you... In that case, I'm sorry, my fault! My dear fellow, forgive the first violin! I didn't want to cause offence in the very slightest."

"It's cynical even..." said Brykovich, mollified by Khalyavkin's repentant tone of voice. "There are things people don't talk about in that way..."

"All right, all right... I won't! My dear fellow, I won't! Your hand!"

"Particularly as I gave no occasion to..." continued Brykovich, in a hurt voice, completely mollified, and now stretching out his hand. "I never did you any harm."

"True enough, I shouldn't have ra... raised this ticklish problem... I let it slip off my tongue, like a fool, in my cups... Sorry, old man! I really am a brute! I'll now pour cold water on my head and get sober."

"It's a foul life, as it is, loathsome, and you add to it all with your insults!" Brykovich was saying, as he paced the room in his excitement. "No one sees the truth and everyone thinks and babbles as he likes. I can imagine what is being said behind one's back in these rooms! I can just imagine it! True I was wrong, it was my fault: it was silly of me to attack you in the middle of the night because of money; my fault, but... after all, you must excuse me, enter into my position, and yet... you throw filthy hints into my face!"

"My dear fellow, I'm drunk, don't you see! I repent and feel for you. Honest to God I do. And I'll let you have the money, old boy! As soon as I get it on the first of the month, I'll let you have it! Peace and harmony, then! Hurrah! Oh, my dear fellow, I love educated people! I studied myself once, in the Musical Acadecademy... can't say it right, damn!..."

Tears welled up in Khalyavkin's eyes, he caught Brykovich by the sleeve as the latter was pacing up and down, and kissed him on the cheek... "Ah, my dear friend, I'm as drunk as a coot, but I can see it all. Tell the floor-waiter to bring the first violin a samovar, old boy! You have a strict rule here – No walking about the corridor and no ordering of samovars after eleven o'clock; but it's something terrible how thirsty one is after the theatre!"

Brykovich pressed the bell-button. "Timofei, bring a samovar for Mr Khalyavkin!" he said to the floor-waiter who had now appeared.

"Can't be done, sir!" boomed out Timofei in a deep bass. "Madame has told us not to serve up samovars after eleven o'clock."

"Well then, I order you to!" shouted Brykovich, turning pale.

"No use ordering, if we are told not to…" grumbled the floor-waiter, leaving the room. "Can't be done if we are told not to. And that's that!"

Brykovich bit his lip, turned his head away and looked out of the window.

"What a position to be in!" sighed Khalyavkin. "Er, yes, I must say… Oh well, no use my feeling embarrassed, I understand, you know… your innermost self. All that psychology, I know it all… Well then, there's nothing to be done, you have to drink vodka, willy-nilly, if they don't give you tea! Will you have some vodka, eh?"

Khalyavkin got a bottle of vodka and a sausage from the window sill and made himself comfortable on the sofa to start on his drink and his snacks. Brykovich sadly contemplated the sot and listened to his endless prattle. Perhaps because at the sight of that tousled head, the half-pint bottle and the cheap sausage, he remembered his recent past, when he was just as poor, but free, and the expression on his face became yet gloomier, and he felt he wanted a drink. He came up to the table, emptied a glass and coughed.

"It's a horrid life!" he said and shook his head. "Foul! You see – you've just insulted me, the floor-waiter has insulted me… and so it goes on!… And why? Just like that, for no reason really…"

After his third, Brykovich sat down on the sofa and became thoughtful, propping up his head in his hands, then he sighed sadly and said:

"I made a big mistake! Oh, what a mistake! I've sold my youth and career and principles – that's why life is taking its revenge on me now. A desperate revenge."

The vodka and the sad thoughts made him very pale and even seemed to have made him thinner, several times he clutched his head in despair and said: "Oh, what a life, if you only knew!"

"Admit now, tell me honestly," he said, peering into Khalyavkin's face, "Tell me in all conscience, what do people here in general... think of me? What do the students living in these rooms say? I'm sure you've heard..."

"I have..."

"Well, what?"

"They don't say anything, they just despise you."

The new friends talked no more. They did not separate till dawn, when the servants began lighting stoves in the corridor.

"Don't you pay her... anything..." Brykovich was muttering as he left. "Don't pay her a penny! Let it be..."

Khalyavkin fell on the sofa, put his head on the violin case and snored loudly.

The following midnight they met again...

Having partaken of the joys of friendly libations, Brykovich never misses a single night now, and if he finds Khalyavkin is out, he goes into someone else's room, where he bemoans his fate and drinks, drinks and bemoans it again – and this he does every night.

The Dream

A Christmas Story

SOMETIMES THE WEATHER IN WINTER, as if vexed by human infirmity, enlists grim autumn's help and works in co-operation with it. Snow and rain whirl about in the gloomy, foggy air. The wind – raw, cold and piercing – knocks at the windows and roofs with violent fury. It howls in the chimneys and weeps in the ventilators. Dejection hangs in the air, which is black as soot... Nature feels sick... Everything is raw, cold and uncanny...

It was just that sort of weather on Christmas Eve 1882, before I became a convict, when I was working as a valuer in the pawnshop of Tupayev, a retired captain.

It was midnight. The storeroom – in which, at the boss's wish, I had my night abode and acted as a watchdog – was weakly lit by the blue flame of a small wick floating in oil. It was a large, square room, cluttered up with bundles, trunks, whatnots... On the grey wooden walls – from the chinks of which peeped out bits of tow – hung hare-skin and cloth coats, guns, pictures, a sconce, a guitar... As it was my duty to guard all this property at night, I lay behind the showcase on a big red trunk full of valuables, and looked thoughtfully at the flame of the lamp.

For some reason I felt frightened. Things kept in the storeroom of a pawnshop are frightening... At night-time, in the dim light of the lamp, they seem alive... And that evening, while the rain muttered outside the window, and the wind howled mournfully in the stove and above the ceiling, it seemed to me as if they too were howling.

Before they had turned up here, they had all had to pass through the valuer's hands – that is, through mine – so I knew everything about every one of them... I knew, for instance, that powders for a consumptive cough had been bought with the money obtained for that guitar... I knew that a drunkard had shot himself with that revolver; his wife had hidden the revolver from the police, pawned it at our shop, and bought a coffin. A bracelet which was looking at me from the showcase had been pawned by the man who had stolen it... Two lace chemises, marked No. 178, had been pawned by a girl who needed a rouble to get into a salon where she intended to earn some money... In a word, on each article I read hopeless sorrow, illness, crime, venal debauch...

On Christmas Eve these things were somehow particularly eloquent.

"Let us go home!..." it seemed to me that they were weeping with the wind. "Let us go!"

But it was not only the things that provoked a feeling of terror in me. Whenever I raised my head above the showcase and threw a timid glance at the dark, misted window, it seemed to me that human faces were looking into the storeroom from the street.

"What nonsense!" I nerved myself. "What silly sentimentality."

The fact was that a man endowed by nature with the nerves of a valuer was, on Christmas Eve, tormented by his conscience – an incredible and almost fantastic occurrence. The only conscience allowed in pawnshops is a pawned conscience; there it is understood to be an article that can be bought and sold – no other functions for it are recognized. Where on earth could I have got it from? I tossed from side to side on my hard trunk and, screwing up my eyes against the flickering lamp, I tried with all my strength to smother this new and unbidden feeling within me. But my efforts remained vain...

Of course, physical and mental exhaustion after a heavy day's work was partly to blame. On Christmas Eve the poor used to press into the pawnshop in crowds. On an important feast day, and in foul weather into the bargain, poverty is no crime, but a terrible misfortune! At such a time the poor look for a crumb in the pawnshop and receive a stone in its stead... On Christmas Eve so many people came to see us that we had to take three-quarters of the pawned goods into the barn because we had no room in the storeroom. From early morning till late at night, without stopping for a moment, I had haggled with paupers, squeezed pennies and half-pennies out of them, seen their tears, listened to their vain entreaties... By the end of the day I could hardly stand on my feet: I was tired out, body and soul. It was not surprising that I could not sleep now, that I was tossing from side to side and feeling frightened...

Someone knocked cautiously on my door... After the knock I heard the boss's voice:

"Are you asleep, Pyotr Demyanych?"

"No, not yet. Why?"

"You know, I've been thinking, shouldn't we open the doors early tomorrow morning? It's Christmas Day, and the weather's awful. The poor will rush to us, like flies to honey. So you'd better not go to mass tomorrow, but sit at the till… Goodnight!"

"I feel frightened," I decided when the boss had left, "because the lamp is flickering… I must put it out…"

I got out of bed and went to the corner where the lamp was hanging. The little blue flame spluttered weakly and flickered, and was clearly in the throes of death. Each flicker lit up the icon, the walls, the bundles, the dark window for an instant… And through the window two pale faces, pressed against the glass, were looking into the storeroom.

"There's no one there…" I argued. "I'm imagining it."

When, after blowing out the light, I was groping my way to the bed, something odd happened which had a considerable influence on my subsequent mood. A loud, shrill twang suddenly and unexpectedly resounded above my head, but lasted no more than a second. Something cracked and gave a loud whine, as if in great pain.

A string had broken on the guitar, but I was seized by panic fear and, stuffing up my ears, ran like a madman to the bed, tripping over the trunks and bundles… I buried my head in the pillow and listened, hardly daring to breathe, my heart in my mouth.

"Let us go!" howled the wind and the things together. "Let us go, for Christmas's sake! After all, you're a pauper too, you understand! You too have been through hunger and cold! Let us go!"

Yes, I had been a pauper too, and I knew what hunger and cold were like. Poverty had pushed me into the damned job of being a valuer, poverty had forced me to despise grief and tears for the sake of a crust of bread. If it had not been for poverty, would I have had sufficient courage to value in pence what is worth health, warmth, holiday joys? Of what, then, was the wind accusing me? Why was my conscience tormenting me?

But no matter how hard my heart was beating, no matter how fear and a gnawing conscience tormented me, exhaustion won the day. I fell asleep. I slept lightly… I heard the boss again knocking at my door, I heard the bells ringing for midnight mass… I heard the wind howling and the rain beating on the roof. My eyes were closed, but I saw the things in the storeroom, the showcase, the dark window, the icon. The things crowded round me and winked and asked me to let them go home. One after another the strings of the guitar snapped with a whine, snapped endlessly… Through the window looked beggars, old women, prostitutes, waiting for me to open up the shop and give them back their things.

Through my sleep I heard something scratching like a mouse. It scratched for a long time monotonously. I turned over and hunched myself up because of a strong blast of cold and damp. As I pulled up the bedclothes I heard a rustle and whispering voices.

What a bad dream! I thought. How uncanny! I wish I would wake up!

Some glass thing fell and broke. A flame flashed behind the showcase, and a light played on the ceiling.

"Don't stamp!" a whisper could be heard. "You'll wake up that old devil over there… Take off your boots!"

Someone came up to the showcase, looked at me and touched the padlock. It was a bearded old man, pale and hollow-cheeked, wearing a torn soldier's greatcoat and shoes tied up with string. He was joined by a tall, thin young fellow with frightfully long arms, dressed in a shirt which he wore outside his trousers, and a short, tattered jacket. They both whispered something, and fiddled about by the showcase.

Burglars! it flashed through my mind.

Although I was asleep, I remembered that a revolver always lay under my pillow. I felt for it quietly, and squeezed it in my hand. Glass tinkled in the showcase.

"Quiet, you'll wake him! Then we'll have to bump him off!"

Then I dreamt I gave a loud, wild cry and, frightened by my own voice, jumped up. The old man and the young fellow, spreading wide their arms, fell on me, but stepped backwards on seeing the revolver. I remember, a moment later they stood before me, pale and tearfully blinking their eyes, and begged me to let them go. The strong wind came through the half-broken window and played with the flame of the candle which the thieves had lit.

"Your honour!" somebody said in a tearful voice from outside the window. "Kind sir! Kind friend!"

I looked out of the window and saw the pale, emaciated face of an old woman, drenched with rain.

"Don't touch them! Let them go!" she wept, looking at me with beseeching eyes. "Why, it's poverty!"

"Poverty!" repeated the old man.

"Poverty!" sang the wind.

My heart ached, and I pinched myself in order to wake up... But instead of waking up I stood by the showcase, took the things out of it, and convulsively pushed them into the pockets of the old man and the lad.

"Take them, quick!" I gasped. "It's Christmas tomorrow, and you're paupers! Take them!"

When I had crammed the paupers' pockets full, I tied up the remaining valuables in a bundle and flung them to the old woman. Through the window I gave the old woman a fur coat, a bundle with a black suit, the lace chemises, and the guitar into the bargain. What odd dreams one does have! Then, I remember, the door creaked. The boss, constables and police officers appeared before me, just as if they had sprung out of the ground. The boss stood beside me, but I went on tying up the bundles, as if I did not see him.

"What are you doing, you scoundrel?"

"It's Christmas tomorrow," I answered. "They must have something to eat."

Here the curtain falls, and when it rises again it does so on a new setting. I am no longer in the storeroom, but in some other place. A policeman comes up to me, gives me a jug of water for the night, and mutters: "You're a one, you are! What a thing to try to do on Christmas Eve!" When I woke up it was already light. The rain was no longer beating against the window, the wind was not howling. Bright sunshine was playing gaily on the wall. The first to give me the compliments of the season was a police officer.

"And a happy house-warming to you..." he added.

I was tried a month later. For what? I assured the judges that it had been a dream, that it was unfair to try a man for a nightmare. Judge for yourselves – could I have given other peoples' belongings to robbers and scoundrels for no reason at all? And besides, who has ever heard of pawned things being given back without being redeemed first? But the court took my dream for reality, and sentenced me. I am a convict, as you see. Couldn't you put in a word for me somewhere, your honour? I'm not guilty, honest to God I'm not.

Out of Sheer Boredom

A Holiday Love Story

NIKOLAI ANDREYEVICH KAPITONOV, a lawyer, had his dinner, finished his cigar and went up to his bedroom to have a rest. He lay down, covered himself with a piece of muslin to keep off mosquitoes, and shut his eyes, but could not go to sleep. The onion he had had in his soup gave him such heartburn that sleep was out of the question.

"No," he decided after turning over from one side to another half a dozen times. "I'll never fall asleep today. Let's have a look at the papers."

Nikolai Andreyevich got up, threw a dressing gown over his shoulders and went, in his stockinged feet, to his study to get the newspapers. He could have no intimation that a sight far more interesting than heartburn and newspapers was awaiting him in the study.

As he crossed the threshold of the study, the following picture met his gaze; half-lying on a plush-covered sofa, with her feet on a little footstool, was his wife, Anna Semyonovna, a lady of thirty-three; her careless and languid pose resembled that in which Cleopatra of Egypt is usually depicted in the act of applying poisonous snakes to herself. The Kapitonovs' tutor, Vanya Stchupaltsev, a first-year engineering student, pink, clean-shaven, aged about nineteen or twenty, was kneeling by her side on one knee. The meaning of this *tableau vivant* was not difficult to grasp: just before the lawyer came in, the lips of the youth and the lady had fused in a long-drawn-out, sultry and languorous kiss.

Nikolai Andreyevich stopped dead in his tracks, held his breath and waited for what would happen next, but could not contain himself and coughed. At that the engineering student looked round and, seeing the lawyer, was seized with a momentary paralysis, then blushed, jumped up and ran out of the study. Anna Semyonovna looked embarrassed.

"Charming! Sweet!" began the husband, bowing and spreading his arms. "Congratulations! Sweet and lovely!"

"It's sweet of you, too, to eavesdrop!" mumbled Anna Semyonovna, trying to regain her composure.

"*Merci*! Wonderful!" continued the lawyer, grinning broadly. "It's all so nice, old dear, that I'd give a hundred roubles to see it again."

"There was absolutely nothing… You just thought… Silly, even…"

"All right, but who was kissing?"

"We were kissing, that's true, but as to anything more… I cannot follow what you mean."

Nikolai Andreyevich smiled ironically at his wife's embarrassed expression and shook his head.

"So you've developed a taste for fresh cucumbers in your old age, eh!" he began in a sing-song voice. "Tired of sturgeon, so it's sardines you want. You have no sense of shame! However, it's natural, I suppose! A Balzacian age! There's nothing can be done about it! I understand! I understand and sympathize!"

Nikolai Andreyevich sat down by the window and drummed with his fingers on the window sill.

"And carry on in the same way…" he said with a yawn.

"Don't be silly!" said Anna Semyonovna.

"The weather's damn hot! You ought to have ordered some lemonade or something. Yes, madam, I understand and sympathize. All these kisses, moans and sighs – oh, the heartburn! – it's all sweet and lovely, only you should not turn a boy's head, old dear. You shouldn't, you know. He is a nice, kind boy… a good brain and worthy of a better fate. You ought to have pity on him."

"You don't understand anything. The boy fell head over heels in love with me, and I wanted to give him this pleasure. I allowed him to kiss me."

"Fell in love…" mocked Nikolai Andreyevich. "You must have laid a hundred snares and mouse traps for him before he fell in love."

The lawyer yawned and stretched.

"An extraordinary thing!" he grumbled, looking out of the window. "If I were to kiss a girl as innocently as you have just done, I'd have God knows what heaped on my head: Villain! Seducer! Corrupter! But you, Balzacian ladies, you always get away with it. They mustn't put onion in the soup next time, or I shall die of heartburn… Ugh! Quick, look at the object of your love! Running along the drive, the poor mutt, like a scalded cat, without looking back. Imagines, I suppose, that I'll challenge him to a duel for the sake of a treasure such as you. Lecherous as a cat and timid as a hare. You wait, you mutt, I'll give you a fright! You'll be running about all right!"

"Oh, no, please don't say anything to him!" said Anna Semyonovna. "Don't give him a dressing down, he's not to blame in the slightest."

"I won't give him a dressing down, only just like that... for fun."

The lawyer yawned, collected the newspapers, picked up the skirts of his dressing gown, and wandered off to his bedroom. Nikolai Andreyevich lay on the bed for about an hour and a half, read all the newspapers, then dressed and went out for a walk. He walked round the garden cheerfully whisking his cane, but on catching sight of Stchupaltsev some distance off, he folded his arms, frowned and strode on like a provincial tragedian getting ready to meet his rival. Stchupaltsev was sitting on a bench under an ash and, pale and trembling, was preparing for a difficult explanation. He was trying to be brave, wore a grave expression, but was twisting himself into knots, as the saying goes. On seeing the lawyer, he grew even paler, heaved a deep sigh and meekly tucked his feet under the bench. Nikolai Andreyevich came up to him sideways, stood for a bit in silence and, without looking at him, began:

"Of course, my dear sir, you know what I want to talk to you about. After what I have seen, we can no longer remain friends. No, indeed! Emotion makes it difficult for me to speak... but you will understand without any words from me that you and I cannot live under the same roof. It is you or I!"

"I understand you," muttered the student, breathing heavily.

"This villa belongs to my wife, and you, therefore, will remain here, and I... I'll go. I have not come here to reproach you, oh no! Reproaches and tears will not bring back what has been irretrievably lost. I have come to ask you what your intentions are..." (Pause.) "Of course it is no business of mine to interfere in your private affairs, but you must agree that the desire to know about the future fate of a woman so passionately loved is not something you can interpret as interference. Do you intend to live with my wife?"

"But, how do you mean?" said the engineer, abashed, and tucking his feet even further under the bench. "I... I don't know. It's all rather strange."

"I see you are trying to evade giving a straight answer," growled the lawyer sullenly. "Well then, let me tell you straight out: either you take the woman you have seduced and provide her with the necessary means of existence, or else we have a duel. Love creates certain responsibilities, my dear sir, and as a man of honour you must see this! I am going in a week's time, and Anna and the family will come under your wing. I'll pay a certain regular sum for the upkeep of the children."

"If Anna Semyonovna so wishes," mumbled the young man. "I... I, as a man of honour, I'll assume... but I'm poor, you know! Although..."

"You are a man of honour!" said the lawyer in a hoarse voice, shaking the engineer's hand. "Thank you! Anyway, I'm giving you a week for reflection. Think it over!"

The lawyer sat down by the side of the engineer and covered his face with his hands.

"But what have you done to me!" he moaned. "You have shattered my life... you have taken away the woman I loved more than life. Oh no, I shall not survive this blow!"

The young man looked at him with anguish and scratched his forehead. He was frightened.

"You have yourself to blame, Nikolai Andreych!" he said with a sigh. "It's no use crying over spilt milk. Remember, you married Anna entirely for her money... then all your life you failed to understand her, tyrannized over her... disregarded the purest noblest impulses of her heart."

"She told you that?" asked Nikolai Andreyevich, suddenly taking his hands away from his face.

"She did. I know the whole of her life, and... and believe me, I became fond not so much of the woman in her as of the martyr."

"You are a man of honour..." sighed the lawyer, getting up. "Goodbye and be happy. I hope that all that has been said here will remain between us."

Nikolai Andreyevich heaved another sigh and strode homewards.

Halfway to the house he met Anna Semyonovna.

"Looking for your mutt are you?" he asked. "Go and have a look at the way I made him sweat!... So you've had time to make a confession to him! Strange ways you have, you Balzacian ladies, I must say! Can't use beauty and freshness as a bait, so you come up with confessions and pathetic little speeches! Stuffed him up with lies, you have! I married for money and I never understood you and I've tyrannized over you and this and that and a damn sight more..."

"I never said anything to him!" exclaimed Anna Semyonovna, blushing crimson.

"All right, all right... I'm being understanding, don't you know, putting myself in your place. Only I'm sorry for the boy. Such a nice boy, honest, sincere."

When evening came and twilight shrouded the earth, the lawyer went for another walk. It was a glorious evening. The trees were sleeping and looked as if no storm could wake them from their young, springtime slumber. The drowsy stars looked down on the earth. Frogs croaked and an owl screeched somewhere behind the garden. The short, jerky whistles of a nightingale's song could be heard from afar.

As he was passing under a spreading lime tree in the dark, Nikolai Andreyevich stumbled on Stchupaltsev.

"Why are you standing here?" he asked.

"Nikolai Andreyevich!" began Stchupaltsev, his voice trembling with emotion. "I agree to all your conditions, but... it's all so strange, some-how. Here you are unhappy all of a sudden... you suffer and say that your life is shattered."

"Yes. What then?"

"If you feel that you have been wronged, well then... then I can give you satisfaction, even though I do not believe in duels. If a duel will ease your mind however slightly, I can assure you, I am ready... a hundred duels if need be..."

The lawyer laughed and put an arm round the student's waist.

"There, there... enough of that! I was only being funny, my dear chap!" he said. "That is all rot and nonsense. That trashy, contemptible woman is not worth you wasting your words on and getting excited about. Enough, young man! Let us go for a walk."

"I... I don't understand you..."

"There is nothing to understand. A trashy, bad bit of fluff – that's all she is! You have no taste, my dear chap. Why have you stopped? Surprised I am saying things like that about my wife? Of course I shouldn't be saying this to you, but as you are in a way an interested party, it is no use concealing things from you. I'm telling you frankly: drop it! The game's not worth the candle! She told you nothing but lies, and as a 'martyr' she isn't worth a farthing. A hysterical Balzacian lady. Stupid and tells a lot of lies. I give you my word, my dear chap! I'm being serious..."

"But she is your wife!" said the student in surprise.

"Agreed! I was the same as you and got married, and now would be glad to get unmarried, but – woa!... Drop it, my dear fellow! It's not love, only mischief and boredom. If you want to flirt, well then there's Nastya just coming... Hullo, Nastya, where are you going to?"

"To get some kvas, sir!" they heard a woman's voice.

"I can understand that," continued the lawyer, "but all these hysterical women, martyrs... to hell with them! Nastya is a fool, but at least she has no pretensions... Shall we go on?"

The lawyer and the student came out of the garden, glanced back, both heaved a sigh, and went through the field.

A Disagreeable Experience

"CABBY, YOU'VE A HEART OF STONE. You've never been in love, my man, so you can't understand my psychology. This rain can no more put out the fire in my heart than the fire brigade can put out the sun. Damn it, how poetically I do express myself! You're not a poet by any chance, are you, cabby?"

"No, sir!"

"Well, you see…"

After groping in his pocket for it for some time, Zhirkov at last found his purse and began to settle with the driver.

"We agreed, my friend, on one rouble, twenty-five copecks. Receive your fee. Here's a rouble for you, and here's thirty copecks… Five copecks tip… Farewell, and remember me. But first take this basket and put it in the porch. Carefully now, the basket contains the evening dress of the woman I love more than life itself."

The driver sighed and reluctantly climbed off the box. After trying to keep his balance in the dark as he splashed through the mud, he succeeded in getting the basket to the front door, and put it down on the steps.

"What weather!" he grumbled reproachfully; and grunting and sighing, he reluctantly clambered back on the box, sniffing as he did so.

He clicked his tongue, and his little horse splashed off through the mud with some hesitation.

"I think I've got everything I need with me," reflected Zhirkov as he felt with his hand along the doorpost, searching for the bell. "Nadya asked me to go to the dress shop and fetch a dress – I've got it; she asked for sweets and cheese – I've got them; flowers – I've got them. 'All hail thou dwelling chaste…'" he sang. "But where's the bell, damn it?"

Zhirkov was in the complacent mood of a man who has just had supper, who has had a good many drinks, and who knows perfectly well that he will not have to get up early the next day. Moreover, after an hour and half's drive from town through mud and rain, warmth and

95

a young woman were awaiting him... It is pleasant to be chilled and soaked if you know that you will soon get warm again.

Zhirkov caught hold of the bell-button in the dark and pushed it twice. He could hear footsteps behind the door.

"Is that you, Dmitry Grigorych?" asked a female whisper.

"It's me, entrancing Dunyasha!" answered Zhirkov. "Open the door quickly, or I shall be soaked to the skin!"

"Oh, my goodness!" whispered Dunyasha, the maid, anxiously, as she opened the door. "Don't talk so loud and don't make a noise with your feet. The master has arrived from Paris, you know! He came back this evening!"

At the words "the master" Zhirkov backed away from the door, and for a moment was gripped by cowardice and a purely boyish terror, such as even very brave men experience when they are unexpectedly confronted with the possibility of meeting the husband.

What a to do! he thought, as he listened to Dunyasha closing the door very carefully and going back along the passage. What is this? Does it mean I must retrace my steps? Thanks very much, that's a bit unexpected!

And he suddenly thought it funny and amusing. His journey from town to country house to see her, in the dead of night and in torrential rain, seemed to him an amusing adventure; and now that he had run into her husband, the adventure seemed to him even more curious.

"A most entertaining business, it really is!" he said to himself aloud. "Where on earth can I go to now? Shall I drive back?"

It was raining and a strong wind was roaring in the trees, but in the dark neither rain nor trees could be seen. Water babbled in the drains and gutters, and seemed to be chuckling and teasing him maliciously. The porch in which Zhirkov was standing had no roof, so that he really was getting drenched.

He would come in weather like this, he thought, laughing. The devil take all husbands!

His love affair with Nadezhda Osipovna had started a month ago, but he did not yet know her husband. He only knew that her husband was a Frenchman by origin, that his surname was Boisot, and that by profession he was a dealer. Judging from the photograph which Zhirkov had seen, he was a hefty bourgeois of about forty with a moustache and a typical French soldier's face; looking at it, one wanted, for some reason, to give the moustache and the little Napoleon beard a tug and ask: "Well, what's the news, monsieur le sergeant?"

Stumbling and splashing through the liquid mud, Zhirkov walked a little way away and shouted:

"Cabby! Cabby!"

No answer came.

"Not a voice, not a groan," muttered Zhirkov, groping his way back to the porch. "I've sent my cabby away, and this isn't the sort of place you'd find a cab in – not even by day. What a fix! I shall have to wait till morning! Oh, damn, the basket will get wet through and the dress'll be spoilt. It cost two hundred roubles!! What a situation to be in!"

While he was thinking out where he and his basket could shelter from the rain, he remembered that, at the edge of the village, there was an open-air dance place and a covered bandstand next to it.

"Shall I make for the bandstand?" he asked himself. "It's an idea! But can I drag the basket there? It's so cumbersome, damn it... The cheese and the flowers can go to hell!"

He picked up the basket, but then immediately remembered that while he was going to the bandstand the basket would have time to be soaked half a dozen times.

"Oh, what a problem!" he laughed. "Lord, the water's gone down my neck! Brrr... Soaked, chilled, drunk, no cab... it only remains for the husband to jump out into the street and give me a sound beating with his stick. But what am I to do? I can't stand here all night, and anyway the dress would be ruined... I know... I'll ring again and give the things to Dunyasha, and then I'll go to the bandstand."

Zhirkov rang cautiously. A moment later he could hear steps behind the door and a light flashed through the keyhole.

"Oo ees Zaire?" asked a raucous male voice with a foreign accent.

Heavens, it must be her husband, thought Zhirkov. I must concoct some story...

"Excuse me, do the Zlyuchkins live here?" he asked.

"Zaire aren't any Zlyushkins here, damn you. Go to hell, you and your Zlyushkins!"

For some reason Zhirkov felt embarrassed, gave a guilty cough, and left the porch. As he stepped into a puddle and filled his galosh with water he spat angrily, but then immediately began to laugh again. At every turn his adventure was becoming more and more odd. He took great pleasure in thinking of how the next day he would describe his adventure to his friends and to Nadya herself, how he would imitate her husband's voice and the squelching of his own galoshes... His friends would certainly split their sides with laughter.

There's only one bad thing: the dress will get soaked! he thought. If it wasn't for the dress I'd have been asleep in that bandstand long ago.

He sat down on the basket to shield it from the rain, but more water fell from his soaked cape and hat than did from the sky.

"Oh, damn it!"

When he had been standing in the rain for half an hour he remembered his health.

That's the way to catch a fever, I'm afraid, he thought. What an extraordinary situation! Shall I ring again? Eh? I'll ring, yes, I think I will... If her husband opens the door, then I'll cook up some lie and give him the dress... After all, I can't sit here till morning! Well, come what may! Ring!

Full of schoolboy cheek, Zhirkov put out his tongue at the door and the darkness, and pushed the button. A minute's silence followed; he pushed it again.

"Oo eez zaire?" asked an angry voice with a foreign accent.

"Does Madame Boisot live here?" asked Zhirkov in a respectful tone of voice.

"Eh? What the devil d'you want?"

"Madame Katish the dressmaker has sent a dress to Madame Boisot. I'm sorry that it's so late, but Madame Boisot wanted the dress to be sent as soon as possible... by the morning... I left town in the evening, but... it's shocking weather... I could hardly get here... I didn't..."

Zhirkov did not finish what he was saying, because the door opened in front of him, and on the threshold, in the swaying light of the lamp, appeared Monsieur Boisot – precisely the same as he was on the photograph, with a soldier's face and a long moustache; however, in the photograph he was portrayed as a dandy, whereas now he was wearing nothing but a nightshirt.

"I wouldn't have bothered you," Zhirkov continued, "but Madame Boisot asked for the dress to be sent as quickly as possible. I'm Madame Katish's brother... and... and besides, the weather's shocking."

"Very good," said Boisot sullenly, his eyebrows twitching as he took the basket, "I sank your sister. My vife she vaited for zee dress till after tvelve. Some monsieur had promised to bring it 'er."

"And would you be so kind as to give your wife the cheese and flowers which she forgot at Madame Katish's?"

Boisot took the cheese and flowers, sniffed both of them and, without closing the door, stood still as if expecting something. He looked at Zhirkov, and Zhirkov looked at him. A minute passed in silence. Zhirkov remembered his friends, to whom he would recount his adventure the next day, and felt a desire to play some silly joke as the finishing touch to the whole odd business. But he could not think of a joke, while the Frenchman was standing and waiting for him to go.

"It's dreadful weather," muttered Zhirkov. "Dark, dirty and wet. I'm soaked through."

"Yes, monsieur, you are quite vet."

"And what's more, my cabby is gone. I don't know where to go. It would be very kind of you if you would let me stay here in the hall for a bit, until the rain stops."

"*Eh bien, monsieur*, take off your galoshes and come here. That's all right, you can."

The Frenchman closed the door and led Zhirkov into a small drawing room with which he was very familiar. Nothing was changed in the room, except that there was a bottle of red wine on the table, and that on some chairs, which were arranged in a row in the middle of the room, lay a very skimpy, narrow little mattress.

"It's cold," said Boisot, putting the lamp on the table. "I only arrived from Paris yesterday. Everyvere it's fine and varm, but here in Russia it's cold and these moustiquos... mistiquos... *les cousins*. Zey bite like 'ell."

Boisot poured out half a glass of wine, made a very angry face, and drank.

"I haven't slept all night," he said, sitting down on the little mattress. "*Les cousins*, and then some svine kept on ringing and asking for Zlyushkin."

The Frenchman fell silent and dropped his head, presumably waiting for the rain to stop. Zhirkov decided that good manners required that he should make conversation.

"You must have been in Paris at a very interesting time," he said. "Boulanger* retired while you were there."

Zhirkov went on talking about Grévy, Déroulède, Zola,* and discovered that the Frenchman was hearing all these names for the first time. In Paris Boisot knew only a few business firms, his aunt Madame Blessor, and not another soul. The conversation about politics and literature ended with Boisot once more making an angry face, drinking some wine, and lying down full length on his skimpy mattress.

Well, this husband's rights can't be particularly extensive, thought Zhirkov. The mattress is like nothing on earth!

The Frenchman closed his eyes; when he had lain there quietly for a quarter of an hour he suddenly jumped up, fixed his leaden eyes dully on his guest, as if in complete lack of comprehension, then once more made an angry face and drank some wine.

"Zese damned moustiques," he grumbled and, rubbing one hairy leg against the other, he went out of the room.

Zhirkov heard him waking someone up and saying:

"*Il y a là un monsieur roux qui t'a apporté une robe.*"*

Soon he returned and once more applied himself to the bottle.

"My vife she just coming," he said, yawning. "I understand, you vant some money?

From bad to worse, thought Zhirkov. It's very odd! Nadezhda Osipovna will appear in a moment. Of course, I shall pretend that I don't know her.

The rustle of a skirt was heard, the door opened slightly, and Zhirkov saw a familiar curly head, cheeks and sleepy eyes.

"Who is it from – Madame Katish?" asked Nadezhda Osipovna, but immediately afterwards, recognizing Zhirkov, she gave a cry, laughed and came into the room.

"It's you?" she asked. "What's all this pretence for? But how did you get so muddy?"

Zhirkov blushed, put on a stern expression and, at a complete loss as to how to behave, looked askance at Boisot.

"Oh, I understand!" guessed the lady. "You were probably frightened of Jacques? I forgot to warn Dunyasha... Do you know each other? This is my husband, Jacques, and this is Stepan Andreych... You brought the dress? Well, *merci*, my friend... Come, or else I shall fall asleep. Sleep well, Jacques..." she said to her husband. "You're tired after your journey."

Jacques looked at Zhirkov in amazement, shrugged his shoulders, and with an angry expression reached for the bottle. Zhirkov also shrugged his shoulders, and followed Nadezhda Osipovna.

He looked at the dull sky and at the muddy road, and thought:

How dirty! What strange places an intelligent man can get to!

And he thought of morality and immorality, of cleanliness and uncleanliness. As often happens to people who find themselves in some evil place, he remembered nostalgically both his study and the papers on his desk, and he longed to go home.

He walked quietly through the drawing room, past the sleeping Jacques.

He was silent all the way home, tried not to think of Jacques, who for some reason he could not get out of his head, and no longer talked to the cabby. His heart was as upset as his stomach.

His First Appearance

PYATERKIN, A JUNIOR BARRISTER, was returning in a simple peasant cart from the small provincial town of N***, where he had gone to defend a shopkeeper on a charge of arson. In his heart of hearts he felt more depressed than he had ever been. Humiliation, failure and insult had, he felt, been heaped upon him. He felt that that day, the day of his first appearance in court, for which he had waited so long and from which he had expected so much, had entirely ruined his career, his faith in mankind and his conception of the world.

To begin with, the accused had shamelessly and cruelly deceived him. Before the trial the shopkeeper had blinked his eyes in such obvious sincerity and had so frankly and simply protested his innocence that, in the eyes of a psychologist and physiognomist (both of which the young lawyer considered himself to be) all evidence against him appeared shamelessly far-fetched, mere fault-finding and prejudice. But at the trial itself the shopkeeper had turned out to be a swindler and a scoundrel, and the wretched psychology went to hell.

Secondly, it seemed to him that his, Pyaterkin's, behaviour at this trial had been impossible. He had stuttered, had muddled his questions, had stood up in front of witnesses and flushed stupidly. His tongue had altogether refused to obey him and had stumbled in ordinary speech as if it had been trying to get round a tongue-twister. He had spoken desultorily, as if in a coma, looking over the heads of the jury. And as he spoke he had the impression that the jury were looking at him with derision and contempt.

In the third place, and worst of all, both the public prosecutor, an old, experienced lawyer, and the opposing barrister had behaved in an unfriendly way. He had the impression that they had agreed beforehand to ignore counsel for the defence, and if they did glance up at him, it was only to make him the butt of their off-handedness, to scoff at him and to make a brilliant repartee at his expense. Irony and condescension were apparent in their speeches. As they spoke they gave the impression of apologizing for the fact that counsel was such an innocent little nincompoop. Finally Pyaterkin could bear it no longer. During the interval he rushed up to the opposing barrister and, trembling in every limb, reeled off a lot of rude remarks. Then, when the session was over, he caught up with the public prosecutor on the staircase and gave him a piece of his mind too.

Fourthly... But the enumeration of all that was troubling our hero and gnawing at his vitals would need a "fifthly", a "sixthly" and so on inclusive of "in the hundredth place"...

It's a disgrace... it's abominable! he thought, as he sat in the cart, with his ears sunk in his collar, eating his heart out. Finished! To hell with the bar! I'll go and hide myself in the backwoods, I'll go into seclusion... as far as possible from these gentlemen... as far as possible from these squabbles! "Get a move on, damn you!" he turned on the driver. "You're not driving a corpse to its wedding! Go on, faster!"

"Faster... faster!" mimicked the driver. "Can't you see what the road's like? Would tire the devil out if you tried to make him go faster. This weather's sheer punishment, God knows!"

The weather was abominable. It seemed to share Pyaterkin's indignation, hatred and suffering. It was as dark as soot and a cold, damp wind blew and whistled on every note. The rain was pouring down. A mixture of snow and sticky mud squelched underneath the wheels. Gullies and potholes and little bridges, half washed away, succeeded each other without end.

"Can't see a thing..." continued the driver. "Shan't get there by morning at this rate. We'll have to spend the night at Luke's."

"Who's Luke?"

"An old man who lives further along the road in the wood here. He's taken the forester's place. Ah, there's his cottage."

They could hear the hoarse barking of dogs, and a dim light flickered through the naked branches.

If ever on a dark and rainy night you see a light in a wood, you are sure to feel a desire for company, however misanthropic you may be. And so it was with Pyaterkin. When the cart stopped at the cottage with the light welcoming them shyly through the single small window, he felt better.

"Good evening, granddad!" he said kindly to Luke, who was standing in the passage just inside the cottage and was scratching his belly with both hands. "May we spend the night here?"

"You m… may," growled Luke. "There are two others here as it is… Come into the living room, please."

Pyaterkin stooped, stepped into the living-room and… his misanthropy came back with a vengeance. At a small table lit up by a tallow candle sat the two men who had had such a powerful influence on his mood: von Pach, the public prosecutor, and Semechkin the opposing barrister. Like Pyaterkin, they too had been returning from N***, and like him had landed up at Luke's. On seeing counsel for the defence coming in, they were both pleasantly surprised, and jumped up.

"Hullo! How did you get here?" they began. "The bad weather has driven you in here as well? Welcome! Do come and sit with us!"

Pyaterkin had thought that as soon as they saw him they would turn away in awkward silence, and therefore interpreted this friendly welcome at best as insolence.

"I don't understand," he muttered, shrugging his shoulders with dignity. "After what has passed between us, I… I am even surprised!"

Von Pach looked at Pyaterkin in surprise, shrugged his shoulders and, turning to Semechkin, continued the interrupted conversation:

"Well, I was reading the report… and you know, old boy, that report was just a mass of contradictions… The police inspector wrote, for instance, that the deceased woman Ivanova was dead drunk when she left the party and died after she had gone two miles on foot. How could she have gone two miles on foot if she had been dead drunk? Now, isn't that a contradiction? Eh?"

While von Pach was thus perorating, Pyaterkin sat down on a bench and began to examine his temporary abode… A light in a wood is romantic only at a distance – at close quarters it is sorry prose… Here it lit up a small, grey cubbyhole of a room with slanting walls and a sooty ceiling. In the corner on the right hung a dark icon, in the corner on the left stood a clumsy-looking stove, gloomy and for all the world like a tree with a hollow in it. On the ceiling a long pole, from which a cradle must once have hung, was stretched across the rafters. A ramshackle table and two narrow, rickety benches made up all the furniture. It was dark, stuffy and cold. There was a smell of rot and burnt candle grease.

The swine… thought Pyaterkin with a sidelong glance at his enemies. They've insulted a man, trampled him in the mire, and now they're carrying on a conversation as if nothing had happened! "I say," he turned to Luke. "Have you got another room by any chance? I can't stay here."

"There's the passage, but it's cold there, sir."

"Damned cold…" growled Semechkin, "had I known, I'd have brought drinks and cards with me. Shall we have some tea, what do you think? Heat us up a samovar, granddad!"

Half an hour later Luke served up a dirty samovar, a teapot with a broken spout and three cups.

"I have some tea…" said von Pach. "All we want now is sugar… Give us some sugar, granddad!"

"Mercy on us! Sugar!" said Luke, who was standing in the passage grinning. "You want sugar right in the middle of the forest! You're not in town, you know!"

"All right then, let's drink it without sugar," von Pach decided.

Semechkin made the tea and poured out three cups.

They've poured some out for me as well… thought Pyaterkin. I don't want their tea! Spit in my face and then offer me tea! They simply have no self-respect, these people. I'll ask Luke to give me another cup and I'll just drink hot water. Besides, I've got some sugar.

Luke did not have a fourth cup. Pyaterkin poured the tea out of the third cup, filled it up again with hot water and began to sip it, giving an occasional bite at the sugar. Hearing the loud scrunching, his enemies exchanged glances and burst out laughing.

"It's delightful, honestly!" prattled on von Pach. "We have no sugar, he has no tea… Ha-ha… Jolly, isn't it! What a child he still is. A great lout like that, and yet he's kept himself young enough to be able to sulk like a schoolgirl… Here, my friend!" he said, turning to Pyaterkin. "You shouldn't snub our tea… It isn't one of the cheaper sort… And if you don't drink it because you're too proud, remember you could pay for the tea with your sugar."

Pyaterkin made no answer.

Cads… he thought. They've insulted me and slandered me, and now they're trying to thrust their friendship on me. And these are known as humans! It means they simply don't care about all the ruderies I told them after the trial… I shan't pay any attention to them… I'll lie down.

A sheepskin coat was stretched out on the floor next to the stove… At the head of it lay a long bolster filled with straw… Pyaterkin stretched himself out on the sheepskin coat, put his burning head on the bolster, and covered himself with his fur coat.

"What a bore!" yawned Semechkin. "Too cold and dark to read, nowhere to sleep... Brr!... Tell me, Osip Osipych, if Luke, say, were to have a dinner in a restaurant and not pay for it, what would that be: larceny or fraud?"

"Neither one nor the other... simply a case for civil action..."

An argument started which went on for an hour and a half; Pyaterkin listened and shook with rage. Half a dozen times he was overwhelmed with the desire to jump up and join in the argument.

What nonsense! he thought, suffering torments as he listened to them. How out of date they are! How illogical!

The argument ended with von Pach lying down next to Pyaterkin, covering himself with his fur coat and saying:

"That's enough, now... All this arguing of ours is not letting counsel for the defence sleep. Lie down..."

"He's asleep already, I think..." said Semechkin, lying down on the other side of Pyaterkin. "Are you asleep, my friend?"

They can't leave me alone... thought Pyaterkin. The swine!

"He doesn't answer, so he must be asleep..." muttered von Pach. "He's managed to fall asleep in this pigsty... They say lawyers lead an armchair sort of life... It's not an armchair sort of life, it's a dog's life... Just look at this damned place we've landed up in. You know, I rather like our neighbour... what's his name? Shestyorkin? Full of zeal and fire..."

"Mm, yes... He'll be a good lawyer in a years' time... He has a way with him, that young man... Hardly out of his nappies, yet he speaks with a flourish and likes letting off fireworks... Only he shouldn't have dragged in Hamlet in his speech."

The close proximity of his enemies and their cool, indifferent tone were choking Pyaterkin. He was ready to burst from rage and shame.

"And that business with the sugar," von Pach grinned. "A regular schoolgirl! What's he offended with us for? Do you know?"

"I'm damned if I do..."

Pyaterkin could bear it no longer. He jumped up and opened his mouth to say something, but all the suffering he had endured in the course of the day was too much for him: words did not come, but hysterical weeping instead.

"What's the matter with him?" exclaimed von Pach in distress. "My dear man, what's the matter with you?"

"Are you... are you ill?" said Semechkin, jumping up. "What's the matter with you? Have you got no money? What is it?"

"It's mean... vile! The whole day... the whole day!"

"My dear boy, what is vile and mean? Osip Osipych, get me some water! My dear fellow, what's the matter? Why are you in such a bad temper today? Today you were probably entrusted with the defence for the first time? Were you? Well then, it's understandable. You have a good cry, my dear fellow... In my day I wanted to go and hang myself, but crying is better than hanging. You cry – you'll feel better."

"Vile... mean!"

"But nothing was vile! It was all as it should have been. You spoke well and you were listened to well. It's over-anxiety, old fellow. I remember the first time I undertook someone's defence. I had brown trousers on and a musician had lent me his miserable-looking tails. There I sat, and thought the public was laughing at my trousers. The accused had fooled me, so it seemed to me, and the prosecutor was making fun of me, and anyway I was stupid. I suppose you have decided that the bar can go to hell? This happens to everyone. You are not the first nor the last. One's first appearance in court certainly costs one dear."

"And who was jeering? Who was making fun of me?"

"Nobody was. You only imagined it. All beginners imagine it. Didn't you think too that the jury was looking at you with contempt? You did? Well, there you are. Have a drink of water, old boy. Cover yourself up."

Pyaterkin's enemies covered him up with fur coats and looked after him all night as if he were a child. His sufferings of a whole day were nothing but a bubble.

Holy Simplicity

F ATHER SAVVA ZHEZLOV, THE AGED PRIOR of Holy Trinity Church in P***, received an unexpected visit from his son, Alexander, a well-known Moscow lawyer. When the lonely old widower caught sight of his only child, whom he had not seen since he went to the university some twelve or fifteen years before, he grew pale, shook and stood rooted to the ground. Their joy and delight knew no bounds.

That evening, father and son talked. The lawyer ate, drank and was visibly moved.

"How nice and pleasant it is here," he said, going into raptures as he fidgeted on his chair. "It's cosy and warm, and there's a sort of patriarchal smell here. It really is nice!"

Father Savva, obviously giving himself airs in front of the old cook for having such a grown-up and gallant son, walked round the table with his hands behind his back, and tried to make himself appear "learned" in order to please his guest.

"It's a fact, my boy," he said. "It's turned out precisely as I hoped in my heart: both you and I – we both went in for learning. Now you went to the university, and I was educated at the Kiev Academy... So we both followed the same path... We understand each other... Only I don't know what they do in the academies nowadays. In my day they laid great stress on the classics, and even taught ancient Hebrew. What do they do now?"

"Don't know. But you've got marvellous sturgeon, Father. I'm full already, but I'll eat some more all the same."

"You eat, you eat. You should eat more because you do brain work, not physical work... mm... not physical work. You're a graduate, you have to use your brains. Are you staying long?"

"I didn't come to stay. I came to see you quite by chance, Father, like a deus ex machina. I came here on tour, to defend your ex-mayor... You probably know there's to be a trial here tomorrow."

"I see. So you're presumably in the legal profession? A lawyer?"

"Yes, I'm a barrister."

"I see. May God give you His blessing. What's your rank?"

"Honestly, I don't know, Father."

I'd like to ask about his salary, thought Father Savva, but they think a question like that is indiscreet. Judging by his clothes and by that gold watch there, I should think he must get more than a thousand roubles.

The old man and the lawyer fell silent.

"I didn't know you had such sturgeon, or I'd have come to see you last year," the son said. "I wasn't far from here last year, in your provincial capital. What funny towns you have here!"

"That's just what they are... funny... nothing in them!" Father Savva agreed. "Nothing to be done! They're far away from intellectual centres... steeped in prejudice. Civilization hasn't seeped through to them yet..."

"That's not the point... You just listen to a funny story that happened to me. While I was in your provincial capital, I went to the theatre. I asked for a ticket at the box office, but they said to me: there will be no performance, because not a single ticket has been sold yet! So I asked them: what are your takings if there's a full house? They said: three hundred roubles! So I said: tell them to put the show on, I'll pay three hundred... I paid three hundred roubles because I was bored, but when I began to watch their harrowing drama, I was even more bored... Ha-ha..."

Father Savva glanced incredulously at his son, glanced at the cook, and sniggered behind his hand.

What a fib! he thought. "Where did you get those three hundred roubles from, Sashenka?" he asked timidly.

"What d'you mean, where from? From my pocket, of course..."

"Mm... forgive me for an indiscreet question, but what salary do you get?"

"It depends... One year I would earn about thirty thousand, another year I don't even scrape up twenty thousand... Years vary."

What a fib! Ho-ho-ho! What a fib!... thought Father Savva, roaring with laughter and looking lovingly at his son's somewhat drunken face. How youth does brag! Ho-ho-ho! Thirty thousand – he certainly lays it on a bit thick! "It's incredible, Sashenka!" he said. "I'm sorry, but... ho-ho-ho... thirty thousand! One could build two houses with that amount of money..."

"Don't you believe me?"

"It's not that I don't believe you exactly, but... how shall I express it... You're awfully sort of... er... ho-ho-ho... Well, if you get such a lot of money, what do you do with it all?"

"I spend it, Father... Life in the capital simply eats up money. For every thousand you spend here you have to spend five there. I keep horses, play cards... sometimes I go out on the spree."

"I see... But you should save!"

"Can't be done... Haven't got the right kind of nerves for saving..." (The lawyer sighed.) "There's nothing to be done with me. Last year I bought myself a house on the Polyanka for sixty thousand. After all, it might be a help in my old age! And what d'you think? Less than two months after I'd bought it, I had to mortgage it. I mortgaged it, and all the cash went – pouf! I lost some of it at cards, and some of it went on drink."

"Ho-ho-ho! He's fibbing, he is!" the old man tittered. "How amusingly he fibs!"

"I'm not fibbing, Father."

"But you can't lose a house at cards or through drink."

"You can drink away not only a house, but the whole globe! Tomorrow I'll take five thousand away from here, but I've a feeling that these five thousand won't get me as far as Moscow. It's the planetoid I was born under."

"Not planetoid, planet," Father Savva corrected him, then coughed and looked with dignity at the old cook. "I'm sorry, Sashenka, but I doubt what you say. Why, what do you get such sums for?"

"For my talent..."

"Mm... Perhaps you do get about three thousand, but as to thirty thousand or, let's say, buying houses, I'm sorry... I have my doubts. But let's drop this argument. Now tell me, how are things in Moscow? Are you having a good time? Have you a lot of friends?"

"A great many. The whole of Moscow knows me."

"Ho-ho-ho! He's fibbing, he is! Ho-ho! All these wonders you're telling me, my boy!"

Father and son went on conversing in this way for a long time. The lawyer also told him about his marriage (with a dowry of forty thousand roubles), he described his journeys to Nizhni Novgorod, and his divorce which cost him ten thousand roubles. The old man listened, gasped, and roared with laughter.

"He's fibbing, he is! Ho-ho-ho! Why, Sashenka, I never knew you had such a gift of the gab! Ho-ho-ho! I'm not saying that as a reproach. I enjoy listening to you. Go on, go on."

"But I've been talking too much," said the lawyer at last, getting up from the table. "The trial's tomorrow, and I haven't read the case yet. Goodnight."

When he had taken his son to his own room, Father Savva abandoned himself to delight.

"You saw what he's like, eh? You did?" he whispered to the cook. "That's what he is... A university man, a humanist, emancipated, but not ashamed to visit his old man. Forgot his father and suddenly remembered him again. Just like that – remembered him again, the old stick-in-the-mud," he said to himself. "Ho-ho-ho! He's a good son! A kind son! And did you notice? He treats me as an equal... sees a fellow scholar in me. So he understands me, that means. Pity we didn't call the deacon round to have a look at him!"

When he had poured out his soul to the cook, Father Savva went to his bedroom on tiptoe and peeped through the keyhole. The lawyer was lying on the bed smoking a cigar and reading a voluminous notebook. Beside him on a small table stood a bottle of wine, which Father Savva had not previously seen.

"I've just come in for a moment... to see if you're comfortable," mumbled the old man, going into his son's room. "Comfortable? Is the bed soft enough? Why don't you undress?"

The lawyer gave a grunt and frowned. Father Savva sat at the foot of the bed and was plunged in thought.

"Oh, yes..." he began, after a short pause. "I keep on thinking about all you've said. On the one hand, I'm grateful to you for amusing an old man, but on the other hand, as your father and... and an educated man, I can't keep quiet and refrain from passing certain remarks. I know you were joking at dinner, but after all, you know, both science and faith condemn lies even in joke. Hrm... I've got a cough. Hrm... Forgive me, but I'm speaking as a father. Where did you get that wine from?"

"I brought it with me. D'you want some? It's good wine, eight roubles a bottle."

"Ei-ght? That's a fib, that is!" Father Savva threw up his hands. "Ho-ho-ho! But why should you pay eight roubles for this? Ho-ho-ho! I'll buy you the very best wine for a rouble! Ho-ho-ho!"

"Well, quick march, old man, you're preventing me from working. So long!"

The old man left the room, tittering and throwing up his hands, and quietly closed the door behind him. At midnight, when he had read his breviary and given orders to the cook for the next day's dinner, Father Savva looked into his son's room again.

His son was still reading, drinking and smoking.

"It's time to go to bed... get undressed and put out the candle," the old man said, bringing with him into his son's room a smell of incense and burning candles. "It's midnight already... Is that your second bottle? Oho!"

"Can't do anything without wine, Father... There can be no work without a stimulant."

Savva sat down on the bed, was silent for a moment, and then began:

"It's like this, my boy... Mm, yes... I don't know if I'll be alive... if I'll see you again, so it's better if I instruct you about my will today... You see... During the whole forty years that I've been in orders I've saved up about fifteen hundred roubles. When I die, take it, but..."

Father Savva solemnly blew his nose and continued:

"But don't squander it, keep it... And I'd ask you, after my death, to send a hundred roubles to my niece Varenka. And if you're not short, send Zinaida twenty roubles too. They're orphans."

"You send them the whole fifteen hundred... I don't need it, Father..."

"You're fibbing?"

"Seriously... I'd just squander it, anyway."

"Mm... After all, I did save it up!" Savva was offended. "I put aside every single copeck for you..."

"Well, I'll put your money in a glass case as a sign of parental love, but as I don't need it... Fifteen hundred – pah!"

"Well, as you like... Had I known, I wouldn't have saved, wouldn't have been so careful... You go to sleep!"

Father Savva made the sign of the cross over the lawyer and left the room. He was rather offended... His son's perfunctory and indifferent attitude to his forty years' savings had abashed him. But the feeling of affront and embarrassment soon passed. The old man once again felt an urge to go and chat with his son, to talk "learnedly" and recall the past, but he could no longer muster sufficient courage to bother the busy lawyer. He walked and walked through the dark rooms, thought and thought, and went into the hall to look at his son's fur coat. Forgetting himself in parental delight, he seized the coat with both hands and hugged and kissed it, and made the sign of the cross over it, as if it was no fur coat, but his own son, the "university graduate". Sleep he could not.

The Diplomat

A Scene

ANNA LVOVNA KUVALDIN, the wife of a principal in the Civil Service, breathed her last.

Her friends and relations conferred among themselves. "Well, what's to be done now?" they asked. "Her husband should be informed. He loved the dead woman all the same, even though he didn't live with her. He came to see her the other day, crawled on his knees to her and kept on saying: 'Annochka, won't you ever forgive me one momentary impulse?' and other things of the same sort, you know. He must be told…"

"Aristarkh Ivanych!" a tearful aunt turned to Colonel Piskarev, who was taking part in the family council. "You're Mikhail Petrovich's friend. Do us a favour, go and see him at the office and tell him about this misfortune… Only don't tell him all at once, my dear, don't stun him, or else anything might happen to him. His health's not strong. Prepare him first, and only then…"

Colonel Piskarev put on his cap and went off to the head office of the railway where the newly widowed man worked. He found him working out a balance sheet.

"Mikhail Petrovich," he began, sitting down at Kuvaldin's table and wiping the sweat from his brow. "Good morning, old man! Goodness, how dusty the streets are! You go on writing, go on, I won't bother you… I'll sit here a moment and then go… I was passing by, you know, and thought: why, this is where Misha works! Let's drop in on him! Besides, there's also a little matter…"

"Sit down for a bit, Aristarkh Ivanych… Wait a little… I shall be finished in a quarter of an hour, and then we can talk…"

"You go on writing, go on… I just dropped in like that… As I was passing… I'll just say a couple of words and then – off I go!"

Kuvaldin put down his pen and prepared to listen. The Colonel scratched himself behind the collar and continued:

"It's stuffy in here, but it's simply heavenly outside... Sunshine, a little breeze, you know... birds... Spring, in fact. There I was, going along the street and feeling really fine, you know... I'm an independent man, a widower... I can go wherever I want to... I can go to the pub if I want to, or take a ride in a tram, and there's no one to stop me, no one to scream at me at home... A bachelor's life, old boy, is the best life in the world... You can do what you like! You're free! You can breathe, and you feel that you do! In a moment I'll go home, and that'll be that... No one will dare ask me where I've been... I'm my own master... You know, old boy, a lot of people praise family life, but in my opinion it's worse than hard labour... All those fashions, bustles, gossip, screaming... visitors all the time... children crawling into God's world one after another... expense... faugh!"

"In a minute," said Kuvaldin, taking up his pen, "I'll be finished, and then..."

"You go on writing, go on... It's all right if you chance on a wife who doesn't happen to be a devil, but what if she's Satan in skirts? What if she's the sort that jabbers and nags for days on end?... Anyone would scream! Why, take yourself for example... While you were single you looked like a man, but as soon as you married you just faded away – always in the dumps, you were... She disgraced you all over town... drove you out of the house... Well, what's good about that? You can't pity a wife like that..."

"I was to blame for the break-up of our marriage, not her," sighed Kuvaldin.

"Oh, drop that, do! I know her! Bad-tempered, self-willed, cunning! Every word a poisoned barb, every look a sharp knife... And she was more spiteful than words can say, the deceased was!"

"What do you mean – 'the deceased'?" said Kuvaldin, all round-eyed.

"Why, did I really say 'the deceased'?" Piskarev checked himself, blushing. "I didn't say that at all... What on earth's the matter with you... You've gone quite pale! Ha-ha... You should use your ears!"

"Did you visit Anyuta today?"

"I dropped in in the morning... She was in bed... Bullying the servants... This was wrong and that was wrong... An unbearable woman! I don't understand what you love her for, drat her... I wish she'd set you free... You'd live in freedom, enjoy yourself... Marry someone else... All right, all right, I won't say any more! Don't look so cross! I'm only speaking as an old man... You can do what you like so far as I'm concerned... Love her if you want to, or don't... but I'm only saying it like that... for your own good... She doesn't live with you, doesn't want to know you... what sort of a wife is that? She's ugly, sickly, ill-natured... Nothing to regret her for. If only..."

"It's all very well for you to talk, Aristarkh Ivanych!" sighed Kuvaldin. "But you can't just pull love out, like a hair of your head."

"But what is there to love! Spite was all she ever gave you. You must forgive me, I'm an old man, but I didn't like her... Couldn't bear her! Whenever I drove past her flat I used to shut my eyes so as not to see her... Oh, it doesn't matter now. God rest her soul and give her peace, but... I didn't like her, though it might have been my fault."

"Listen, Aristarkh Ivanych..." said Kuvaldin, going pale. "That's the second time you've let it out... Has she died, or what?"

"What d'you mean, who's died? No one's died, it's just that I didn't like the deceased... Oh, bother, I don't mean the deceased, but what's her name... your Anita..."

"But is she dead, or what? Aristarkh Ivanych, don't torture me! You're somehow strangely excited, talk in a confused way... You sing the praises of a single life... She's dead? Is that it?"

"Hold on, who's dead?" muttered Piskarev, coughing. "How you do jump to conclusions, old man... And what if she is dead? We'll all die one day, and she'll have to die too like the rest of us... You'll die and I'll die..."

Kuvaldin's eyes reddened and filled with tears. "At what time?" he asked quietly.

"Not at any time... There you go, snivelling already! But she hasn't died! Who told you that she's died?"

"Aristarkh Ivanych, I... I beg you, don't spare me!"

"It doesn't seem to be any use talking to you, old boy, you're just like a child. I never told you that she'd passed on? I never did, did I? What are you slobbering about then? You go and have a look at her – alive and kicking! When I dropped in to see her she was quarrelling with her aunt... There was Father Matvei, saying the requiem, and she was shouting so the whole house could hear."

"What requiem? Why was it being said?"

"What, the requiem? Oh, just like that... kind of instead of mass... I mean, there wasn't any requiem, but something... there wasn't anything."

Aristarkh Ivanych was thoroughly muddled. He stood up, turned to face the window and coughed.

"I've got a cough, old man... I don't know where I can have caught it..."

Kuvaldin got up too, and walked round the table in great agitation.

"You're not being straightforward with me," he said, pulling at his beard with trembling fingers. "Now it's clear... It's all clear. What's all this diplomacy for, I'd like to know? Why not say things straight out? She is dead, isn't she?"

"Mm... Well, how shall I put it?" Piskarev shrugged his shoulders. "Not dead, exactly, but... Now there you are, crying already! After all, we'll all die! She's not the only one to be mortal, we'll all finish up in the next world! Rather than cry in public like that, you'd do better to say a prayer... You might at least make the sign of the cross!"

Kuvaldin looked dully at Piskarev for a moment, then turned terribly pale, flopped into an armchair and broke into hysterical tears... His colleagues leapt up from their places and dashed to his assistance. Piskarev scratched the back of his head and frowned.

"What a business it is, with people like that, honestly!" he grumbled, in despair. "He's howling – and why's he howling, I ask you? Misha, are you in your right mind? Misha!" he said, nudging Kuvaldin. "She's not dead yet, I tell you! Who told you she was dead? On the contrary, the doctors say there's hope yet. Misha, hey, Misha! I tell you she's not dead! Would you like us to go and see her together? We'll just get there in time for the requiem... I mean... what am I saying? Not for the requiem, but for dinner, Mishenka! I assure you, she's still alive! I'll be damned if she isn't! May I be struck dumb! Don't you believe me? Let's go to her, then... You can call me all the names in the world then if... And where could he have got the idea from, I can't understand? I was at the deceased's house today, that's to say, not at the deceased's but... Oh, bother!"

The colonel made a gesture with his hand, gave up, and left the office. When he arrived back at the dead woman's house, he flung himself on the sofa and tore his hair.

"You go and see him yourselves!" he said in despair. "You prepare him for the news yourselves, but leave me out of it! I don't want to do it! I just said a couple of words to him... I only just gave a slight hint, and you see what's happened to him! In a faint, he is! Dying! I wouldn't do it again for anything in the world! You go yourselves!..."

Mutual Superiority

"NOW, MES ENFANTS, YOU MUST BE SURE to call on Baroness Scheppling (with two 'p's)…" my mother-in-law repeated for the hundredth time, as she settled me and my young bride in the carriage. "The Baroness is a very old friend of mine… And while you're about it, go and see General Zherebchikov's wife too… she'll be offended if you don't call on her."

We climbed into the carriage and drove off to pay our first calls after our marriage. It seemed to me that my wife's face adopted a pompous expression, whereas I hung my head and was sunk in melancholy… My wife and I had many dissimilarities, but none of them caused me more spiritual torment than the dissimilarity between our friends and connections. My wife's list of friends shone with a motley assortment of colonels' and generals' wives, Baroness Scheppling (with two "p"s), Count Derzai-Chertovchinov, and a whole swarm of aristocratic school friends; whereas, on my side, there was nothing but a mass of *mauvais ton*:* an uncle who was a retired prison inspector, a cousin who kept a dress-making business, my fellow Civil Servants – all drunkards and good-for-nothings, and none of them higher than a principal in the Civil Service – Plevkov (a merchant), and so on. I felt a sense of shame. To escape ignominy it would have been better not to visit my friends at all, but this would have meant laying up a lot of trouble and bother for myself. My cousin might perhaps have been crossed off the list, but the calls on my uncle and on Plevkov were unavoidable. I had borrowed money from my uncle for the wedding expenses, and I owed Plevkov for the furniture.

"Very soon, my sweetie," said I to my spouse by way of preparing the ground, "we shall arrive at my uncle Pupkin's. He's from a very ancient, noble family… his uncle was a suffragan in some diocese or other, but he's an eccentric and lives like a pig; I don't mean the vicar lives like a pig, but Pupkin does… I'm taking you there so that you can have a good laugh… he's an awful silly ass…"

The carriage stopped outside a small, three-windowed cottage, with grey, rusty shutters. We got out of the carriage and rang the bell… We

could hear a dog barking loudly, then a reprimand: "Sh! Damn you!"
– then a yelp, a scuffle behind the door... After a prolonged scuffle the
door opened, and we went into the hall... We were met by my cousin
Masha, a little girl with a dirty nose, wearing her mother's cardigan.
I pretended not to recognize her and went to the coat stand where,
together with my uncle's fox-fur coat, hung someone's trousers and a
starched skirt. I took off my galoshes and gave a furtive look at the
drawing room. There, at the table, sat my uncle in his dressing gown,
and with slippers on his bare feet. The hope that we might not find him
at home turned to dust and ashes... Screwing up his eyes and wheezing
so that it could be heard all over the house, he was taking orange peel
out of a vodka decanter with a piece of wire. He had the preoccupied
and concentrated look of an inventor at work. We went in. As soon as
he saw us, Pupkin became covered with embarrassment, dropped his
wire and, gathering up the skirts of his dressing gown, he dashed out
of the room.

"I'm just coming!" he shouted.

"He's taken to flight..." I laughed, consumed with shame and afraid
to look at my wife. "Isn't it funny, Sonya? He really is frightfully eccentric... And just look what furniture! A three-legged table, a paralytic
piano, a cuckoo clock... Honestly, it's like prehistoric monsters living
here rather than human beings..."

"What's that drawing?" my wife asked, looking at the pictures which
were hung pell-mell with photographs.

"That's St Seraphim feeding a bear in the Sarov hermitage... And
that's a portrait of the suffragan, when he was still an inspector in a
seminary... Look, you see he's got the order of St Anne... An estimable
man... I..." (I blew my nose.)

But nothing made me feel so ashamed as the smell... There was a
smell of vodka, of bad oranges, of the turpentine with which my uncle
defended himself against moth, of coffee grounds – all this together
gave out an acutely sour odour... My cousin Mitya, a small schoolboy
with large, sticking-out ears, came into the room and clicked his heels...
When he had picked up the orange peel, he took a cushion off the sofa,
wiped the dust from the piano with his sleeve, and left the room... He
had obviously been sent to "tidy up".

"Well, here I am!" said my uncle at last, coming in and buttoning up
his waistcoat. "Well, here I am! I'm very pleased... extremely! Please sit

down! Only don't sit on the sofa, the back leg is broken. Do sit down, Senya!"

We sat down... There was a silence, during which Pupkin stroked his knee, while I felt embarrassed and tried not to look at my wife.

"Mm, yes..." my uncle began, lighting a cigar (he always smokes cigars when he has guests). "So you're married now... That's how it is... It's a good thing in a way... You have your dear one with you, love, romance; on the other hand, there's children – as soon as they start to appear you'll be howling your head off! Boots for one, trousers for another, school bills for the third... Good God Almighty! Thank God, my wife produced dead ones – half of them!"

"How have you been keeping?" I asked, hoping to change the subject.

"Badly, my boy! The other day I was prostrate all day... My chest bursting, shivering fits, temperature... My wife says: 'Take quinine and don't lose your temper...'

"But how can I help losing my temper? Only this morning I ordered the snow to be cleared from the porch a bit, and d'you think anyone's done anything? None of these beggars would lift his little finger... I couldn't clean it myself, could I? I'm ailing, weak... I've got concealed piles."

I was embarrassed and blew my nose loudly.

"Or perhaps I got it from the baths..." my uncle went on, looking thoughtfully out of the window. "Perhaps! You know, I went to the baths on Thursday... I steamed myself for about three hours. But the steam makes the piles break out all the more. The doctors say that baths aren't good for the health... That's wrong, madam... I've been used to them from childhood because my father kept baths in Kiev, in the Kreshchatik... Sometimes I used to steam myself all day long... Particularly as I didn't have to pay..."

I could not bear the shame of it any longer. I stood up and began to stammer out my goodbyes.

"Why, where are you off to?" said my uncle, surprised, and he seized me by the sleeve. "Your auntie's just coming! Let's have a bite of what's going, we'll have some liqueur!... There's some salted beef, Mitya's run off to fetch some sausage... How you do stand on ceremony, really! Snooty, Senya, that's what you are. That's bad, that is! You didn't order the wedding dress from Gasha! You know, madam, my daughter has a dress-making business... I know Madame Stepanid made your dress, but Stepanidka can't touch us. And what's more, we'd have done it cheaper..."

I cannot remember how I took leave of my uncle, how I reached the carriage... I felt that I was crushed, humiliated, and every minute I expected to hear the contemptuous laugh of my well-educated wife...

God, what vulgarity we're in for at Plevkov's! I thought, going cold with horror. If only we can get it over as quickly as possible, to hell with them all! And what a misfortune – I don't know a single general! I do know one retired colonel, and he keeps a pub! Oh, I really have no luck! "Sonechka," I said to my wife in a tearful voice. "Forgive me for taking you to that pigsty just now... I thought I'd give you something to laugh about, that you'd have a chance to observe some odd types... It's not my fault that it turned out to be so vulgar, so disgusting... I'm sorry..."

I looked shyly at my wife, and saw that my worst fears were confirmed. My wife's eyes were full of tears, a blush either of shame or anger burned on her cheeks, her hands convulsively plucked at the fringe of the carriage window... I was thrown into a fever and shuddered from fear...

Well, this is where my ignominy begins! I thought, feeling my hands and feet turning to lead. "But I'm really not to blame, Sonya!" A wail broke from me. "How silly of you, really! Of course they're pigs, vulgar, but after all it wasn't me who made them my relations!"

"If you don't like your common relations," Sonya sobbed, looking at me with imploring eyes, "then you certainly won't like mine... I'm ashamed, and I can't bring myself to make a clean breast of it... Darling, my sweet... In a moment Baroness Scheppling will start telling you how Mummy worked as her housekeeper, and how ungrateful Mummy and I are for not showing our gratitude for her past kindness to us now that she has fallen on hard times... But please don't believe her! The old tartar's a liar... I swear to you that we send her a sugar-loaf and a pound of tea on every holiday!..."

"But you're not serious, Sonya, are you?" I said in amazement, and felt the lead leaving my limbs and my whole body regaining its buoyancy. "You give sugar and a pound of tea to the Baroness!... Gosh!"

"And when you meet General Zherebchikov's wife, don't laugh at her, darling. She's so unfortunate! If she cries all the time and talks nonsense, it's because Count Derzai-Chertovchinov has robbed her. She'll complain about her fate and will ask you for a loan; but you – don't give her anything... It would be all right if she were to spend it on herself, but she'll just give it to the Count."

"Sweetie... angel!" And I set about embracing my wife from sheer delight. "My ducky-wucky! This really is a surprise! If you were to tell me that your Baroness Scheppling (with two 'p's) walks about the streets stark naked, you'd have done me an even greater favour! Give me your little hand!"

And suddenly I was sorry that I had refused my uncle's salted beef, that I had not strummed on his paralytic piano, had not drunk his liqueur... But then I remembered that at Plevkov's they served good brandy, and sucking pig with horseradish.

"Off to Plevkov's!" I shouted to the driver at the top of my voice.

Tædium Vitæ

It has been observed by experienced people that neither do recluses
*part with this life easily; besides, they often reveal what is so typical
for people of their age – avarice and greed, as well as mistrustfulness,
pusillanimity, stubbornness, discontent, etc.*

(*Practical Manual for Priests* by P. Nechayev)

ANNA MIKHAILOVNA LEBEDEV, a colonel's wife, lost her only daughter, a young girl who was engaged to be married. This death brought with it another death: the old woman, stunned by God's visitation, felt that all her past had irrevocably died and that now a new life was beginning for her – a life which had very little in common with the first one...

She bustled about aimlessly, without any system. To begin with, she sent one thousand roubles to a Mount Athos monastery and donated half the household silver to the cemetery church. After a little while she gave up smoking, and made a vow not to eat meat. But none of this made her feel any better – on the contrary, the feeling of old age and the nearness of death became all the sharper and more emphatic. Then Anna Mikhailovna sold her town house for a mere song, and hurried away to her country house without any definite aim in view.

As soon as someone consciously begins to question the point of existence – in no matter what way – and feels an acute need to look beyond the grave, then neither sacrifices, nor fasting, nor knocking about from place to place will satisfy him. But fortunately for Anna Mikhailovna, just as she arrived at Jenino, Fate brought her face to face with an occurrence which made her forget about old age and the nearness of death for a long time. It so happened that on the day of her arrival Martyn, the cook, spilt boiling water on both his feet. Someone galloped off to fetch the local doctor, but he was not at home. Then Anna Mikhailovna, who was fastidious and sensitive, washed Martyn's wounds with her own hands, put ointment on them and bandaged both feet. She sat up all night by the cook's bedside. When, thanks to her efforts, Martyn ceased to groan and fell asleep, something – as she later recounted – "dawned" in her heart. It suddenly seemed to her that her aim in life was revealed, and was as clear as daylight... Pale, with swimming eyes, she reverently kissed Martyn's forehead as he slept, and began to pray.

After that Madame Lebedev took up medical work. In the days of her sinful, slipshod life – which she now remembered only with abhorrence – she had undergone a good deal of medical treatment herself, because she had had nothing else to do.

Besides, doctors had been numbered among her lovers, and she had learnt a bit from them. Both these facts stood her in good stead now. She ordered a medicine chest, some books and a journal called *The Doctor*, and bravely set about giving people medical treatment. At first only the inhabitants of Jenino came to her for treatment, but later on people started to flock to her from all the villages around.

"Just imagine, my dear!" she boasted to the priest's wife about three months after her arrival. "Yesterday I had sixteen patients, and today I had a whole twenty of them! They tired me out so much that I can scarcely stand on my feet. Do you know, I've run out of laudanum! There's an epidemic of dysentery in Gourino."

Every morning when she woke up, she remembered that there were patients waiting for her, and her heart gave an agreeable shiver. When she had dressed and hurriedly drunk her tea, she would begin to receive patients. The procedure of receiving them gave her inexpressible delight. First, as if wishing to prolong this delight, she would slowly enter the patients' names in an exercise book, and then she would call each one in turn. The greater the suffering of the patient and the dirtier and more disgusting his ailment, the sweeter her work seemed to her. Nothing gave her so much pleasure as the thought that she was struggling against her fastidiousness and not sparing herself, and she purposely tried to take more time in rummaging in suppurating wounds. There were moments when, as if enraptured by the hideousness and stench of a wound, she would fall into a sort of ecstatic cynicism, when she felt an uncontrollable desire to force her nature – and in these moments it seemed to her that she was at the summit of her vocation. She adored her patients. Sentiment suggested that they were her saviours, but reason made her want to see them not as individual personalities, not as peasants, but as something abstract – the people! That is why she was unusually soft and timid with them, blushed in front of them for her mistakes and, while she was receiving them, always had a guilty appearance...

After each reception of patients, which took up more than half a day, weary, red from strain and sick, she would hasten to pass the time by reading. She used to read medical books, or those Russian authors who most closely accorded with her mood.

Having thus begun a new life, Anna Mikhailovna felt fresh, satisfied and almost happy. She did not even desire a fuller life. And then, just as if to crown her happiness, a kind of dessert after a good meal, it so turned out that she became reconciled with her husband, towards whom she had a deep feeling of guilt. Seventeen years before, shortly after the birth of her daughter, she had been unfaithful to her husband, Arkady Petrovich, and they had had to separate. She had not seen him since then. He was serving somewhere in the south in the artillery as battery commander, and now and again – about twice a year – he used to send his daughter letters, which she would carefully hide from her mother. Then, after their daughter's death, Anna Mikhailovna unexpectedly received a long letter from him. In elderly, feeble handwriting he wrote to her that, with the death of his only daughter, he had lost the last thing that bound him to life, that he was old, ill and longing for death, of which, at the same time, he was afraid. He complained that he was fed up with everything, sick of everything, that he no longer got on well with people, and that he could hardly wait for the time when he would hand over the battery and get as far away as possible from petty gossip. In conclusion, he asked his wife for God's sake to pray for him, to take care of herself, and not to give way to despondency. An assiduous correspondence between the old people ensued. So far as it was possible to judge from subsequent letters – which were all equally tearful and gloomy – the colonel was not only distressed by disease and the loss of his daughter: he had run into debt, quarrelled with his superiors and with his brother officers, neglected his battery to such an extent that it was impossible to hand it over, and so on. This correspondence between husband and wife went on for about two years, and ended up with the old man retiring and coming to live at Jenino.

He arrived one February afternoon, when the buildings of Jenino were hidden by deep snowdrifts, and in the clear, blue air, in addition to the sharp, hard frost, there was a death-like silence.

Watching him from the window as he got out of the sleigh, Anna Mikhailovna did not recognize her husband. He was a small, bent old man, who was now quite decrepit and unbalanced. What struck Anna

Mikhailovna first were the elderly folds on his long neck, and his thin legs with stiffly bending knees, like artificial legs. As he paid the driver he made a long statement to him about something or other, and finally spat angrily.

"It disgusts me even to talk to you!" Anna Mikhailovna overheard his elderly grumbling. "You should realize that it's immoral to ask for a tip! Everyone should only get what he's earned – that's how it is!"

When he came into the hall, Anna Mikhailovna saw a yellow face – which even the frost had not coloured – with protuberant prawn-like eyes and a scanty beard in which grey hairs were mixed with red ones. Arkady Petrovich embraced his wife with one arm and kissed her on the forehead. As they looked at each other, the old people somehow felt afraid of something and were terribly embarrassed, just as if they were ashamed of their old age.

"You're just in time!" Anna Mikhailovna hastened to say. "Dinner is just ready. You must be hungry after your journey!"

They sat down to dinner. The first course was eaten in silence. Arkady Petrovich took a fat notebook out of his pocket and looked at some notes, while his wife studiously prepared the salad. They both of them had plenty of material for conversation, but neither of them drew on it. They both felt that memories of their daughter would cause acute pain and tears, while from the past, as from a deep, vinegary barrel, wafted stuffiness and murk...

"But you're not eating any meat!" remarked Arkady Petrovich.

"No, I made a vow not to eat any..." his wife answered quietly.

"Why? It isn't bad for your health... If you analyse it chemically, then fish and all Lenten fare is made up of the same elements as meat. In actual fact, there's no such thing as Lenten fare..." (Why am I saying this? thought the old man.) "For example, this cucumber is no more Lenten fare than chicken..."

"Oh, yes it is. When I eat a cucumber, then I know that they didn't deprive it of life, that blood wasn't shed..."

"That, my dear, is an optical illusion. You eat a great deal of infusoria with a cucumber – and wasn't the cucumber itself alive? Plants are organisms too! And what about fish?"

What am I talking this nonsense for? thought Arkady Petrovich again, and quickly began to talk about the advances being made in chemistry.

"It's really a miracle!" he said, chewing his bread with difficulty. "They'll soon be making milk chemically, and I dare say they'll get as far as making meat! Yes! In a thousand years time instead of a kitchen there'll be a chemical laboratory in every house where, from gases and so forth that don't cost anything, they'll make everything you want!"

Anna Mikhailovna looked at his uneasily restless, prawn-like eyes, and listened. She felt that the old man was talking about chemistry only so as not to talk about anything else, but nevertheless his theory about Lenten and non-Lenten fare interested her.

"You retired as a general?" she asked, when he suddenly fell silent and began blowing his nose.

"Yes, as a general... 'Your Excellency'..."

The General talked all through dinner without stopping, thus displaying his inordinate garrulity – a characteristic which, long ago in their youth, Anna Mikhailovna had not noticed in him. The old woman's head began to ache from his chattering.

After dinner he went to his room for a rest, but though tired, he did not succeed in falling asleep. When, before the evening tea, the old woman went in to him, he was lying hunched up under the blanket, goggling at the ceiling, and emitting occasional sighs.

"What's the matter with you, Arkady?" said Anna Mikhailovna in horror, looking at his grey and drawn face.

"N-nothing..." he said. "Rheumatism."

"Why didn't you say so? I might be able to help you!"

"You can't help..."

"If it's rheumatism, then you should paint yourself with iodine and take sodium salicylate internally..."

"That's all rubbish... I've been having treatment for eight years... Don't stamp your feet like that!" the General suddenly shouted at the old maidservant, angrily opening his eyes wide as he looked at her. "She's stamping like a horse!"

Anna Mikhailovna and the maid, who had long ago become un-accustomed to such a tone of voice, looked at each other and blushed. Noticing their confusion, the General frowned and turned towards the wall.

"I must warn you, Anyuta..." he groaned, "I've got an insufferable temper! I've become irritable in my old age..."

"You should try to overcome it..." sighed Anna Mikhailovna.

"It's easy enough to say 'you should'! And I shouldn't have any pain, either, but then Nature doesn't pay any heed to our 'shoulds'. Ow! But you go away, Anyuta... When the pains come on I find the presence of people trying... It's difficult to talk..."

Days, weeks, months elapsed, and little by little Arkady Petrovich began to feel at home in his new place: he became used to it, and people became used to him. At first he lived in the house without ever going out, but his old age and the burden of his intolerable temper were felt throughout Jenino. He usually woke up very early, at about four o'clock in the morning; his day started with a shrill, elderly cough which woke up Anna Mikhailovna and all the servants. So as somehow to kill the long time from early morning till dinner, if his legs were not fettered by rheumatism he would wander through all the rooms and carp at the untidiness which he thought he saw everywhere. Everything annoyed him: the laziness of the servants, loud footsteps, cocks crowing, smoke from the kitchen, church bells... He grumbled, swore, harried the servants – but after every swear word he would clutch his head and say in a tearful voice:

"God, what a temper I've got! An insufferable temper!"

But at dinner he would eat a great deal and chatter incessantly. He talked about socialism, about new military reforms, about hygiene, and Anna Mikhailovna would listen to him and feel that he was saying all this only so as not to talk about their daughter and about the past. In each other's presence they still felt awkward and as if they were ashamed of something. It was only in the evenings, when darkness filled the rooms and a cricket chirped despondently behind the stove, that this awkwardness disappeared. They sat side by side in silence, and on those occasions it was just as if their souls were whispering about the thing that neither of them could bring themselves to say aloud. On those occasions, warming each other with the remains of life's fire, each of them understood perfectly what the other was thinking about. But no sooner did the maid bring in the lamp than the old man would again fall to chattering or grumbling about the untidiness. He had absolutely nothing to do. Anna Mikhailovna had wanted to draw him into her medical work, but at the very first reception of patients he had yawned and looked bored. Nor did she succeed in making him interested in reading. Used as he had been to reading at odd moments when he was in the army, he did not know how to read for a long time, for hours at a stretch. It was enough for him to read five or six short pages to become tired and take his glasses off.

But spring came, and the General abruptly changed his way of life. When newly trodden paths ran from the garden to the green field and the village, and birds began to stir in the trees in front of the window, quite unexpectedly for Anna Mikhailovna, he took to going to church. He went to church not only on feast days, but on weekdays too. This religious zeal started with the mass which the old man had ordered for his daughter, without telling his wife. He knelt throughout the mass, bowed himself to the ground, wept and, it seemed to him, prayed fervently. But it was not a prayer that he said. Giving himself up to his fatherly feeling and calling up his beloved daughter's face in his memory, he looked at the icons and whispered:

"Shurochka! My darling child! My angel!"

It was a paroxysm of elderly grief, but the old man imagined that a reaction, a radical change was taking place in him. Next day he again felt drawn to go to church, on the day after too... He used to come back from church fresh, radiant, with a smile all over his face. During dinner religion and theological questions began to serve him as a theme for his incessant chatter. On entering his room Anna Mikhailovna several times caught him turning over the pages of the gospels. But unfortunately this religious fervour did not last long. After one particularly sharp attack of rheumatism, which lasted for a whole week, he stopped going to church: he somehow did not remember that he had to go to mass...

He suddenly felt a desire for company.

"I can't understand how one can live like that, without seeing anyone!" he began to grumble. "I must go and pay calls on the neighbours. It may be stupid, futile, but while I'm alive I must submit to the laws of society!"

Anna Mikhailovna offered him the horses. He paid calls on the neighbours, but did not go to see them a second time. The necessity for seeing people was satisfied by him trotting about the village and finding fault with the peasants.

One morning he was sitting in the dining room before an open window and drinking tea. In the little front garden outside the window the peasants who had come to Anna Mikhailovna for treatment were sitting on benches beside the lilac and gooseberry bushes. The old man screwed his eyes up at them for a long time, then grumbled:

"*Ces* muzhiks!... Objects of civic sorrow... Rather than trying to cure your illnesses, you'd do better to go and get treated for all your moral filth and rottenness."

Anna Mikhailovna, who adored her patients, stopped pouring out the tea and looked at the old man in dumb amazement. The patients, who had never met with anything but kindness and warm sympathy in the Lebedev house, were also astonished, and got up from their seats.

"Yes, my dear sirs... *ces* muzhiks..." the General went on. "You surprise me. You surprise me very much! Well, aren't they animals?" the old man turned to Anna Mikhailovna. "The local authorities gave them an advance so that they could sow oats, and they just went and drank their oats away! It wasn't only one or two of them who spent it all on drink, but all of them! The pub-keepers didn't have enough storeroom for all the oats... Was that right?" the General turned to the peasants. "Eh? Was it?"

"Don't, Arkady!" whispered Anna Mikhailovna.

"Do you think the local authorities got those oats for nothing? What sort of citizens are you after that, if you don't respect either your own property, or anyone else's, or public property? You drank away those oats... you cut down the wood, and drank that away too. You steal everything... My wife gives you treatment, and you went and stole her fence... Was that right?"

"That's enough!" groaned the General's wife.

"It's time you pulled yourselves together..." Lebedev went on grumbling. "You are a disgrace to look at! You there, with the red hair, you came for treatment – your feet hurt? – but you didn't bother to wash your feet at home... The dirt's an inch thick! You boor, you hope it'll be washed here? They got it into their heads that they... *ces* muzhiks... just imagine that they can ride roughshod over people. The priest married a certain Fyodor, the local carpenter. The carpenter didn't pay him a penny. 'Too poor!' he says. 'I can't!' Well, all right. Only the priest ordered a little bookshelf from Fyodor... And what d'you think? He went five or six times to the priest to collect his money! Eh? Well, wasn't he a swine? He didn't pay the priest himself, but..."

"The priest's got plenty of money without that..." boomed one of the patients sullenly.

"And how do you know?" the General burst out, jumping up and hanging out of the window. "Have you looked in the priest's pocket? And even if he were a millionaire, you shouldn't take advantage of his work without paying! You don't work for nothing yourself, so don't take something for nothing. You can't imagine how disgusting they are!" The General turned to Anna Mikhailovna. "You should have seen some of them in court, or at their meetings! They're brigands!"

The General did not even calm down when the reception of patients began. He nagged and mimicked every patient, and explained all their illnesses as the result of drunkenness and debauch.

"Look how thin you are!" he prodded one man in the ribs with his finger. "And why? Nothing to eat! You've drunk it all away. Didn't you drink away all the local authorities' oats?"

"There are no two ways about it," sighed the sick man, "we lived better as serfs…"

"Rot! You're lying!" the General exploded. "Why, you're not sincere about it, you're only saying it to flatter!"

Next day the General once more sat at the window and told off the peasants. This occupation fascinated him, and he took to sitting by the window every day. When Anna Mikhailovna saw that her husband was not calming down, she began to receive her patients in the barn, but the General found his way to the barn as well. The old woman bore this "trial" submissively, and only expressed a protest by blushing and distributing money to the patients who had been sworn at; but when the patients, who had taken a strong dislike to the General, began coming to her more and more rarely, she could not contain herself. One day at dinner, when the General made some sort of joke about the patients, her eyes became bloodshot and her face twitched.

"I'd beg you to leave my patients in peace…" she said sternly. "If you feel a need to vent your temper on someone, then you can give me a dressing down, but leave them alone… Thanks to you, they've stopped coming for treatment."

"Aha! They've stopped coming!" the General smirked. "They're offended! By Jove, if someone's angry it means he's in the wrong. Ha, ha… But it's a good thing, Anyuta, that they've stopped coming. I'm very glad… Why, your treatment doesn't do anything but harm! Instead of going to be treated scientifically by a doctor at the rural hospital, they go to you to be treated with soda and castor oil, whatever illness they may have. It does great harm!"

Anna Mikhailovna looked at the old man intently, thought a minute, and suddenly went pale.

"Of course," the General went on jabbering. "In medicine knowledge is necessary above all, but philanthropy without any knowledge is quackery. And what's more, according to the law you haven't the right to treat people. In my opinion, you'll do much more good to a sick man if you shove him off roughly to see the doctor than if you treat him yourself."

The General was silent for a moment, and then continued:

"If you don't like the way I talk to them, well, then I won't speak to them any more, although, as a matter of fact... in all conscience it's much better to be frank with them than to keep silent and worship them. Alexander of Macedon was a great man, but there's no need to go and make a song and dance about it, and it's the same with the Russian people – it's a great people, but it doesn't follow that you can't tell it the truth to its face. You can't make a lapdog of the people. These *ces* muzhiks are human beings just like you and me, with the same shortcomings, and therefore you shouldn't worship them, nor coddle them, but you should teach them, reform them... inspire them..."

"It's not for us to teach them..." the General's wife muttered. "We can learn something from them."

"What can we learn?"

"Lots of things. For instance... how to work hard..."

"How to work hard? Eh? You said: 'How to work hard'?"

The General choked, jumped up from the table, and began to pace the room.

"And I haven't worked hard?" he burst out. "And anyway... I'm an intellectual, and not a muzhik, why should I work hard? I... I'm an intellectual!"

The old man was really offended, and his face bore a boyishly peeved expression.

"Thousands of soldiers passed through my hands... I rotted away in the war, caught rheumatism for the rest of my life and... and I didn't work hard! Perhaps you'll tell me I can learn how to suffer from that people of yours? Of course, it isn't as if I'd ever suffered? I lost my own daughter... the only thing that still tied me to life in this damned old age! And I haven't suffered!"

At this sudden memory of their daughter the old people all at once began to weep and to wipe their eyes with their table napkins.

"And we aren't suffering!" whimpered the General, giving himself up to his tears. "They have an aim in life... faith, whereas we have nothing but problems... problems and horror! We don't suffer!"

The old people both felt sorry for each other. They sat side by side, sympathized with each other and wept together for two hours. After this they could at last look each other openly in the face, and boldly talk about their daughter, about the past, and about the threatening future.

That evening they both went to bed in the same room. The old man talked incessantly, and prevented his wife from sleeping.

"God, what a temper I've got!" he said. "Now why did I say all that to you? Why, those were illusions, and it's natural for man to live on illusions, especially in old age. With my jabbering I took your last consolation away from you. You would have gone on treating the peasants till your dying day and eating no meat, but no – the Devil prompted me. It's impossible without illusions... Sometimes whole states live on illusions... Famous writers are clever if anyone is, but they can't get along without illusions either. Why, that favourite of yours wrote seven volumes on 'the people'!"

An hour later the General turned over and said:

"And why is it precisely in old age that people pay attention to their feelings and criticize their actions? Why don't they pay any attention to it in youth? Old age is unbearable anyway, without that... Yes... In youth the whole of life passes without leaving a trace, scarcely making any impression on consciousness, whereas in old age the slightest feeling is firmly fixed in one's head and raises a heap of problems..."

The old people fell asleep late, but got up early. In general, after Anna Mikhailovna gave up her medical work, they slept little and badly, and as a result life seemed twice as long to them... They shortened their nights with conversation, and spent their days loafing about the rooms or the garden, and casting questioning glances into each other's eyes.

Towards the end of the summer Fate sent the old people one more "illusion". Once, when Anna Mikhailovna went into her husband's room, she found him engrossed in an interesting occupation: he was sitting at the table and greedily eating grated radish and hemp oil. The muscles of his face were working, and saliva was dripping round the corners of his mouth.

"Have some, Anyuta!" he offered. "It's splendid!"

Anna Mikhailovna tried the radish with some hesitation, and began to eat. Soon an expression of greed appeared on her face too…

"It would be nice to have some of that… what d'you call it?" the General said that evening as he was going to bed. "It would be nice the way the Jews do it, rip open a pike's belly, take out the roe, fresh, you know, and some spring onions…"

"Well, why not? It's not difficult to catch a pike!"

The General, undressed as he was and barefoot, went off to the kitchen, woke up the cook and ordered him to catch a pike. In the morning Anna Mikhailovna suddenly felt like having some smoked sturgeon, and Martyn had to gallop off to town for it.

"Oh!" the old woman said in alarm. "I forgot to tell him to get some peppermint cakes while he is about it! I'd like to have something sweet…"

The old people gave themselves up to gustatory sensations. They never left the kitchen, and competed with each other at thinking up new dishes. The General wracked his brains, remembered his bachelor camp life, when he had had some culinary experience himself, and invented… Among the dishes they invented they especially liked one prepared from rice, grated cheese, eggs and the gravy from overdone meat. This dish requires a great deal of pepper and bay leaves.

The last "illusion" ended with this spicy dish. It fell to its lot to be the last delight of both lives.

"It looks like rain…" said the General, who was working up for a stroke, one September night. "I don't think I should have eaten so much of that rice today… I feel very heavy."

The General's wife was spread out on the bed, breathing heavily. She felt stifled… She, like the old man, had a stomach ache.

"And what's more, my legs are itching, damn them…" grumbled the old man. "I've got some sort of itch from the soles of my feet to my knees… It hurts and it itches… it's unbearable, damn it! But I'm keeping you awake… I'm sorry…"

More than an hour passed in silence. Little by little Anna Mikhailovna became used to the heaviness in her stomach, and dozed off. The old man sat up in bed, put his head on his knees and sat like that for a long time. Then he began to scratch his shins. The more assiduously his nails worked, the worse the itch became.

After a little while the wretched old man climbed off the bed and hobbled about the room. He looked out of the window... There, outside the window, in bright moonlight, the cold of autumn was gradually shackling dying nature. He could see the cold, grey fog shrouding the withering grass, and the freezing wood awake and shuddering with what remained of its yellow leaves.

The General sat down on the floor, grasped his knees and put his head on them.

"Anyuta!" he called.

The old woman, who was a light sleeper, turned over and opened her eyes.

"You know what I was thinking, Anyuta?" the old man began. "You're not asleep? I was thinking that the most natural interest in old age should be children... What do you think? But if there aren't any children, then people have to take an interest in something else... It would be a good thing to be a writer... or an artist... or a scholar... when one's old... They say that when Gladstone has nothing to do he studies the ancient classics and – it absorbs him. So that if he is thrown out of office, he'll have something to fill up his life. And in the same way it would be a good thing to go in for mysticism... or... or..."

The old man scratched his legs and went on:

"But it also happens that old people fall into second childhood – you know, when they want to plant trees, wear medals... take up spiritualism..."

A light snore came from the old woman. The General stood up and again looked out of the window. The cold morosely asked to be let in, and the fog had already crept up to the wood and was shrouding the tree trunks.

How many more months to spring? thought the old man, pressing his forehead against the cold glass. October... November... December... six months!

And these six months somehow appeared to him as something endlessly long, as long as his old age. He limped round the room and sat down on the bed.

"Anyuta!" he called.

"Well?"

"Is your medicine chest locked?"

"No, why?"

"Nothing. I want to put some iodine on my legs."

Silence ensued once more.

"Anyuta!" The old man woke up his wife.

"What?"

"Are the bottles labelled?"

"Yes, yes."

The General slowly lit a candle, and went out of the room.

For a long time the sleepy Anna Mikhailovna could hear his bare feet dragging and the tinkling of medicine bottles. Finally he came back, groaned, and lay down.

He did not wake up in the morning. Whether he just died, or whether it was because he had been to the medicine chest, Anna Mikhailovna did not know. And anyway, she was too shaken to inquire into the causes of his death...

Once more she began to bustle about aimlessly, nervously, without any system. Donations, fasts, vows, collections for pilgrimages began again...

"I want to go to a convent!" she whispered, pressing herself in fear to the old maidservant. "To a convent!"

Other People's Trouble

IT WAS HARDLY SIX O'CLOCK IN THE MORNING when Kovalyov, a newly fledged lawyer, got into the carriage with his young wife and drove off along a country lane. He and his wife had never got up early before, and now the splendour of the quiet summer morning seemed to them like something out of a fairy tale. The earth, clad in green and besprinkled with diamonds of dew, looked beautiful and happy. Sun rays were falling in bright patches on the wood, were quivering in the sparkling river, and in the unusually clear blue air there was such freshness that it seemed as if the whole of God's world had just had a bath, and become younger and healthier in consequence.

For the Kovalyovs – as they themselves acknowledged later – this was the happiest morning of their honeymoon, and therefore of their whole lives. They chattered without stopping, sang, roared with laughter for no reason, and played the fool to such an extent that finally they felt ashamed of behaving like that in front of the coachman. Not only in the present, but in the future, too, it seemed that happiness would be theirs: they were going to buy an estate – a little "romantic spot" of which they had been dreaming since the day they were married. The future held the most brilliant expectations for them both. He dreamt of his future work in rural self-government, of rational methods of agriculture, of the work of his own hands and other blessings about which he had read and heard so much, while she was attracted by the purely romantic side of the business: shady avenues, fishing, fragrant nights...

What with laughter and conversation they did not notice that they had driven twelve miles. Court Councillor Mikhailov's estate, which they were going to look at, stood on a high and steep river bank, and was hidden behind a birch grove... The red roof was hardly visible because of the thick green, and all the clay bank was planted with young saplings.

"The view's not bad!" said Kovalyov, as the carriage drove through a ford to the other side of the river. "The house is on the hill, and at the foot of the hill there's a river! It's damn attractive! Only, you know, Verochka, those steps don't fit in at all... they spoil the whole view, they're so clumsy... If we buy this estate then we must certainly put some wrought-iron steps..."

Verochka liked the view too. Laughing loudly, and with affectation in every limb, she ran up the steps with her husband after her, and both of them, dishevelled and out of breath, went into the coppice. The first person to meet them near the house was a big peasant, sleepy, hairy and morose. He was sitting by a little porch and cleaning a child's boot.

"Is Mr Mikhailov at home?" Kovalyov asked him. "Go and tell him that some prospective buyers have come to see the estate."

The peasant looked at the Kovalyovs with dumb amazement and ambled off slowly – not to the house, but to the kitchen, which was at the side of the house. At the same instant faces – each one sleepier and more astonished than the last – flashed for a moment at the kitchen window.

"Prospective buyers have arrived!" a whisper could be heard. "Good Heavens! Mikhalkovo is being sold! Look, how young they are!"

Somewhere a dog barked, and an angry wail could be heard, such as cats give when their tails are stepped on. The servants' agitation was soon also communicated to the chickens, geese and turkeys, which were peacefully pacing up and down the paths. Soon a lad who looked like a servant darted out of the kitchen; he peered at the Kovalyovs and ran to the house, putting his coat on as he went... The Kovalyovs thought this commotion very funny, and they could hardly contain their laughter.

"What funny faces!" said Kovalyov, exchanging a glance with his wife. "They look at us as if we were savages!"

At last a little man with a clean-shaven, elderly face and dishevelled hair came out of the house... He clicked his heels – he was wearing ragged slippers embroidered with gold – smiled sourly, and fixed a stony stare on his unbidden guests...

"Mr Mikhailov?" Kovalyov began, raising his hat. "How do you do?... My wife here and I read the land bank's advertisement about the sale of your estate, and now we have come to have a look at it... We may buy it... Would you be kind enough to show it us?..."

Mikhailov gave another sour smile, became embarrassed, and blinked his eyes. In his confusion he made his hair even more dishevelled, and such a comical expression of shame and bewilderment appeared on his clean-shaven face that Kovalyov and his Verochka looked at each other and could not refrain from smiling.

"Very pleased to meet you, sir," he mumbled. "At your service... Have you come a long way, sir?"

"From Konkov... We're living in a villa there."

"In a villa... Are you?... Extraordinary business! Welcome! You must forgive us, but we've only just got up, and it's not very tidy."

Smiling sourly and rubbing his hands, Mikhailov led his guests to the other side of the house. Kovalyov put on his glasses and, with the look of an expert tourist surveying the sights, began to inspect the estate. He saw first a big stone house of old-fashioned, heavy design, and covered with coats of arms, lions and peeling stucco. The roof had not been painted for a long time, the windows had iridescent glass, grass was growing in the chinks between the steps. Everything was dilapidated and neglected, but on the whole they liked the house. It looked romantic, modest and benign, like an old maiden aunt. In front of it, a few paces from the front door, shone a pond, on which floated two ducks and a toy boat. Birch trees, all of the same height and thickness, grew round the pond.

"Aha! And there's a pond too!" said Kovalyov, screwing up his eyes against the sun. "That's very attractive. Are there any crucians in it?"

"Yes, sir... There used to be carp in it too once, but then when they stopped cleaning the pond, the carp all died." "A pity," said Kovalyov in the tone of a mentor. "A pond should be cleaned as often as possible – all the more so as slime and waterweeds make splendid fertilizer for the fields. You know what, Vera? When we buy this estate, let's build a summerhouse on piles in the middle of the pond, with a little bridge leading to it. I saw a summerhouse like that at Prince Afrontov's."

"We could have tea in the summerhouse..." Verochka sighed sweetly.

"Yes... But what's that tower there with a steeple?"

"That's the visitors' annexe," Mikhailov answered.

"How out of place it is, sticking up there! We'll pull it down. In general, a great deal will have to be pulled down. A very great deal!"

Suddenly they heard, clearly and distinctly, the sound of a woman weeping. The Kovalyovs looked round at the house, but at the same time one of the windows banged, and through the opalescent glass two big eyes, wet with tears, flashed only for a moment. The person who was weeping was obviously ashamed of her tears and, slamming the window, had hidden behind the curtain.

"Wouldn't you like to look at the garden and the outhouses?" said Mikhailov quickly, wrinkling his face – wrinkled enough as it was – into a sour smile. "Come along... after all, the most important thing is not the house but... but the rest..."

The Kovalyovs went off to look at the stables and barns. The lawyer made the round of each barn, looked about, sniffed everything and showed off his knowledge of agriculture. He enquired how many acres the estate had and how many head of cattle, criticized Russia for cutting down her forests, reproached Mikhailov for letting so much manure be wasted, and so on. As he was talking he kept on glancing at his Verochka, who did not take her loving eyes off him for a moment, and thought: how clever he is!

While they were inspecting the cattle sheds they once more heard someone crying.

"Listen, who is that crying there?" asked Verochka.

Mikhailov made a gesture with his hand and turned away.

"Odd," murmured Verochka, when the whimpering changed to interminable hysterical weeping. "It's just as if someone was being beaten or slaughtered."

"It's my wife, don't take any notice of her..." said Mikhailov.

"Why on earth is she crying?"

"She's a weak woman, madam! She can't bear to see her family home being sold."

"Well, why are you selling it?" asked Verochka.

"We're not selling it, madam, it's the bank..."

"That's strange, why do you let them?"

Mikhailov glanced in amazement at Verochka's pink face and shrugged his shoulders.

"We have to pay the interest," he said. "Two thousand one hundred roubles every year! And where can we get it from? It's enough to make anyone howl. Women are weak, of course. There she is, sorry about her family home, sorry for the children and for me... and ashamed in front of the servants... When you said just now, over there by the pond, that this would have to be pulled down and that would have to be built, it was just like a knife in her heart."

When they went back past the house, the Kovalyovs saw a schoolboy with close-cropped hair and two little girls – Mikhailov's children – at the windows. What were the children thinking, as they looked at the prospective buyers? Verochka probably understood their thoughts... When she took her seat in the carriage to drive home, the fresh morning and her dreams of a "romantic spot" no longer had any charm for her.

"How unpleasant it all is!" she said to her husband. "Really, we should give them two thousand one hundred roubles! Let them go on living on their estate..."

"You're a clever one, aren't you!" laughed Kovalyov. "Of course, one's sorry for them, but after all they have themselves to blame. Why did they mortgage the estate? Why have they neglected it so? One shouldn't even waste any pity on them. If that estate were intelligently developed, if one were to introduce rational methods of agriculture... go in for cattle-breeding and so on... one could make a good living out of it. But they didn't do a thing, the swine... He's probably a sot and a gambler – did you see his silly face? – and she's probably just interested in clothes, and extravagant. I know their sort!"

"How can you know them, Styopa?"

"I do! They complain they haven't anything to pay the interest with. How is it they can't find that two thousand, I'd like to know? If they were to introduce rational methods of agriculture, apply fertilizers to the soil and go in for cattle breeding... In general, if you consider the climatic and economic conditions, you could make a living out of just a couple of acres!"

Styopa went on chattering all the way home, and his wife listened to him and believed every word, but she did not recover her former mood. She could not get out of her head either Mikhailov's sour smile or the eyes filled with tears that for a moment had flashed at the window. When later the happy Styopa drove over twice to the auction and finally bought Mikhalkovo with the money of her dowry, she felt terribly uneasy. Her imagination kept conjuring up visions of Mikhailov and his family getting into the carriage and weeping as they left their beloved home. And the more gloomily and sentimentally her imagination worked, the more Styopa showed off. With the most obstinate self-assurance he discoursed on rational methods of agriculture, ordered a ton of books and magazines, ridiculed the Mikhailovs – and finally his agricultural dreams turned into the most shameless, audacious boasting...

"You just see!" he said. "I'm not Mikhailov, I'll show you how things should be run! Oh, yes!"

When the Kovalyovs moved into the deserted Mikhalkovo, the first things that caught Verochka's eye were the traces left by the previous inhabitants: a school timetable written in childish handwriting, a headless doll, a tomtit which flew in for crumbs, an inscription on a wall – "Natasha is a fool" – and so on. A great deal had to be repainted, repapered and pulled down before they could forget about other people's trouble.

A Reporter's Dream

"YOU ARE URGENTLY REQUESTED TO ATTEND the French colony's ball today. I have no one else to send but you. Write a paragraph, with as much detail as possible. If, for any reason, you are unable to attend the ball, please inform me immediately. I shall ask someone else to go. Ticket enclosed herewith. Yours..." (followed by the editor's signature).

"PS: There is to be a raffle. The prize will be a vase, which has been given by the President of the French Republic. I hope you'll win it."

When he had read this letter, Pyotr Semyonych, a reporter, lay down on the sofa, smoked a cigarette, and patted his chest and stomach with self-satisfaction. (He had just had dinner.)

"I hope you'll win it," he mimicked the editor. "And where shall I get the money from to buy a ticket? He won't give me any money for expenses, the swine. He's as stingy as Plyushkin. He ought to take example from the foreign papers... They know how to value people. For instance, you, Stanley, are going to search for Livingstone? Fine. Take so many thousand pounds! You, John Bull, are going to search for 'Jeanette'? Fine, take ten thousand! You're going to write up the French colony's ball? Fine. Take... about fifty thousand... That's how they do it abroad! But he just sends me one ticket, and then he'll pay five copecks a line and he imagines... the swine!"

Pyotr Semyonych closed his eyes and was plunged in thought. A multitude of thoughts, great and small, crawled about in his head. But soon all these thoughts became covered with a sort of agreeable pink mist. A jelly, semi-transparent and soft, began to ooze in every direction, from every crevice, hole and window... The ceiling began to sink... Little men, little horses with ducks' heads ran about, some creature's large, soft wing waved, a river began to flow... A little compositor went past carrying some very big letters, and smiled... Then everything was drowned in his smile, and Pyotr Semyonych began to dream.

He put on a tailcoat and white gloves, and went out into the street. A carriage bearing the editor's monogram on it had been waiting for him at the entrance for a long time. A liveried footman leapt from the coach box and helped him into the carriage, helped him into his seat just as if he were an aristocratic lady.

About a minute later the carriage stopped at the entrance of the Assembly Rooms. Frowning, he gave up his overcoat, and pompously went up a richly ornamented and illuminated staircase. (Terrific luxury.) Tropical plants, flowers from Nice, dresses costing thousands…

"It's the correspondent…" a whisper ran through the crowd of many thousands of people. "It is he…"

A little old man with a solicitous expression and wearing decorations ran up to him.

"I beg your pardon!" he said to Pyotr Semyonych. "Oh, I beg your pardon!"

"Oh, don't mention it! Really, you embarrass me…" said the reporter.

And suddenly, to his great amazement, he began to chatter in French. Before he had only known one word – *"merci"* – but now – just listen! Like that, with any luck, one could learn to speak Chinese.

Pyotr Semyonych took a flower and threw down a hundred roubles, and just at that moment a telegram from the editor was brought to him: "Win the President of the French Republic's gift, and write your impressions. Reply paid for a thousand words. Don't worry about expense." He went to the raffle and began to take tickets. He took one… two… ten… Finally he took a hundred, a thousand, and received a Sèvres porcelain vase. Seizing the vase with both hands, he hurried on.

A little lady with luxurious flaxen hair and blue eyes came to meet him. Her dress was remarkable, above all criticism. A crowd followed her.

"Who is this?" the reporter asked.

"This is an illustrious Frenchwoman. She was ordered from Nice with the flowers…"

Pyotr Semyonych went up to her and introduced himself. A moment later he took her arm, and walked on and on… He had so many questions to ask the French girl, so many… She was so delightful!

She's mine! he thought. But where shall I put the vase in my room? he wondered, admiring the French girl. His room was small, but the vase was growing and growing, and had grown so much that it would not even get into the room. He was on the point of tears.

"A-a-a... so you love the vase more than me, do you?" the French girl said to him suddenly, out of the blue; and bang! she hit the vase with her fist.

The valuable vessel cracked loudly and flew into pieces. The French girl laughed, and ran away somewhere into a mist, into a cloud. All the newspaper men stood round laughing... Pyotr Semyonych, furious, foaming at the mouth, ran after them, and suddenly, finding himself in the Bolshoi Theatre, fell head-downwards from the sixth tier.

Pyotr Semyonych opened his eyes, and saw that he was lying on the floor beside his own sofa. His bruised back and elbow ached.

Thank God there's no French girl! he thought, rubbing his eyes. So the vase isn't broken. It's a good thing I'm not married, if I were, I dare say the children would start romping, and would break the vase.

But when he had rubbed his eyes thoroughly, of course he did not see the vase either.

It's all a dream, he thought. "Still, it's one o'clock in the morning already. The ball must have started ages ago... it's time I went... I'll just lie here a little bit longer, and then – off I go!"

But when he had lain there a little bit longer he stretched and... fell asleep – and so he never got to the French colony's ball.

"Well?" the editor asked him next day. "Did you go to the ball? Did you enjoy it?"

"So-so... Nothing special," he said, making a bored face. "Tame. Dull. I wrote it up in two hundred lines. I scolded our society a bit for not knowing how to have a good time." When he had said this, he turned towards the window and thought of the editor:

"The s-w-i-n-e!!"

One Man's Meat

I T WAS AFTER TWO O'CLOCK IN THE MORNING. The Fibrovs, husband and wife, were not asleep. He was tossing from side to side, constantly spitting, while she – a small, thin brunette – was lying motionless and looking thoughtfully at the open window, through which peeped the dour and unsociable dawn…

"I can't sleep!" she sighed. "Do you feel sick?"

"Yes, a bit."

"I can't understand, Vasya, why you aren't fed up with coming home every day in such a state! There's not a single night without you feeling ill. You ought to be ashamed of yourself!"

"Well, I'm sorry… I don't do it on purpose. I drank a bottle of beer at the editor's office, then I had a drop more at the 'Arkadia'. Forgive me."

"Oh, what is there to forgive? You ought to think it repulsive and disgusting yourself. Spitting, hiccuping… You look like nothing on earth. Why, it's every night, every night! I can't remember when you came home sober."

"I don't want to drink, but somehow it just goes down of its own accord. It's such a damn awful job – you rush about town all day. You have a glass of vodka somewhere, beer somewhere else, and in yet another place you meet a friend who's having a drink, you see… it's impossible not to drink. Another time you can't get any information without splitting a bottle of vodka with some swine or other. For example, today at that fire I couldn't very well not have a drink with the agent."

"Yes, it's an awful job!" the brunette sighed. "You should give it up, Vasya!"

"Give it up? How can I!"

"Of course you can. It would be all right if you were a real writer, if you wrote good poetry or stories, but as it is you're just a reporter, writing about thefts and fires. You write such nonsense – makes one ashamed to read it sometimes. It wouldn't be so bad if you earned a lot, two or three hundred roubles a month say, but you get a miserable fifty roubles, and even that's not regular. The flat's poor and dirty, and it stinks of laundry, and we're surrounded by workmen and loose women. You hear nothing but vulgar words and songs all day. We haven't any furniture or linen. You're miserably dressed, like a pauper, so that the landlady calls you by your Christian name, while I'm worse than any milliner. We don't eat half as well as workmen... You eat some mess or other, somewhere in town, in pubs, and you probably don't even pay for that yourself, I... God alone knows what I eat! If we were working class, uneducated, then I'd be reconciled to this existence, but after all you're from a good family, went to the university, you speak French. I went to a good school, I'm used to being pampered."

"You wait, Katyusha, they'll ask me to run the gossip column in the *Night-Blindness* – then we'll live differently. I'll take a flat then."

"You've been promising me that for three years now. And what's the point anyway, even if they do ask you? However much you get, you'll just drink it all away. It isn't as if you'd give up going about with your writers and actors! But d'you know what, Vasya? I ought to write to my uncle Dmitry Fyodorych in Tula. He'd find you a splendid job somewhere in a bank or a government office. It would be fine, Vasya! You'd go to the office like other people, on the twentieth of every month you'd get your salary – and no worry! We'd rent a detached house with its own yard and sheds and a hayloft. You can rent a splendid house there for two hundred a year. We'd buy furniture, china, tablecloths, we'd have a cook and have dinner every day. You'd come back from the office at three, glance at the table, and it would be laid ever so neat, and there'd be radishes and all sorts of different kinds of snacks. We'd get chickens, ducks, pigeons, we'd buy a cow. In the provinces, if you don't live luxuriously and drink your money away, you could have all that on a thousand roubles a year. And our children wouldn't die of damp, like they do now, and I wouldn't have to drag myself to the hospital all the time. Vasya, I beg you, for heaven's sake let's go and live in the provinces."

"I'd die of boredom with the savages there."

"Well, is it so lively here? We've no social life, we don't know anyone... Clean or fairly decent people you only have a business acquaintanceship with, but you don't know anyone's family. Who comes to see us? Well, who? That Cleopatra Sergeyevna... You think she's a celebrity, she writes musical feuilletons, but I think – she's a kept woman, a loose woman. Well, how can a woman drink vodka and take her corsets off with men looking on? She writes articles, talks about honesty all the time, but she borrowed a rouble from me last year, and hasn't paid it back to this day. Then there's that beloved poet of yours that comes to see you. You pride yourself on knowing such a famous man, but tell me honestly, is he worth it?"

"You couldn't have a more honest man!"

"But he isn't much fun. He only comes here to get drunk. He drinks and tells smutty stories. The day before yesterday, for example, he got sozzled and slept the whole night here on the floor. And the actors! When I was a girl I worshipped those celebrities, but since I married you it riles me just to look at a theatre. They're always drunk and coarse, they don't know how to behave in female company, they're supercilious, they go about in dirty jackboots. Terribly trying people! I can't understand what you find funny in those stories of theirs, which they tell with loud, raucous laughter! And you look at them somehow ingratiatingly, just as if those celebrities were doing you a favour by knowing you... Ugh!"

"Oh stop it, please!"

"But there, in the provinces, Civil Servants would come to see us, school teachers, officers. Educated, gentle people they all are, without pretensions. They'd have a cup of tea, and a glass of vodka if they were offered it, and go home. No noise, no stories, it would be dignified like that, considerate. You know, they'd be sitting in armchairs and on the sofa, discussing all sorts of things, and then the maid would hand tea round, with jam and biscuits. After tea they'd play the piano, sing, dance. It would be so nice, Vasya! At about midnight there'd be a light snack: sausage, cheese, the roast left over from dinner. After supper you'd see the ladies to their homes, and I'd stay at home and tidy up."

"It would be boring, Katyusha!"

"If it was boring at home, then you could go to the club, or for a walk... If you go for a walk here you don't meet a soul you know, you take to drink willy-nilly, but there you'd know everyone you met. You could talk to whoever you felt like talking to... teachers, lawyers, doctors – there'd be plenty of people to say an intelligent word to. They take a great interest in educated people there, Vasya! You'd be one of the leading lights there."

And Katyusha went on dreaming aloud for a long time. The lead-grey light outside the window gradually changed to white... The silence of night yielded its place imperceptibly to the bustle of morning. The reporter was not asleep, but listening and constantly raising his heavy head to spit. Suddenly, when Katyusha was least expecting it, he sat up sharply and leapt out of bed... His face was pale, there was sweat on his forehead...

"I feel deuced sick," he interrupted Katyusha's dreaming. "Wait a moment, I'm just coming..."

He covered his shoulders with a blanket, and ran quickly out of the room. He was a victim to that unpleasant occurrence which is so well-known to drunkards in the morning. About two minutes later he returned, pale and languid... His walk was unsteady... His face bore an expression of disgust, of despair, almost of terror, as if he had only just understood all the outward unsightliness of his way of life. The daylight lit up all the poverty and dirt of his room for him, and the expression of hopelessness on his face became more acute.

"Katyusha, write to your uncle!" he muttered.

"Really? You agree?" exclaimed the brunette in triumph. "I'll write tomorrow, and I give you my word of honour that you'll get a splendid job! Vasya, you... you are being serious?"

"Please, Katyusha, do... for God's sake."

And Katyusha once more began to dream aloud. Lulled by the sound of her own voice, she soon fell asleep. She dreamt of a detached house, of a farmyard in which her own ducks and hens were sedately pacing. She saw pigeons looking at her from a dormer window, and heard the cow mooing. Around all was quiet; there were no fellow lodgers, no raucous laughter, not even the hateful, hurried squeak of pens could be heard. Vasya, a picture of dignity and decorum, was striding through the front garden to the gate. He was going to the office. And her heart was filled with that feeling of peace which is undisturbed by desire and thought...

At midday she woke up in a capital frame of mind. Sleep had had a salutary effect on her. But then she rubbed her eyes and looked at the place where, not long ago, Vasya had been tossing and turning, and the joy which had seized her fell away from her like a piece of lead. Vasya was gone, to came back late at night drunk, as he had come back yesterday, the day before... always... Again she would daydream, again a look of disgust would flash across his face.

"There's no point in writing to Uncle!" she sighed.

The Guest

A Scene

ZELTERSKY, A SOLICITOR, COULD NOT KEEP his eyes open. Nature was plunged in darkness. "The breeze had fallen, the choirs of birds were silent, and the herds were lying down." Zeltersky's wife had gone to bed long ago, the servants were sleeping too, all the livestock was asleep, only Zelterski himself could not go to his bedroom, although his eyelids weighed a ton. The fact was that he had a guest, a retired Colonel called Peregarin, who lived in a neighbouring country villa. He had arrived after dinner, had sat down on the sofa, and had not once moved since then, just as if he was stuck to it. He was sitting there and recounting in a hoarse, nasal voice how he had been bitten by a mad dog in Kremenchug in 1842. He finished telling the story, and then began it from the beginning all over again. Zeltersky was in despair. He would have done anything to get rid of his guest! He frequently looked at his watch, said that his head ached, and often left the room where his guest was sitting – but it was all of no avail. His guest did not understand, and went on talking about the mad dog.

Zeltersky was furious. The old fool will sit here till morning! he thought. What a blockhead! Well, if he doesn't understand ordinary hints, stronger measures will have to be taken. "Listen," he said aloud. "Do you know what I like about country life?"

"What?"

"The fact that one can lead a regular life here. In town it's difficult to keep to a regular regime, whereas here it's just the opposite. We get up at nine, dine at three, have supper at ten, and by midnight we're asleep. I'm always in bed by twelve. Heaven forbid that I should go to bed later. I can't get rid of my migraine the next day if I do!"

"You don't say! Of course, it depends on what you're used to. You know, I used to have a friend called Klyushkin, a captain. I got to know him in Serpukhovo. Well now, this Klyushkin…"

And the Colonel, hiccuping, smacking his lips and gesticulating with plump fingers, began to tell him about Klyushkin. It had already struck midnight, the hand of the clock was reaching towards half-past twelve, but he still went on telling his story. Zeltersky was thrown into a sweat.

He doesn't understand! The silly ass! he thought, irritated. Does he really think that his visit gives me pleasure? Now, how can I get rid of him? "Listen," he interrupted the Colonel. "What should I do? My throat hurts terribly! I don't know what the hell possessed me this morning – I went to see a friend whose child is ill with diphtheria, I've probably caught it. Yes, I feel I've caught it. I've got diphtheria!"

"It does happen!" said Peregarin imperturbably, in a nasal voice.

"It's a dangerous illness! It's not only that I'm ill myself, but I can give it to other people too. The illness is infectious to the highest degree. I only hope that I won't give it to you, Parfeni Savvych!"

"To me? Ha-ha! I've lived in fever hospitals and didn't catch anything – and you think I'll catch it from you! ha-ha… No, old chap, an old fogey like me won't catch any illnesses. Old men are tough. We had a little old man in our brigade, a Colonel Trébien… He was of French origin. Well now, this Trébien…"

And Peregarin began to describe how tough Trébien had been. The clock struck half-past twelve.

"Forgive me for interrupting you, Parfeni Savvych," groaned Zeltersky. "At what time do you go to bed?"

"Sometimes at two, sometimes at three, and sometimes I don't go to bed at all, especially if I'm in good company, or if my rheumatism's bothering me. Today, for example, I shall go to bed at about four, because I had a good sleep before dinner, I can do without sleep altogether. During the war we sometimes didn't go to bed for weeks on end. I remember once, we were stationed near Akhaltsykh…"

"Excuse me, but I always go to bed at twelve. I get up at nine, so I have to go to bed early, willy-nilly."

"Of course. It's good for the health, too, to get up early. Well, it was like this… we were stationed near Akhaltsykh…"

"It's the very devil… I feel shivery, feverish. It's always like that with me before one of my fits. I should tell you that I sometimes have strange, nervous fits. At about one o'clock in the morning… the fits never occur in the daytime… suddenly a noise starts in my head: buzz-buzz-buzz… I lose my senses, leap up and start throwing whatever household utensils there may be lying about. If there's a knife near – I throw the knife, if there's a chair – I throw that. I feel shivery now, it's probably a fit coming on. It always begins with shivering."

"Did you ever! You should have treatment for it!"

"I've had treatment, it doesn't help... I just confine myself to warning my friends and the household that they should go away shortly before a fit, but I've given up having treatment ages ago."

"Pss... What illnesses one does come across in this world! Plague, and cholera, and all sorts of fits..."

The Colonel shook his head and was plunged in thought. Silence fell.

How would it be if I read him my book? the thought occurred to Zeltersky. I've got that novel of mine lying about somewhere, I wrote it when I was still at school... It might be of service now... "Oh, by the way," Zeltersky interrupted Peregarin's reflections, "wouldn't you like me to read you something I've written? I concocted something in my leisure hours. A novel in five parts, with a prologue and epilogue."

And without waiting for an answer, Zeltersky jumped up and fished out from the drawer of his table an old, yellow manuscript, on which was written in large letters: "The Swell: A Novel in Five Parts".

Now he'll surely go away, mused Zeltersky, turning over the pages of his youthful peccadillo. I'll go on reading to him till he howls... "Well, now listen, Parfeni Savvych..."

"With pleasure... I like it..."

Zeltersky began to read. The Colonel crossed his legs, settled himself more comfortably, and made a serious face, evidently preparing himself to listen conscientiously and for a long time. The reader began with a description of nature. When the clock struck one, nature yielded its place to a description of the castle in which lived the hero of the novel. Count Valentin Blensky.

"I'd like to live in a castle like that!" sighed Peregarin. "And it's so well written! I could sit and listen to it for ages!"

You wait a bit! thought Zeltersky. You'll howl soon!

At half-past one the castle gave way to a description of the hero's handsome personal appearance... Precisely at two o'clock the reader read in a quiet, subdued voice:

"'You ask, what do I desire? Oh, I desire that there, far away, beneath the vaults of the southern sky, your little hand should languidly tremble in my hand... There, only there, will my heart throb stronger beneath

the vaults of my spiritual edifice… Love, love!' No, Parfeni Savvych…
I can't go on… I'm at the end of my tether!"

"Well, drop it. You'll finish it tomorrow, but let's talk now… Well
now, I haven't told you yet what happened at Akhaltsykh…"

Zeltersky, worn out, threw himself back in the sofa and, closing his
eyes, began to listen…

I've tried everything, he thought. Not a single bullet has pierced this
mammoth hide. Now he'll sit here till four o'clock… Lord, I'd give a
hundred roubles now to flop into bed this very instant… Ah! Let's ask
him for a loan! That's an excellent method… "Parfeni Savvych," he
interrupted the Colonel. "I'm interrupting you again. I want to ask
you a little favour… The fact is that lately, living here in the country,
I've been spending an awful lot. I simply haven't got a penny, but I'm
expecting some money at the end of August."

"But… I've stayed too long…" snorted Peregarin, looking round for
his cap. "It's after two already… What's that you were saying?"

"I'd like to borrow two or three hundred roubles from someone…
You don't know anyone who could lend me that?"

"How should I? Still… it's time you went to bye-byes… Goodbye…
Remember me to your wife…"

The Colonel took his cap and made a step towards the door.

"Where are you off to?" said Zeltersky in triumph. "And I wanted to
ask you… Knowing your kindness, I hoped…"

"Tomorrow, but now – off to my wife – quick march! She's probably
been waiting up for her loved one… Ha-ha-ha! Goodbye, my dear
fellow… Off to bed!"

Peregarin pressed Zeltersky's hand quickly, put on his cap, and went
out. His host was triumphant.

Wife for Sale

I

GROHOLSKY EMBRACED LISA, kissed every one of her fingers, with their rosy, bitten nails, and seated her on the couch covered with cheap velvet. Lisa crossed her legs, placed her hands behind her head and lay down.

Groholsky sat down on a chair beside her, and bent down, enthralled by the vision before him.

How pretty she seemed to him lit in the rays of the setting sun! It hung full in the window, golden, with a dainty purple aureole, momentarily covering the entire drawing room, and Lisa herself, in a flush of soft, amber light...

Groholsky was enchanted, although, Heaven knows, Lisa was no great beauty. True, her thin, curly hair was black as soot, and her small, cat-like face, with its grey eyes and turned-up nose, was fresh, and even piquant, and her lithe, graceful, well-proportioned body was like an electric eel's, but generally speaking... Setting my own prejudices aside, however: Groholsky, who had been thoroughly spoilt by women, and had loved and unloved many in his time, considered her beautiful. But then he loved her, and a blind love will find an ideal beauty everywhere.

"Listen," he began, gazing straight into her eyes, "I came to talk things over, my sweet. Love cannot abide the vague or indefinite... Indefinite relationships which... I spoke to you previously, Lisa. We must try to find an answer to the question I raised yesterday. Let's try to find a solution together. What are we going to do?"

Lisa yawned. Wrinkling her face, she withdrew her right hand from under her head.

"What are we going to do?" she repeated, barely audible after Groholsky.

"Why, yes, what are we going to do? You decide, you have a clever little head... I love you, and a man who loves cannot dissemble. He is more of an egoist. I cannot share you with your husband. I tear him into shreds mentally, each time I think he also loves you. And secondly, you love me. Love demands conditions of unalloyed freedom. But are you free? Aren't you tormented by the thought of this man everlastingly on your conscience? A man whom you do not love, and quite possibly, and quite naturally, might even hate… So much for the second point. Now thirdly… What was the third point? Ah, yes… We are deceiving him, Lisa… And that isn't honest. Truth above all things, Lisa, truth. Enough of lies!"

"Well, what can one do?"

"You should be able to guess. I think it's imperative that you tell him about our liaison, leave him and be free again. You must do both these things as quickly as possible, this evening for example. Explain to him and be done with it. Aren't you tired of this stolen, surreptitious love?"

"What? Explain – explain to Vanya?"

"Yes, of course!"

"That's impossible! I told you last night – Michele – it's impossible!"

"Why so?"

"He'll be offended, and start shouting, and doing all sorts of nasty things. As if you don't know what he's like! Heaven forbid! No explanations! What an idea!"

Groholsky mopped his forehead and sighed.

"Yes," he said, "he's bound to take it badly… After all, I'm taking away the man's happiness. Does he love you?"

"He loves me. Very much."

"That's a fine pickle! Don't know which end to begin. It's dishonest to hide it from him – yet an explanation might kill him! The devil only knows. What shall we do?"

Groholsky thought for a while, his pale face in a scowl.

"We can always go on as we are," said Lisa. "Let him find out, if he wants to."

"But that's… that's sinful… After all, you're mine, and no one has the right to think that you don't belong to me, but to someone else! You're mine! I won't share you with anyone! I'm sorry for him. God knows, I'm sorry, Lisa. It hurts me to look at him! But… but what is one to do, ultimately? You don't love him, do you? Why bother with him then? You must explain, tell him everything and come away with me. You're my wife, not his. He ought to know. He'll get over it somehow... He's not the first, nor the last... Will you run away? Eh? Tell me quickly! Will you?"

Lisa sat up and looked questioningly at Groholsky.

"Should I run away?"

"Why, yes... to my estate... then afterwards to the Crimea. We can explain by letter... We can go tonight. There's a train at one thirty. What do you say?"

Lisa scratched the bridge of her nose thoughtfully.

"Very well," she said, and burst into tears.

Her eyes suffused, small reddish marks appeared on her cheeks, as tears cascaded down her cat-like little face...

"What are you crying for?" Groholsky sounded alarmed. "Lisa! What's it all about? Sweetheart, dearest..."

Lisa stretched out her arms to Groholsky and hung round his neck, sobbing.

"I'm sorry for him," she murmured. "So sorry for him..."

"Whom are you sorry for?"

"For Va...Vanya."

"And aren't I sorry for him? We'll make him suffer... He'll suffer and curse us... But is it our fault that we love each other?"

Having said this, Groholsky leapt away from Lisa as if stung, and sat down in an armchair. She disengaged herself immediately from his neck, and quickly seated herself on the couch.

They both blushed horribly, lowered their eyes and coughed.

A tall, broad-shouldered man of around thirty, wearing Civil Service uniform, entered the drawing room unnoticed. Only the noise of a chair into which he had stumbled on entering heralded his arrival, and forced the two lovers to look round. This was the husband.

But they had looked round too late. He had seen how Groholsky had held Lisa around her waist, and how she had clung to Groholsky's white, aristocratic neck.

"He's seen us!" thought Lisa and Groholsky at the same moment, trying to hide their leaden arms and confused eyes...

The stupefied husband's rosy face turned white.

A strange, choking, soul-searing silence lasted for three minutes. And what a three minutes! Groholsky remembers them to this very day.

The first to stir and break the silence was the husband. He marched over to Groholsky, wearing an inane grimace, which resembled a smile, on his face, and held out his hand. Groholsky squeezed the soft, sweaty hand lightly, and shuddered as if he had crushed a cold frog in his fist.

"How do you do?" he mumbled.

"And how are you?" wheezed the husband, barely audible, as he sat down opposite Groholsky, and straightened the back of his collar...

Another exhausting silence followed. But this was more tolerable... The worse moment had already passed.

It only remained for one of the two to withdraw to look for some matches or some other nonsense. They both wanted desperately to leave. But they both sat tugging at their beards, cudgelling their brains to find a way out of the awkward situation. They sweated. They suffered unendurably and devoured themselves with hatred. They wanted to come to grips, but how, and who was to begin? If only she would leave the room!

"I saw you at the gathering last night," muttered Bugrov (that was the husband's name).

"I was there... At the ball. Did you dance?"

"Hmm... yes, with Lyukotskaya, the youngest one. She's heavy on her feet. Dances terribly, but talks a lot." (Pause.) "Babbles all the time."

"Yes... it was pretty boring. I observed you..."

Groholsky looked up accidentally at Bugrov... His eyes met the deceived husband's errant eyes, and he could stand it no longer. He rose hurriedly, quickly caught Bugrov's hand, squeezed it, grabbed his hat and made for the door with an uncomfortable sensation in the middle of his back. He felt as if a thousand eyes were riveted to his spine, rather like an actor who is booed off the stage, or a fop who has been knocked on the head and dragged off by the police...

As soon as Groholsky's footsteps had faded and the door had creaked shut in the hall, Bugrov jumped up, circled the room a few times and advanced on his wife. She wrinkled her kitten face, blinked her eyes as if expecting a casual slap. Her husband came up to her, trod on her dress, jostled her with his knee, trembling all over, his face white and distorted with anger.

"If you ever let him in here again, you trash," he said in a hollow, tearful voice, "so much as a step, I'll kill you! You understand? You worthless object! You tremble, do you? You hideous creature!"

Bugrov seized her by the elbow, shook her and hurled her like an india-rubber ball towards the window.

"You've no shame, you vulgar creature!"

Lisa flew to the window, barely touching the floor with her feet, and clutched the curtains.

"Silence!" he roared, stamping his foot, his eyes blazing with fury.

She remained silent. She looked up at the ceiling and sighed, like a penitent child waiting to be punished.

"So that's how it is? You've taken up with that good-for-nothing? Excellent! And what about your marriage vows? A fine wife and mother you've turned out to be! Silence!"

He struck her across her pretty, fragile shoulders.

"Keep quiet, you scum! I haven't even begun. If I ever catch this blackguard in here... Listen to me! If ever I see you with him, don't ask for mercy! I'll kill you. And him. I don't care a damn if they send me to Siberia! Now get out of here. I'm sick of the sight of you!"

Bugrov wiped his eyes and forehead on his coat sleeve and paced round the drawing room. Lisa continued to sob, louder and still louder, twitching her shoulders and her turned-up little nose, and began to examine the lacework on the curtains.

"So you want to fool around?" shouted her husband. "You're head's stuffed full of nonsense! It's all a lot of rubbish! And I don't like any of it, friend Lizaveta. This isn't a brothel. I won't stand for it. If you must engage in this dirty business, you'd better clear out. There's no place in my house for you, so quick march! But if you want to be a wife, forget these fancy gentry, banish them from your mind and don't talk about it again! Love your husband. You were given a husband, well, love him then, or is one not enough? Is that it? Get along with you now, tormentors, all of you!"

Bugrov paused, and then shouted:

"I told you to clear out! Go into the nursery! What are you yowling about? It's her own fault and she howls! Last year you hung around Petyka Totchkov – and now – God forgive – it's this devil... pfoo! It's time you realized who you are, a wife and mother! So much unpleasantness last year, and now it's going to start all over again... pfoo!"

Bugrov sighed loudly, leaving an aroma of sherry in the air. He had just dined, and was a little tipsy...

"Don't you know your responsibilities? No! Then you'll have to be taught! You're still ignorant! Your mother ran around and you... Go on, cry! Howl!"

Bugrov came up to his wife and pulled the curtain out of her hand.

"Don't stand by the window... People can see you crying... Don't let it happen another time. Petting will get you into trouble and land you in a mess. Do you think I like wearing horns? That's what will happen if you go around with these types... Now that's enough... Another time, I'll... After all, I... Lisa... that's enough."

Bugrov sighed, enveloping Lisa in his sherry-ladened breath.

"You're young: you don't understand anything. I'm never at home, so they take advantage of it. You must be clever, use your common sense. They'll only make a fool of you. And that I couldn't stand. *Finis*. I might as well lie down and die then. I'd be capable of anything. Just you betray me, my girl, and I'll beat the life out of you and throw you out. Go to those blackguards then."

And Bugrov wiped the fickle Lisa's wet, tear-stained face with his large, soft palm (horrible dictum!). He treated his twenty-year-old wife like a child.

"Now, that's enough. I'll forgive you this time, but never again. It's the fifth time. But I won't forgive you the sixth. As God is holy. Even He wouldn't forgive such tricks!"

Bugrov bent down and stretched his shiny lips to kiss Lisa's little head.

But kiss her he did not.

Doors slammed in the hallway, the dining room and the salon, and Groholsky flew into the sitting room like a hurricane. He was pale and shivering. He was waving his hands, kneading his expensive hat. His frock coat hung on him like on a clothes' hanger. He was the epitome of fever itself. Bugrov saw him, left his wife and went to stare out of another window. Groholsky ran up to him, waving his hands and breathing heavily and, without looking at anyone, began to speak in a trembling voice:

"Enough of this play-acting, Ivan Petrovich! Let's stop fooling each other! Enough, I can't stand it any longer. Do what you like, but I can't go on like this. It's scandalous and unnerving, that's what it is!"

Groholsky choked and spluttered.

"My code won't allow it. I'm an honest man. I love her. I love her more than anything on earth. I'm bound to tell you... surely you've observed this and..."

"What am I going to say to him?" thought Ivan Petrovich.

"We must put an end to this comedy. It cannot go on much longer. It must be decided somehow."

Groholsky drew in a deep breath of air and continued:

"I cannot live without her. And she feels the same. You're an educated man, you'll understand that family life under these circumstances becomes impossible. This woman does not belong to you. That is... In a word, I ask you to be humane and indulgent, Ivan Petrovich! You must appreciate that I love her, I love her more than myself, above everything on earth, and I am really in no condition to fight against this love!"

"And what about her?" asked Bugrov in a sullen, somewhat mocking tone.

"Well, ask her. Ask her yourself, then. Ask her what it's like to live with you, a man she does not love, while loving another...Why it's – it's – sheer torture!"

"And what about her feelings?" Bugrov repeated, this time without any trace of mockery in his voice.

"She... she loves me! We fell in love with each other, Ivan Petrovich! Kill us, despise us, condemn us, do what you will, but we cannot hide it any longer from you! Judge us with all the severity of a man from whom we have taken – from whom Fate has taken his happiness!"

Bugrov reddened like an over-cooked lobster and stared at Lisa with one eye. He blinked, his fingers, lips and eyebrows began to tremble. Poor Bugrov, he had only to look into Lisa's tearful eyes to know that Groholsky was right. This was a serious business...

"Well, if that's how things are..." he murmured. "Then you—"

"God knows we feel for you," Groholsky whined in a high-pitched tenor. "Do you think we don't sympathize with you? I know only too well the unhappiness I've caused you. As God is my witness! But I crave your indulgence. We are not to blame! Love is no crime. No amount of will-power can prevail against it. Let me have her, Ivan Petrovich! Let her come away with me! Take what you will in return for your misery, take life itself, but give me Lisa! What can I give – if only in part – for her? I can substitute one kind of happiness with another! Yes, I can, Ivan Petrovich! It would be mean on my part to leave you empty-handed! I fully appreciate your feelings at this moment!"

Bugrov waved his hand as if to say "For God's sake leave me alone!" His eyes watered and filmed over... "They'll see me, and think I'm a crybaby..." he thought.

"I appreciate your feelings, Ivan Petrovich! I can give you another kind of happiness, such as you have never known. What would you like? I'm a rich man, the son of an influential father... Would you like some money? Well, how much would you like?"

Bugrov's heart began to beat wildly. He grasped the window curtains with both hands...

"Will you take... fifty thousand roubles? Ivan Petrovich, I beg you. This is no bribe, no horse-trade... I wish to sacrifice something from my side, to soften, if possible, your own immeasurable loss. Will you accept one hundred thousand? I'm willing. How about one hundred thousand?"

Dear God! Two enormous hammers throbbed inside the wretched Ivan Petrovich's sweating temples... He heard the sound of Russian troikas, with their tinkling bells, in his ears...

"Accept this sacrifice from me!" Groholsky continued. "I implore you. You'll take a great load off my conscience. I beg you!"

Dear Lord! An elegant four-seater carriage, drawn by handsome, well-groomed, spirited bays, sped by the window through which Bugrov was staring. It sped along the glistening causeway sprinkled with May rains. In the carriage sat people in straw hats, with satisfied faces, carrying fishing tackle and hunting bags... A schoolboy in a white cap held a gun in his hand. They were going into the country to fish and hunt, and drink tea in the fresh air. They were going to those delightful places Bugrov knew so well as a child when he ran around the fields, and the woods and the river banks, barefoot and sunburnt. How many thousand times happier was this son of a simple country deacon! How devilishly tempting was this month of May! How fortunate were those who could pull off their heavy service uniforms, and jump into a carriage to fly to the meadows where the quails call and the air smells of new-mown hay!

He was gripped in a pleasant, cold sensation. One hundred thousand roubles! His secret thoughts sped by with the carriage; all the fond dreams he had indulged in during his frustrating clerical career, while sitting in the Governor's chancellery, or in his own stuffy little study... A deep river, filled with fishes, a spacious garden with narrow footpaths, small fountains, shadows, flowers, summer houses, a magnificent country house with towers and terraces, and an Aeolian harp and silver bells. (He knew of the existence of the Aeolian harp from German novels.) A clear blue sky: the air, clean and transparent, saturated with perfume, reminded him of his own barefoot, hungry and careworn childhood... Get up at five, lie down at nine in the evening, catch fish in the daytime, hunt, gossip with the peasants. That was the life!

"Stop torturing me, Ivan Petrovich! Will a hundred thousand do?"

"Hmm... One hundred and fifty thousand," Bugrov bellowed hollowly like a hoarse bull, lowering his eyes shamefacedly as he waited for a reply.

"Done," said Groholsky. "I agree. Thank you, Ivan Petrovich. I won't keep you a moment..."

He leapt up, put on his hat and, making his way backwards, ran out of the drawing room.

Bugrov tightened his grip on the window curtains. He was ashamed of himself. He felt low and stupid, yet at the same time what wonderful prospects flashed through his aching brain. He was rich!

Lisa understood nothing, her only fear was that he would come over to her window and push her aside, so she slipped out of the half-open door into the nursery. She lay down huddled on the nanny's bed shivering with fever.

Bugrov remained alone. Feeling stifled, he opened the window. How delightfully the wind played on his face and neck! How good it would be to breathe this air, sprawled out on carriage cushions... And the air would even be better far from the town, near the woods and country villas. Bugrov even smiled to himself, relishing the idea of the fresh air which would envelop him when he stepped out on the terrace of his country house to admire the view... He pondered for a long time. The sun had already set, but he still stood, lost in meditation, trying desperately to lose Lisa's image, which persistently intruded into all his thoughts.

"I've brought it," Groholsky whispered into Bugrov's ear, having entered unnoticed. "Here it is. You'll find forty thousand in that packet. Be so good as to present this bill of exchange to Valentinov the day after tomorrow and you'll receive twenty... Here's another cheque, and I'll send my bailiff with the remaining thirty thousand in a day or so..."

Groholsky, flushed and excited, laid out a heap of documents and packages in front of Bugrov. It was a sizeable mound. Bugrov had never seen such a large, multicoloured assorted heap in his life before. Bugrov opened his fat fingers and began sorting out credit notes and cheques, without so much as glancing at Groholsky.

Having laid out all the money, Groholsky looked surreptitiously round the room for his newly bought and sold Dulcinea...

Bugrov hastily stuffed his pockets and wallet with money, stuffed the cheques into a desk drawer and, after drinking half a carafe of water, rushed out into the street.

"Cabby!" he cried savagely.

At eleven thirty that night he rolled up to the entrance of the Hotel Paris. He strode up the stairs noisily to the floor where Groholsky had an apartment, knocked and was shown in.

Groholsky was packing his things in a suitcase, while Lisa sat at a table trying on a variety of bracelets. They were both startled to see Bugrov enter their room. They thought he had come to fetch Lisa, as well as to return the money, which he might have taken on impulse, without due reflection. But Bugrov had not come for Lisa.

Ashamed of his new outfit, and feeling horribly awkward, he stood bowing at the doorway like a waiter. His new get-up was magnificent. Bugrov was unrecognizable. Accustomed as his huge body was to Civil Service uniform, he now cut a splendid figure in his brand-new, stylishly designed suit of French tricot. He wore a pair of shiny half-boots, with glittering fasteners. He stood ashamed of his new outfit, trying to hide with his right hand the watch fob for which he had, barely an hour ago, paid three hundred roubles...

"This is what I came about..." he began. "An understanding is more important than money. I shan't give Mischutka up."

"What Mischutka?" asked Groholsky.

"My son."

Groholsky and Lisa exchanged glances. Her eyes brimmed with tears: she flushed, her lips trembling.

"Very well," she said.

She thought of Mischa's warm little bed. It would be cruel to exchange such a bed for a sofa in a cheerless hotel room, so she agreed.

"But I will be able to see him," she said.

Bugrov bowed and left the room. He flew down the stairs elated, cutting the air with an expensive cane.

"Home," he told the driver. "I shall be leaving at five tomorrow morning. Come. If I'm asleep, wake me. We'll drive into the country…"

II

I T WAS A BEAUTIFUL AUGUST EVENING. The sun, covered in a golden, purple haze, stood over the western horizon, ready to sink beyond the distant kurgans.* The shadows and half-shadows had already disappeared from the garden, leaving the air moist. Only the tops of the trees remained touched with pale gold… It was warm. It had rained, adding more freshness to the already transparent, aromatic, exhilarating air.

I am not describing a metropolitan August, with its dark, misty, drizzling and impossibly damp and cold sunsets. Heaven forbid! Nor do I refer to our harsh northern August. I ask the reader to transport himself to the Crimea, on the coastline near Fyodosia, to the exact stop where stands the country house of one of my heroes.

The country house itself was neat and pretty, surrounded by flower beds, shrubs and clipped hedges. A hundred feet or so behind the house was an orchard which is often frequented by the owners and their guests. Groholsky pays a tidy sum for this house, something like a thousand roubles a year… It was not worth the rent, but it was certainly handsome… Tall, elegant, with delicate walls and very delicate balustrades, it was a fragile, refined house, painted light blue, overhung with curtains, draperies and portières, reminding one rather of a charming, delicate, frilly little miss…

On the evening in question, Groholsky and Lisa were sitting on the terrace of this country house. He was reading the *New Times*, drinking milk from a green mug. Standing on a table before him was a siphon of soda water. Groholsky imagined himself stricken with catarrh of the lungs and, on Doctor Dimitrev's advice, devoured enormous quantities of grapes, milk and soda water.

Lisa sat some way off, in an upholstered armchair. Leaning on one of the arms, she cradled her face in her little fists, staring at the house opposite… A blinding reflection from the windows struck her eyes…Beyond the small front garden, through the sparse trees, she could glimpse the immense expanse of the sea, with its dark-blue waves, and gleaming white ship masts… It was all so lovely!

Groholsky, who was reading a feuilleton by Anonymous, looked up every few lines, and stared with his blue eyes at Lisa's back… His eyes burned with all his former passion… His happiness knew no bounds, despite his imaginary catarrh of the lungs… Lisa, who felt his glance at her back, thought of her son's bright future. She was calm, and at peace with herself…

She was less interested in the sea and the blinding reflection which came from the windows of the house opposite than in the procession of carts which came one by one to that house.

Lisa saw the lattice gates and the large glass doors open, as a crowd of removers began to mill around with the furniture. Large armchairs and a settee covered in dark, raspberry-coloured velvet, chairs for the hall, the dining room and the drawing room, as well as a large double bed and a child's cot were carried in through the glass doors. A large, heavy-looking object, covered in sacking, was also brought in…

"It's a grand piano," Lisa thought, with a beating heart.

She had not heard the piano for a long time, and she was very fond of the piano. They did not have a single musical instrument in their country house. Both she and Groholsky were musicians at heart; but that's about all.

After the piano, boxes and crates marked "with care" were brought in.

These were crates with mirrors and crockery. A rich-looking, shiny carriage, drawn by two white swan-like horses, passed through the gates.

"My God! What wealth," thought Lisa, remembering her old pony, which Groholsky, who neither liked riding nor horses, had bought for a hundred roubles. Her pony looked like a flea compared with these swan-like horses. Groholsky, who was afraid of riding too fast, deliberately bought this old nag for Lisa.

"What wealth!" Lisa whispered, thinking to herself, as she watched the noisy furniture movers.

The sun was already hidden behind the hills, and the air had lost its transparency and dryness, but they still continued to mill and bring the furniture into the house. It had even grown too dark for Groholsky to read, but Lisa continued to stare unremittingly.

"Won't you light the lamp?" asked Groholsky, frightened lest a fly should fall into the milk and be swallowed by mistake in the dark. "Lisa, won't you light the lamp? Or do you want to sit in the dark, my angel?"

Lisa did not answer. She was engrossed in the little gig which had driven up to the gates of the house opposite. What a dear little horse had drawn the gig! It was of middle size, not large, but graceful... In the gig sat some gentleman or other in a top hat. A child of about three, apparently a boy, sat on his knees, waving his hands and shouting with delight...

Lisa suddenly squealed and bent forwards with her whole body.

"What's the matter with you?" asked Groholsky.

"Nothing... I merely... It seemed as if..."

The tall, broad-shouldered gentleman in the top hat jumped out of the gig. Taking the boy in his arms, he skipped gaily towards the glass doors.

The doors opened noisily and the two of them disappeared into the dark interior of the house.

A couple of grooms came up to the horse with the gig and respectfully led her through the gates. Lights soon appeared in the house opposite, and one could hear the sound of knives and forks and crockery being laid. The gentleman in the top hat had sat down to dinner, and judging by the unceasing clatter at the table, he must have taken his time about it. Lisa thought she could recognize the smell of chicken soup and roast duck. After dinner the house resounded with the most awful cacophony. The gentleman in the top hat had, in all probability, wished to entertain the lad somehow, and had allowed him to bang away to his heart's content on the piano.

Groholsky came up to Lisa and put his arm around her waist.

"What wonderful weather!" he exclaimed. "What air! Can't you feel it? I'm happy, Lisa, so deliriously happy, that I'm afraid something dreadful will happen. When great emotions are involved, something usually happens. You know what, Lisa? Despite all my happiness, I'm not absolutely at peace with myself. One idea constantly haunts and torments me. It won't give me any peace, day or night..."

"And what idea is that?"

"What idea? It's dreadful, my heart. I'm tortured by the thought of your husband. I've said nothing about this all along. I didn't want to disturb you. But I cannot remain silent any longer. Where is he? What's happened to him? Where's he gone to with all his money? It's awful! He comes like an apparition each night, with his gaunt, suffering, imploring face. Judge for yourself, my angel. We've robbed him of his happiness. We've built our own joy on the ruins of his happiness. Can the money he so generously took ever replace you? After all, he loved you, didn't he?"

"Yes, he did. He loved me very much."

"So, you see! He's either taken to drink, or even… I'm worried about him, terribly worried. Shouldn't we drop him a note, eh? Calm him down a bit. A kind word in time might…"

Groholsky sighed deeply, shook his head and sank down into the armchair, overwhelmed by his gloomy prognostications. He held his head up in his fists, and began to think. Judging by his face, they must have been tormenting thoughts.

"It's time I was in bed," said Lisa.

She went to her room, undressed and fluttered into bed. She went to bed at ten and got up at ten. She liked to look after herself.

She was soon in the arms of Morpheus, dreaming the most beguiling and enchanting dreams the night long. Entire novels, stories, the Arabian Nights passed through her dreams. And the hero of all these dreams was none other than the gentleman in the top hat who had startled her so much that same evening…

The gentleman in the top hat pulled her away from Groholsky, beat her and Groholsky, whipped the little boy under the window, sang, made love declarations and drove her around in the gig! Oh, dreams! One can live through more than one decade of happiness, lying in bed, with closed eyes. And Lisa lived through a great deal of happiness that night, despite the beating she got!

She woke up at eight, threw on her clothes, tidied her hair and, without even putting on her pointed Tatar slippers, ran headlong onto the terrace. Shielding her eyes from the sun with one hand, and holding up her slipping dress with the other, she looked at the house opposite, and her face broke into a smile.

There was no longer any doubt about it. It was he.

On the veranda of the house opposite, in front of the glass doors, stood a table with a bright, glittering tea service, a silver samovar at its head. At the table sat Ivan Petrovich himself. He held a silver glass-holder in his hand, from which he drank tea with enormous gusto, a fact which communicated itself to Lisa's ears by the great champing noises he made. He wore a brown dressing gown, with large, black flowers, with massive great tassels which stretched to the floor. It was the first time in her life that Lisa had seen her husband in a dressing gown, let alone in such an expensive one. Mischutka sat on one knee, doing his best to prevent him from drinking his tea. He kept jumping about, trying to grab at his father's lower lip. After every two or three gulps, his father bent down and kissed the top of his son's head. A grey cat, with its tail raised high, rubbed itself against one of the table legs, miaowing to be fed.

Lisa hid herself behind the door curtains, and looked with unfeigned joy at the members of her former family, her face glowing with happiness...

"Michele..." she whispered. "Mischa! You're here, Mischa. Sweetheart. Dear Lord, how he loves Vanya!"

She burst out laughing when she saw Misha stirring his father's tea with a spoon.

"And look how Vanya loves Mischa! My dear ones!"

Her heart began to beat, she almost fainted from happiness. So she sat down and continued to follow the scene from an armchair.

"How did they get here?" she asked herself, blowing kisses to Mischa. "Who gave them the idea? Heavens, can all this wealth really belong to them? And those swan-like horses, which had driven through the gates, could they really belong to Ivan Petrovich? Ah!"

Having finished his tea, Ivan Petrovich returned to the house. He reappeared on the porch some ten minutes later... and surprised Lisa.

Could this devilishly well-dressed fellow be the same one who barely seven years ago stopped being called by his familiar sobriquet of "Vanya" or "Vanyusha", and who, for a couple of groats, was always ready for a prank?

He wore a wide-brimmed straw hat, fine, shiny riding boots, a piqué waistcoat. A thousand little suns were reflected in his watch chain. In his right hand he elegantly held a pair of gloves and a riding crop.

How much pride and ambition seemed to unite in his heavy-set figure, as he waved a gracious hand to the groom to order the carriage! He sat down in the gig importantly, and ordered the grooms who stood around the carriage to hand him up Mischutka and the fishing rods.

Placing Mischutka by his side, he circled him with his left arm and, with a tug at the reins, set off.

"Oooo…" shouted Mischutka.

Lisa, without realizing it, waved her handkerchief after them. If she had glanced at herself in the mirror, she would have seen her flushed, laughing and simultaneously tearful face. She was upset because she was not riding beside the carefree little boy, and because for some reason she was unable to kiss him at that very moment.

For some reason!

She ran into Groholsky's bedroom and began to wake him.

"Grisha! Grisha! Get up! darling. They've arrived!"

"Who's arrived?" asked Groholsky.

"Our people… Vanya and Mischa. They're here. In the house opposite. I looked out, and there they were, drinking tea, Mischa too. What a lovely little fellow he's become, our Mischa. If only you could have seen him! Mother of God!"

"What are you talking about? Who's arrived? Where?"

"Mischa and Vanya. I looked out at the house opposite, and there they were, drinking tea. Mischa can drink tea by himself already. You remember the people who moved in yesterday? It was they!"

Groholsky scowled, rubbed his forehead and turned white as a sheet.

"You mean – your husband's arrived?" he asked.

"Why, yes…"

"Whatever for?"

"He probably wants to live down here. They don't know we're here, otherwise they'd have looked up at our villa. As it is, they drank tea, and didn't pay the slightest attention…"

"Where is he now? For heavens' sake, talk sense! Where is he?"

"He's gone fishing with Mischa. In a gig. You remember those horses yesterday? Well, they belong to them. To Vanya. He drives around with them. You know what, Grisha? We must invite Mischa to stay with us here, mustn't we? He's such a sweet, lovely child!"

Groholsky grew thoughtful while Lisa chattered and chattered.

"There's an unexpected meeting for you!" said Groholsky, having weighed the matter at great length as usual. "Who'd have thought we'd bump into him here? Well, that's fate for you. It had to happen. I can imagine his discomfiture when he meets us!"

"But we will ask Mischa to stay with us here, won't we?"

"We'll invite Mischa. But it would be deuced awkward to meet the other one. What on earth would I say to him? There's no point in meeting him. If we have to communicate with him, the servants can do it for us... I have the most awful headache, Lisa. My arms and legs ache all over. Is my head warm?"

Lisa ran the palm of her hand across his forehead and found that it was hot.

"I had the most ghastly dreams all night... I'll stay in bed for the day. I must take some quinine. Ask them to bring me up some tea, mamotchka..."*

Groholsky took his quinine, and spent the whole day lolling in bed. He sipped warm water, moaned, changed his bedclothes constantly, whined and bored everyone around him. He was quite unbearable whenever he thought he had a chill. Lisa had to run between his room and her observation post on the terrace, interrupting her fascinating observations. At lunchtime she had to administer mustard plasters. How boring all this would have been, Reader, if my heroine did not have the house opposite as a focal point. As it was, Lisa spent the better part of the day gazing at the house, simply choking with happiness.

At ten, Ivan Petrovich and Mischa returned from fishing, and had breakfast. At two, they had lunch, and at four, they drove off somewhere in their carriage. The white horses carried them off with the speed of lightning. At seven, some male guests arrived. They played cards on a couple of tables set out on the terrace until about midnight. One of the men played the piano superbly. The guests enjoyed themselves, eating, drinking and laughing. Ivan Petrovich yelled so loudly at the top of his voice, telling them an anecdote taken from Armenian life, that he could be heard in all the neighbouring houses. It was very merry! And Mischutka was allowed to stay up until midnight...

"Mischa's so happy; he doesn't cry," thought Lisa. "It means he's forgotten his mama. He's forgotten all about me!"

Lisa's heart was very heavy. She wept the whole night. Tiny pricks of conscience, irritation, boredom and a passionate desire to talk to Mischutka and to kiss him added to her suffering. She awoke next morning with swollen eyes and a headache. Groholsky thought the tears were on his account.

"You mustn't cry, darling," he told her, "I'm feeling better today. True, my chest hurts a little, but it's nothing."

When they came to take tea on the terrace, the people in the house opposite were lunching. Ivan Petrovich looked at his plate and saw nothing, except a slice of goose, oozing with fat.

"I'm very glad," whispered Groholsky, glancing sideways at Bugrov periodically. "I'm delighted he's settled down so nicely. At least he can drown his sorrows in comfort. Don't show yourself, Lisa. They'll see you! I'm in no mood to chat with him. Let him be. Why bother him?"

But lunch was far from private: that "awkward situation" Groholsky feared so much occurred precisely at lunchtime.

Just as the partridges (Groholsky's favourite dish) were being set on the table, Lisa suddenly became agitated, and Groholsky started to wipe his face with a table napkin. They saw Bugrov on the terrace of the house opposite. He stood goggled-eyed, leaning on the garden rail, staring straight at them.

"Go on in, Lisa. Go on," whispered Groholsky. "I told you we should eat inside. You're impossible…"

Bugrov continued to stare and then suddenly yelled out. Groholsky looked back at him and saw his astonished face.

"Is that you?" Ivan Petrovich shouted. "It's you? Are you here, too? How are you?"

Groholsky indicated his shoulder blades as if to emphasize the malady which prevented him from shouting across such a distance. Lisa's heart raced; her eyes grew misty. Bugrov ran down his terrace, crossed the road, and appeared a few seconds later below the terrace where Lisa and Groholsky were lunching. Groholsky had lost all taste for partridges!

"Well, hello," said Bugrov, reddening and thrusting his large hands into his pockets. "So you're here, too?"

"Yes, we're here, too…"

"What brings you here?"

"And what brings you here?"

"What, me? It's quite a long story, old man. Go on and eat, don't mind me. I lived in the Orlovsky district, well, ever since… I rented an estate; a lovely spot! Do go on eating. I lived there from the end of May, and now I've given it up. It was cold up there, so the doctor suggested I should go down to the Crimea."

"Is there really something the matter with you?"

"Well, I've got something rumbling down here…"

On the word "here" Ivan Petrovich indicated with the palm of his hand an area between his neck and the middle of his stomach.

"So you're here. Well, that's very nice. How long have you been down here?"

"Since June."

"Well, and how are you, Lisa? Feeling fit?"

"I'm fine," said Lisa. She grew uncomfortable.

"You must have missed Mischutka? Eh? He's here with me. I'll send Nikofor around with him immediately. Well, it's been very nice, but I must say goodbye to you. I have to go… I met Prince Ter-Gaimazov yesterday. Wonderful fellow, although he's an Armenian! He's having a croquet party. We'll play croquet. Well, goodbye! My carriage is ready."

He flapped around on one spot, shook his head and, waving goodbye with his hand, ran back to his house.

"Poor devil," said Groholsky, following him with his eyes, sighing deeply.

"What's so poor about him?" asked Lisa.

"Because he sees you, but has no right to call you his own!"

Late that afternoon, Lisa kissed and embraced Mischutka, whom Nikofor had brought round. Mischutka's first inclination was to cry, but after he had been offered some cherry jam, he gave a friendly smile.

Lisa and Groholsky saw nothing of Bugrov in the next three days. He used to disappear somewhere, returning home only at night. On the fourth day he turned up once more at lunchtime, shook them both by the hand and sat down at table. He looked serious.

"I've come on business," he said. "Read this."

He held out a letter to Groholsky.

"Read it aloud."

Groholsky read aloud the following:*

"My kind, considerate and never-to-be-forgotten son, Ioaan,* I have received your affectionate and respectful letter in which you invite your aged father to visit the serene and salubrious Crimea, to partake of the exhilarating air and to discover a part of the world unknown to me. I wish to inform you in answer to your letter that I shall come down on my next leave, but not for long. My colleague, Father

Gerasim, is sick and ailing, and cannot be left alone for any length of time. I am extremely touched that you do not forget your parents, your mother and father. You gladden your father with your solicitude, and remember your mother in your prayers, which is as it should be. I expect you to meet me in Fyodosia. What sort of place is this Fyodosia? It will be pleasant to see it. Your godmother, who took you from the christening font, is called Fyodosia. You say the Lord helped you to win 200,000 roubles. I am delighted. But I cannot approve of the fact that having reached the lower ranks of the government service, you now leave it. Even rich men ought to serve. My blessings on you always, now and for ever more. Ilya and Sergei Andronov wish to be remembered to you. Send them ten roubles apiece. They are in great need. Your loving father, Piotr Bugrov (priest)."

When Groholsky had finished reading aloud the letter, both he and Lisa looked questioningly at Bugrov.

"The fact is…" Ivan Petrovich began, stuttering, "I'd like Lisa not to put in an appearance while he's down here. I wrote and told him that you were ill and had gone down to the Caucasus to recuperate. It might be rather awkward if you did meet him, you understand."

"Very well," said Lisa.

"That's not unreasonable," thought Groholsky. "He's made some sacrifices, why shouldn't we?"

"I really would appreciate it. Otherwise there might be an awful rumpus. He's a stickler for rules. He might anathematize you, bell, book and candle. So try to stay indoors, Lisa, and don't come out. That's about all. He won't be here very long, don't worry."

Father Piotr did not long delay his coming. One fine morning, Ivan Petrovich rushed over and said in an awed whisper, "He's arrived! He's asleep now, but please be very careful…"

So Lisa immured herself within four walls: she never once went outside into the yard or onto the veranda, and looked at the sky through curtained windows. As ill luck would have it, Ivan Petrovich's father spent his whole time out of doors and even slept on the veranda at night.

The little priest usually walked around the grounds in his brown cassock, his large hat, with upturned brims, peering through his old-fashioned spectacles at the unfamiliar surroundings. Ivan Petrovich accompanied him, wearing the Order of Stanislavs* in his buttonhole.

He rarely wore this Order. But he liked to impress his relatives, and always put it on in their presence.

Meanwhile Lisa nearly died of boredom, and Groholsky was miserable. He had to go out alone, without his partner; he almost wept. But he accepted his fate manfully. And then, on top of everything, Bugrov would come round each morning, whispering totally unnecessary bulletins regarding his father's health. They were sick of his bulletins!

"He slept well last night!" he would announce. "But he was a bit upset because I didn't have any salt cucumbers in the house. Still, he's taken a great liking to Mischutka; he keeps stroking his head all the time…"

A couple of weeks later, Father Piotr took his last walk round the house and, to Groholsky's unfeigned delight, departed. The old priest had enjoyed himself and went off well satisfied. Groholsky and Lisa returned to their old ways, and Groholsky had already begun to count his blessings, when disaster, in a shape more menacing than Father Piotr's, overtook him!

Ivan Petrovich used to descend on them every day. He was a nice enough chap, but, frankly speaking, a bit of a strain. He would come about lunchtime, eat with them, and would sit for hours on end. That wasn't so bad. But vodka had to be bought specially for him to serve at table, a drink Groholsky could not abide. He would swallow five glasses of vodka and would talk the entire lunch. Even this was not so bad, but he would insist on staying up until two in the morning, preventing them from going to bed. But worst of all, he began to talk of things which were best left unsaid.

At around two in the morning, having drunk his fill of vodka and champagne, Bugrov would take Mischutka into his arms and, weeping, say in front of Lisa and Groholsky:

"Son of my heart, Mikhail! What am I? A scoundrel who sold your mother, sold her for thirty pieces of silver! Punish me, Lord! Mikhail Ivanovich, piglet, where is your mother? She has gone, sold into slavery! I'm a scoundrel, that's what I am…"

These words and tears cut Groholsky to the quick. He watched Lisa's face growing pale, and wrung his hands dumbly.

"Go to bed, Ivan Petrovich," he would say timidly.

"Yes, of course. Let's go, Mischutka. May God be our judge. I can hardly sleep, knowing my wife is a slave. But Groholsky is not to blame. I sold my goods for his money. We all get our deserts!"

Groholsky found Ivan Petrovich equally unbearable by day. To his great horror, Bugrov never once left Lisa's side. He took her fishing, told her stories and went walking with her. He even took advantage of one of Groholsky's chills, to take Lisa in his gig; they drove, Heaven knows where, and returned late at night.

"It's positively outrageous and inhuman," thought Groholsky, biting his lips.

Moreover, Groholsky liked to kiss Lisa frequently. He could hardly survive without these sugary kisses, but with Ivan Petrovich around, he found himself somewhat inhibited. The agony of it! The poor fellow thought he was quite deserted. But Fate took pity on him. Ivan Petrovich suddenly disappeared for one whole week. Some friends had arrived and taken him and Mischutka away with them.

One fine morning Groholsky returned from his walk, beaming, full of good spirits.

"He's returned," he told Lisa, rubbing his hands together. "I couldn't be more pleased. Ha, ha, ha…"

"What's there to laugh about?"

"He has women with him."

"What women?"

"I don't know… but I thoroughly approve of his going around with women. That's fine! After all, he's quite young and active. Come over here, and look for yourself…"

Groholsky escorted Lisa onto the terrace and pointed to the house opposite. They both burst out laughing. It was so funny. Ivan Petrovich stood on the veranda of the house opposite, grinning. Below the veranda stood two unknown brunettes, with Mischutka. The two ladies were talking loudly in French, and laughing.

"French ladies, evidently," Groholsky observed. "The one nearest to us isn't at all bad-looking. They are free and easy, but that doesn't matter. There are some good women among them also. But these look pretty cheeky…"

The whole joke lay in the manner in which Ivan Petrovich stretched down his long arms and grabbed one of the women by her shoulders. He hoisted her, laughing, beside him on the veranda.

Having lifted both the ladies onto the veranda, he picked up Mischutka. The two ladies ran down again, and the game began all over again.

"He seems pretty strong – plenty of muscle," muttered Groholsky, who watched observantly.

This performance was repeated some six times. The ladies were so charming that they were not in the least embarrassed when a strong breeze ruffled their billowing skirts, each time they were hoisted into the air. Only Groholsky lowered his eyes demurely as the ladies threw their legs over the balustrade, on approaching the veranda. Lisa merely looked on and laughed. She had no reason to feel ashamed in front of the men; they were innocent. The fault lay with the two ladies.

Ivan Petrovich rushed round that same evening to announce, a little uncomfortably, that he was now a "family man"…

"You mustn't think they're just of couple of nobodies," he said. "True, they are Frenchwomen, they are a little noisy and drink wine, everyone knows that! That's how they've been brought up. Nothing can be done about it! The Prince let me have them," he added, "almost for nothing… He insisted I should take them. I must introduce you to the Prince sometime. He's an educated man, he keeps writing and writing… But do you know what these ladies are called? One is Fanny, and the other, Isabelle. Ah, Europe! Ha, ha, ha! The West! Well, I must run."

Ivan Petrovich left Groholsky and Lisa alone, and devoted himself exclusively to his two ladies. His house resounded with laughter, chatter, the sound of crockery the whole day long. And lights burned far into the night. Groholsky could relax again after the long and tortuous interval; he could consider himself a happy man, at peace with the world. Ivan Petrovich, with his two women, could never know the joy, which he, Groholsky, had with one… But Fate is merciless – alas! – Groholsky, Lisa, Mischutka and Ivan Petrovich were mere pawns in her hands. And Groholsky once more lost his peace of mind…

A week and a half went by. Then one morning, Groholsky rose later than usual and strolled out onto the terrace. A shocking scene greeted his eyes, which surprised and angered him!

Below the veranda of the house opposite stood the two Frenchwomen, chatting gaily, with Lisa herself between them. She babbled, periodically glancing sideways at her own house, as if to say, "I wonder whether that tyrant, that despot, has woken up yet?" (That is how Groholsky interpreted these glances to himself).

Ivan Petrovich stood on the terrace, in shirt sleeves. He lifted up Fanny, then Isabelle and finally Lisa herself over the balustrade. He seemed to press her a little too closely for Groholsky's comfort. And Lisa also swung her leg over the balustrade. Ah, these women! They are sphinxes, all of them!

When Lisa returned home from her husband, she entered the bedroom on tiptoe, as if nothing had happened. She found Groholsky prostrate in bed, groaning to himself. He was pale, with red patches on his cheeks...

He sprang out of bed the moment he saw Lisa and began pacing around the bedroom...

"So that's how you behave?" he squealed in a high tenor. "That's it, is it? I'm most obliged to you. It's quite scandalous, my dear madam! It's downright immoral! Please grasp that."

Lisa grew pale and, of course, burst into tears.

Women who feel themselves in the right usually quarrel as well as cry; but those who admit they are in the wrong only weep...

"Fine company you keep with these depraved creatures! It's positively indecent! Don't you know who they are? They are bought women, trollops! How can a decent woman like you demean yourself by crawling over there? And that man... he! What does he want? What does he want from me? I don't understand; I gave him half my fortune – no, more than half of it! You know that yourself. I even gave him more than I had: I gave him everything! I have stood his familiarity – he has no right to address you familiarly, I have borne your long walks together, your after-dinner kisses, but this I will not stand. It's either me or him! One of us must go. I cannot live like this any longer. Surely you understand, it must be one or the other? It's as much as I can stand: my cup brims over. I've suffered enough as it is. I'll go over and talk to him immediately, this very minute. Who does he think he is? It's a pity he fancies himself so much..."

Groholsky made a good many other brave and caustic observations, but he did not go over "immediately": he was a little frightened and somewhat crestfallen. He went to see Ivan Petrovich some three days later.

His mouth dropped in astonishment the moment he entered Bugrov's private apartment, and beheld the wealth and luxury with which Bugrov surrounded himself. The velvet draperies and very expensive chairs alone made one hesitate before entering. Groholsky, who had known many a rich man, could recall no one who lived in such crazy luxury.

Entering the salon, with inexplicable trepidation, Groholsky beheld a scene of indescribable chaos: plates filled with breadcrumbs lay around on the grand piano; a tumbler stood propped on a chair and a basket, filled with disreputable-looking rags, peered from under the table. The window sills were strewn with nutshells.

And Bugrov himself looked equally untidy when Groholsky entered the room. He was striding around the salon red-faced, in a state of undress, with his hair uncombed, talking to himself. Something appeared to be worrying him. And Mischutka sat on a divan in this same salon, letting out the most ear-piercing screams.

"It really is awful, Grigory Vasilych!" Bugrov exclaimed the moment he saw Groholsky. "Look at this mess! Just look at it! Do sit down, I beg you. And forgive my state of nudity, won't you? I don't know how people can live in such a mess! The servants won't do what they are told, the climate is dreadful and everything costs so much...Shut up!" Bugrov roared, stopping in front of Mischutka. "Shut up when I tell you, you little beast!"

Bugrov pulled the little boy's ear.

"But this is awful, Ivan Petrovich," Groholsky said tearfully. "How can you strike a little child? You astonish me..."

"Well, why does he keep howling then? Silence! Or I'll give you such a hiding!"

"Now don't cry, Mischa, darling. Daddy won't hit you again. You mustn't, Ivan Petrovich. He's only a baby... Now... now... would you like a little pony? I'll have it sent round. You really are impossible, Ivan Petrovich. You're so hard-hearted."

Groholsky paused a moment, and then enquired, "And how are your ladies, Ivan Petrovich?"

"No how. I threw them out without any nonsense. I might have kept them around, only the boy's growing up. Can't set him a bad example. If I was alone, that'd be another matter. Besides what do I need them for? The whole thing's a joke. I talk to them in Russian; they answer me in French. They don't understand anything. I might as well talk to a brick wall."

"I want to have a word with you, Ivan Petrovich. Oh, it's nothing very important. It just boils down to this: I have a request to make."

"What kind of request?"

"Is there any chance of your going away from here? We're most happy and delighted to have you around, but it is a trifle inconvenient, if you know what I mean? This whole situation is pretty awkward...

177

the uncertainty of the whole thing, added to the strain we feel in each others' company, make it imperative that we part. Yes, indeed. You'll forgive me, but it must be quite obvious to you that life in such close proximity is bound to make one consider that... Perhaps 'consider' isn't the right word, but anyway, it's deuced awkward, whichever way you look at it..."

"Yes, I had very much the same impression. I'll go away."

"We would be most obliged to you. Believe me, Ivan Petrovich, we shall have the warmest recollection of you! This sacrifice which—"

"Good. But what am I going to do with all these things? I say, don't you want to buy this furniture from me? It isn't so expensive. I'll give you all the furniture, the horse carriage and the grand piano for eight... no, ten thousand roubles..."

"Very well. I'll give you ten thousand roubles."

"That's all settled then. I'll leave tomorrow and go to Moscow. I can't go on living here much longer. Everything's so frightfully expensive. Money simply evaporates; I can't take a step without spending a thousand roubles. And that's got to stop; I have my family to consider. Well, thank goodness, you bought the furniture. I'll have something in hand, otherwise I'd be completely bankrupt..."

Groholsky rose from his chair, said goodbye to Bugrov and returned home triumphantly. That same evening he sent him ten thousand roubles.

Bugrov and Mischutka were already in Fyodosia early next morning...

III

S OME MONTHS PASSED. The spring came.
Bright clear days followed the advent of spring and everything on earth seemed pleasant; life itself seemed less gloomy and boring. A warm wind blew from across the sea and the fields. The earth was covered with new grass, and young leaves appeared on the trees. Nature returned to life in her new clothes...

One would imagine that new hopes and desires would awaken in a man's heart with the renewal of nature, when everything was so fresh and so young. But a man's heart will not easily resurrect...

Groholsky still lived in the same country house. His hopes and desires were modest and unpretentious, they still centred on Lisa, and on nothing else. He continued to look adoringly at Lisa, and savouring the thought: "Oh, what a happy fellow I am!" The poor devil actually considered himself very happy. As for Lisa, she continued to sit on the veranda very much as before, gazing dumbly at the house opposite, through whose trees she could glimpse the blue sea... Lisa had grown more silent; she cried frequently, and very rarely gave Groholsky his mustard plasters. A marked change could be detected in her. The canker of regret gnawed inside her. She was full of longings. She missed her son, her former life, and all the happy times she once had. Her old life had not been particularly happy, but it was more exciting than this one. If only rarely, she at least visited her friends, went to the theatre and attended social gatherings, when she lived with her husband... But here with Groholsky everything seemed so quiet, so empty... Here he was, full of complaints, with his sickening kisses, eternally weeping for joy like an octogenarian! It was all so boring! Neither Mikhail Sergeych, who loved to dance the mazurka with her, nor Spiridon Nikolayevich, the son of the editor of *The County Times*, were here. Spiridon Nikolayevich sang beautifully and recited poetry. Nor was there any table laden with *hors d'œuvres*: no Nanny Gerasimovna to grumble at her for eating too much jam... There was no one here at all! She might as well lie down and die of boredom! Yet if Groholsky rejoiced in his solitude, it was all in vain. He paid for his egoism rather earlier than he should have done. At the beginning of May, when the air itself seemed to breathe love and sigh with gladness, Groholsky lost everything: he lost the woman he loved and...

This year Bugrov once again came to the Crimea. He did not rent the house opposite, but shuttled between one town and another with his son, drinking, sleeping and playing cards. He had lost his enthusiasm not only for hunting and fishing, but for Frenchwomen as well. Confidentially, they had robbed him a little.

Bugrov had grown thin and morose, rarely smiled and took to wearing linen suits. The few times he visited Groholsky's dacha he brought Lisa pots of jam, fruit and confectionery, as if trying somehow to dispel her gloom.

Groholsky was not alarmed by these visits. They were not only rare, but of short duration, undertaken more on Mischutka's behalf than anything else; one could hardly deny the child access to his mother.

Bugrov would arrive, spread out his presents, say a few words and go away again. And those few words he would direct to Groholsky, not Lisa. So Groholsky saw no occasion for alarm. He should have remembered the old Russian proverb, of course, which says: "still waters run deep".* The proverb may be a trifle malicious, but very useful in everyday life…

One day, as he was strolling in the garden, Groholsky heard two voices, one male, and the other female. They belonged respectively to Bugrov and Lisa.

Groholsky listened a moment, grew pale as death, and walked stealthily towards the summer house, stopping behind a lilac bush. He watched and listened attentively. Then his hands and feet turned to ice, a cold sweat broke out on his forehead. Feeling faint, he grabbed at some branches on the lilac bush to prevent himself from falling. It was all over!

Bugrov held Lisa around the waist. He was saying:

"What can we possibly do, my darling? Things were bound to work out like this. I was a swine to have sold you. I was driven by greed. Damn the money! What good did it do me? I only showed off and earned myself a packet of trouble. Didn't have any peace, any luck, and got nowhere into the bargain. Stagnated, in fact. You've heard about Andrushka Markusin? He's become Head of Chancellery. That fool! And I just sit like a paralytic! Dear God! I lost you, and that was an end to my happiness. I'm a swine and a scoundrel. Can you imagine what I'll go through on the last dread Day of Judgement! What do you think?"

"Let's get away from here, Vanya." Lisa started to cry. "I can't bear it. I'm dying of boredom."

"There's nothing we can do. Money was paid for you."

"Well, give back the money."

"Gladly, if I could. But it's all gone. I spent it. No, we must resign ourselves. We are justly punished: I for my cupidity, and you for all your nonsense. We'll just have to face up to it. Things are bound to improve in the next world," said Bugrov, raising his eyes heavenwards, overcome with religious fervour.

"But I refuse to stay here! I'm fed up!"

"And what about me? I'm also fed up. You think I enjoy living without you? I'm completely worn out. My chest has started aching. And you, my legal wife, flesh of my flesh, you'll have to learn to grin and bear it. I'll come and visit you from time to time…"

Bugrov bent down and whispered to Lisa loudly enough to be heard some feet away:

"I'll come to you, even at night, Lisa, don't worry. I am staying in Fyodosia; it's not far. I'll stay near you as long as my money lasts. To the very last farthing! And that will soon be gone! It's a hell of a life. And I ache all over. My chest hurts, and my stomach…"

Bugrov lapsed into silence. It was Lisa's turn… And how cruelly she took it! She started to cry, to complain, to list all her lover's shortcomings. And Groholsky, who heard every word she said, felt as if he was robber, murderer and executioner, rolled into one!

"And what's more, he's killing me!" Lisa concluded.

Having kissed Lisa goodbye, Bugrov opened the garden gate and collided with Groholsky. Groholsky had been lying in wait for him.

"I've seen and heard everything, Ivan Petrovich," said Groholsky, in the tone of a dying man. "You aren't being fair. Not that I blame you; you cannot help loving her. But she's mine! Mine! Do you understand? I can't live without her! Why won't you understand that? Let's assume that you suffer, you love her, but haven't I given you something in return for your suffering? Why won't you go away from here, for God's sake! Go away for ever! I beg you! Or you'll be the death of me!"

"But I haven't anywhere to go," said Bugrov hollowly.

"You mean you've spent everything? You are a spendthrift, aren't you? Well, never mind. You go to my estate in the Chernigov county. I'll give you this estate. It's small, but quite delightful. Honestly, it is."

Bugrov gave an enormous grin: he was in the seventh heaven of delight!

"I'll give it to you as a present. I'll write to the bailiff right away to give the necessary instructions. You can tell everyone you bought it. But do go away, for heaven's sake!"

"Very well. I'll go away. I can quite understand."

"Well, let's find a notary, and settle everything immediately," said Groholsky, ordering a carriage. His spirits had revived considerably.

The next evening, while Lisa sat on the garden seat waiting for her customary rendezvous with Ivan Petrovich, Groholsky came up to her silently. He sat down beside her and took her hand.

"Life's pretty boring, isn't it, Lisa?" he said after a slight pause. "You're finding it very dull? Well, why don't we go somewhere? What's the point of always sitting at home? We ought to go out, enjoy ourselves, meet people. Isn't that what you want?"

"I don't want anything," said Lisa, glancing down the garden path along which Bugrov used to come to her. She looked pale and worn.

Groholsky lapsed into thought. He knew whom Lisa expected, whom she wanted.

"Let's go in, Lisa. It's getting damp," he said.

"You go. I'll join you in a moment."

He cogitated again.

"You're waiting for him, aren't you?" he asked, making a face as if red-hot pincers had gripped his heart.

"Yes. I want to give him some socks for Mischa…"

"Well, he won't be here."

"How do you know?"

"He's gone away…"

Lisa looked wide-eyed.

"He's gone – left for my estate in Chernigov county. I gave it to him as a present."

Lisa turned deathly pale; she caught Groholsky's shoulder to save herself from falling.

"I saw him off on the steamer. At three o'clock."

Lisa clutched her head, swayed, and collapsed on the garden seat, shivering violently.

"Vanya!" she cried suddenly. "I'm coming with you, Vanya! Dearest!"

And she had a fit of hysterics.

From this evening forwards until July, the people in the neighbouring house saw two ghost-like figures perambulating in the garden from early morning to night. It was a depressing sight. Groholsky's ghost followed remorselessly in Lisa's shadowy footsteps. I call them ghosts because they had ceased to look like themselves.

They had grown thin and haggard, shrivelled to nothing, resembling ghosts more than living people. They were pining away slowly, like fleas in the classical story about the Jew who sold insecticide powders.

At the beginning of July, Lisa ran away from Groholsky. She left him a note indicating that she would be staying with her "son" for a while… For a while! She had fled in the night while Groholsky was sleeping…

After reading her letter, Groholsky wandered aimlessly like a madman in the grounds of the house for a whole week. He neither ate nor slept. In August he had a bout of recurring fever. In September he ventured abroad. He drank heavily, hoping to find consolation in drink and debauchery.

He squandered his entire fortune, but he was quite unable, poor devil, to erase the image of the beloved woman with the kitten face from his mind. But ones dies neither from happiness, nor unhappiness. Groholsky's hair turned grey, but he survived. In fact, he's alive to this day...

He returned from abroad and decided to take a look at Lisa, but Bugrov, who received him with open arms, persuaded him to remain as his guest for an indeterminate period. And he's remained Bugrov's guest ever since...

* * *

I had occasion this year to go by Bugrov's estate at Groholyevka, and found my hosts at supper. Ivan Petrovich was delighted to see me and insisted I should have a meal with them. He has grown fat and even a little flabby. But his face looks well-fed, pink-cheeked and jolly. And he has not started to get bald.

Lisa has also filled out somewhat, but it does not suit her. Her face is beginning to lose its kittenish appearance; she now looks more like a seal, alas! Her cheeks seem to have filled out in all directions.

The Bugrovs appear to be very comfortable; they have everything they need. The house is well-stocked and full of servants.

After dinner we all sat round and talked. I forgot that Lisa could not play the piano and asked her to give us some tune or another.

"But she can't play," said Bugrov. "She's no musician! Hey, there! Ivan! Tell Grigory Vasilych to come here. What's he up to, anyway?" Bugrov turned to me and added. "Our musician will be here in a moment. He plays the guitar. We keep the piano for Mischutka to practise on."

Some five minutes later, Groholsky entered the dining room, looking sleepy-eyed, unkempt and unshaven. He bowed to me and sat down a little to the side.

"Who's ever heard of anyone going to bed so early?" Bugrov turned to him. "You do nothing but sleep! A regular sleepy-head! Well, come on, play us something cheerful..."

Groholsky tuned the guitar; he plucked at the strings and began to sing: "Yesterday I waited for my lover..."

I listened, staring at Bugrov's satisfied countenance. "What a hideous face!" I thought. I was ready to weep...

After he had finished his song, Groholsky bowed to us all and left the room.

"What am I going to do with him?" asked Bugrov as Groholsky was leaving. "He's a constant worry to me! Broods all day, and moans all night. He's sick or something. And I don't sleep for worrying about him. He's probably going off his head. You'd think he was miserable living here. Why should he be? He eats and drinks with us. Only we don't give him any money. He'd only drink it or throw it around. As if I didn't have enough to worry about! Lord forgive me, sinner that I am."

I was persuaded to stay the night. When I awoke the next morning, I heard Bugrov lecturing someone in the next room.

"Can't you do anything properly, you fool? Who's heard of anyone painting the oars green? Think. Use your head and your common sense! Well, why don't you say something?"

"But... but I made a mistake," a cracked tenor voice said, trying to justify itself. The voice belonged to Groholsky.

Groholsky accompanied me to the railway station.

"He's a dreadful tyrant, a bully," he kept whispering to me the whole way. "He's a decent enough fellow, but an awful slave-driver! He hasn't a heart or a mind, he's completely primitive. Oh, how he tortures me! If it wasn't for that fine noble woman, I'd have left him long ago. But I couldn't leave her here. Somehow it's easier for us to bear things together."

Groholsky sighed and continued:

"She's pregnant; did you notice? The child is actually mine. Yes, mine. She soon realized she'd made a mistake and gave herself to me again. She simply can't stand him..."

"You're completely spineless!" I found myself saying to Groholsky, without being able to hold it back.

"Yes, it's quite true, I have a weak character. Born like that. Do you know how I came into the world? My late father took a dislike to a little clerk: lord, how he bullied and hounded him! He poisoned his entire life! Well, my late mother was a compassionate woman, who came from plain, middle-class folk; she took pity on the clerk and made him welcome. That's how I came to be. How could I, the son of a persecuted man, have any character? Where would I get it from? Well, that's the second bell. Goodbye and do come to visit us again, but don't tell Ivan Petrovich I said anything about him!"

I shook Groholsky by the hand and jumped into the carriage. He bowed in the direction of my carriage and walked towards a bucket filled with water. I suppose he was thirsty...

Notes on the Texts

The stories included in this volume have been collected from several original sources. A breakdown of the bibliographical details of each individual text is provided below.

'The Woman in the Case' (*Roman s Kontrabasom*, literally: 'Romance with a Double Bass'): First printed in the periodical *Oskolki* (1886), under the pseudonym A. Chekhonte. Reprinted, with a few slight changes, in the *Collected Works* (1899).

'A Visit to Friends' (*U Znakomykh*): First published in the *Cosmopolis* (Russian section) IX, No. 2, February (1898). Reprinted in an anthology *A Memorial to A.P. Chekhov: Poetry and Prose*, published in St Petersburg (1906).

'Appropriate Measures' (*Nadlezhashchie Mery*): First published in the journal *Oskolki* (22nd September 1884), with the subtitle: 'A Scene'. Signed: A. Chekhonte. Included in the anthology *Pyostrye Rasskazy* (*Motley Stories*) (1886) and, in a slightly changed version, in the *Collected Works* (1899). The translation is made from the revised text.

'The Boa-Constrictor and the Rabbit' (*Udav i Krolik*): First published in the *Peterburgskaya Gazeta* (20th April 1887). Signed: A. Chekhonte. The story is based on a story written in 1886, which was forbidden by the censor: 'For the Information of Husbands'.

'History of a Business Enterprise' (*Istoriya Odnogo Torgovogo Predpriyatiya*): First published in the magazine *Oskolki* (2nd May 1892), under the pseudonym Grach ("the Rook").

'75,000': First published in the magazine *Budilnik* (13th January 1884). Signed: A. Chekhonte.

'The Mask' (*Maska*): First published in the magazine *Razvlechenie*, (27th October 1884), with the title: '*Noli me tangere* (From the Life of a Provincial Ace)'. Signed: A. Chekhonte. Included, in a greatly revised version, in the *Collected Works* (1900). The translation is made from the revised text.

'An Unpleasant Incident' (*Nepriyatnost*): First published in *Novoye Vremya* (3rd and 7th June 1888). Title: 'A Worrying Trifle'. Signed: An. Chekhov. Included, with new title and some changes, in the anthology *Gloomy People* (St Petersburg 1890). Included, with some changes and omissions, in the *Collected Works* (1901). The translation is made from the text of 1901.

'The Eve of the Trial' (*Noch pered Sudom*): First published in the magazine *Oskolki* (1st February 1886). Subtitle: 'A Case from My Practice as a Quack Doctor). Signed: A. Chekhonte. Published, with slight changes, in the anthology *Innocent Speech* (*Nevinnye Rechi*) (Moscow 1887). Included, with further changes, in the *Collected Works* (1889). The translation is made from the text of 1889. The story was written in 1884, when Chekhov sent it to the magazine *Strekoza* (*The Dragonfly*), but the manuscript was mislaid by the editors. Later on, Chekhov thought of turning the story into a farce, and some notes for it are preserved in Moscow.

'Sinister Night' (*Nedobraya Noch*): First printed in the *Peterburgskaya Gazeta* (3rd November 1886). Signed: A. Chekhonte.

'The Lodger' (*Zhilets*): First printed in the journal *Oskolki* (1st November 1886), where it was called 'The Lodger in No. 31'. Reprinted with considerable changes in *Zhurnal dlya vsekh*, No. 11 (1898). The translation has been made from the revised text.

'The Dream: A Christmas Story' (*Son: Svyatochny Rasskaz*): First published in the *Peterburgskaya Gazeta* (25th December 1885). Signed: A. Chekhonte. The story was written some time in 1884.

'Out of Sheer Boredom' (*Ot nechego delat*): First printed 26th May 1886 in the *Peterburgskaya Gazeta*. Signed: A. Chekhonte.

'A Disagreeable Experience' (*Nepriyatnaya Istoriya*): First published in the *Peterburgskaya Gazeta* (29th June 1887). Signed: A. Chekhonte.

'His First Appearance' (*Pervy Debyut*): First published in the *Peterburgskaya Gazeta* (13th January 1886). Signed: A. Chekhonte.

'Holy Simplicity' (*Svyataya Prostota*): First published in the *Peterburgskaya Gazeta* (9th December 1885). Signed: A. Chekhonte.

'The Diplomat' (*Diplomat*): First published in the *Peterburgskaya Gazeta* (20th May 1885). Signed: A. Chekhonte.

'Mutual Superiority' (*Oba Luchshe*, literally: 'Both Are Better'): First published in the magazine *Oskolki* (30th March 1885). Subtitle: 'A Story'. Signed: A. Chekhonte. Included, without a subtitle and with a few slight changes, in the anthology *Pyostrye Rasskazy* (*Motley Stories*) (St Petersburg, 1886). The translation is made from the revised text.

'Tædium Vitæ' (*Skuka Zhizni*): First printed in *Novoye Vremya* (31st May 1886). Signed: An. Chekhov.

'Other People's Trouble' (*Chuzhaya Beda*): First printed in *Peterburgskaya Gazeta* (28th July 1886). Signed: A. Chekhonte.

'A Reporter's Dream' (*Son Reportera*): First published in the magazine *Budilnik* (18th February 1884). Title: 'The French Ball: A Dream Fantasy'. Signed: A. Chekhonte. Chekhov originally intended to include this story in the *Collected Works* (1899), and he revised the story for this edition and changed the title. In the original version there were references to Moscow journalists and writers, but in the revised version Chekhov omitted personal remarks and proper names. The translation is made from the text (the galley proof) of the revised version. The ball described in the story took place on 17th February 1884.

'One Man's Meat…' (*Kon i Trepetnaya Lan*: literally: 'The Horse and the Tremulous Doe'): Signed: A. Chekhonte. First published in the *Peterburgskaya Gazeta* (12th August 1885). Subtitle: 'A Scene'. Reprinted, with no subtitle and some changes, in the anthology *Pyostrye Rasskazy* (*Motley Stories*) (St Petersburg 1886). The translation is made from the text of 1886.

'The Guest' (*Gost*): First published in the *Peterburgskaya Gazeta*, (5th August 1885). Signed: A. Chekhonte.

'Wife for Sale' (*Zhivoi Tovar*): First published in *Mirski Tolk* (6th–27th August 1882). Signed: A. Chekhonte.

Notes

p. 11, *Jamais de ma vie*: "Never in my life" (French).

p. 15, *Straight lies… how many*: The quoted lines are from 'The Railway' (1864) by Nikolai Nekrasov (1821–78).

p. 20, *And of… queen*: The quotation is from 'The Demon' (1842) by Mikhail Lermontov (1814–41).

p. 33, *Turgenev*: Ivan Turgenev (1818–83), the novelist, playwright and poet.

p. 35, *Mikhailovsky*: Nikolay Konstantinovich Mikhailovsky (1842–1904) was an eminent theorist and a leading exponent of the *Narodnik* (Populist) movement.

p. 35, *Pisarev*: Dmitry Ivanovich Pisarev (1840–68) was a radical Russian thinker whose ideas would influence Lenin's.

p. 44, *Je… trimonrin*: The meaning of this is unclear.

p. 99, *Boulanger*: Georges Boulanger (1837–91), French general and politician.

p. 100, *Grévy, Déroulède, Zola*: Jules Grévy (1807–91), French President; Paul Déroulède (1846–1914), French writer and politician; Émile Zola (1840–1902), French writer and critic.

p. 100, *Il y a… une robe*: "There's a red-headed gentleman here who has brought you a dress" (French).

p. 117, *mauvais ton*: "Bad style" (French).

p. 163, *kurgan*: A tumulus, sepulchral burial ground found in the Crimea and Southern Russia.

p. 169, *mamotchka*: Term of endearment, literally "little mother".

p. 171, *the following*: The letter is written in old-fashioned Church Slavonic.

p. 171, *Ioaan*: Ivan in biblical Russian.

p. 172, *the Order of Stanislavs*: An order awarded to low-ranking Civil Servants.

p. 180, *old Russian proverb*: The proverb in Russian literally translates as: "Do not be afraid of the dog which barks: fear the one that is silent."

Extra Material

on

Anton Chekhov's

The Woman in the Case

Anton Chekhov's Life

Anton Pavlovich Chekhov was born in Taganrog, on the Sea of Azov in southern Russia, on 29th January 1860. He was the third child of Pavel Yegorovich Chekhov and his wife Yevgenia Yakovlevna. He had four brothers – Alexander (born in 1855), Nikolai (1858), Ivan (1861) and Mikhail (1865) – and one sister, Marya, who was born in 1863. Anton's father, the owner of a small shop, was a devout Christian who administered brutal floggings to his children almost on a daily basis. Anton remembered these with bitterness throughout his life, and possibly as a result was always sceptical of organized religion. The shop – a grocery and general-supplies store which sold such goods as lamp oil, tea, coffee, seeds, flour and sugar – was kept by the children during their father's absence. The father also required his children to go with him to church at least once a day. He set up a liturgical choir which practised in his shop, and demanded that his children – whether they had school work to do or not, or whether they had been in the shop all day – should join the rehearsals to provide the higher voice parts.

Chekhov described his home town as filthy and tedious, and the people as drunk, idle, lazy and illiterate. At first, Pavel tried to provide his children with an education by enrolling the two he considered the brightest, Nikolai and Anton, in one of the schools for the descendants of the Greek merchants who had once settled in Taganrog. These provided a more "classical" education than their Russian equivalents, and their standard of teaching was held in high regard. However, the experience was not a successful one, since most of the other pupils spoke Greek among themselves, of which the Chekhovs did not know a single word. Eventually, in 1868, Anton was enrolled in one of the town's Russian high schools. The courses at the Russian school included Church Slavonic, Latin and Greek, and if the entire curriculum was successfully completed, entry to a university was guaranteed. Unfortunately, as the shop was making less and less money, the school fees were often unpaid and lessons were missed. The teaching was generally mediocre, but the religious education teacher, Father Pokrovsky, encouraged his pupils to read the Russian classics and such foreign authors as Shakespeare, Swift and Goethe. Pavel also paid for private French and music lessons for his children.

Every summer the family would travel through the steppe by cart some fifty miles to an estate where their paternal grandfather was chief steward. The impressions gathered on these journeys, and the people encountered, made a profound impression on the young Anton, and later provided material for one of his greatest stories, *The Steppe*.

At the age of thirteen, Anton went to the theatre for the first time, to see Offenbach's operetta *La Belle Hélène* at the Taganrog theatre. He was enchanted by the spectacle, and went as often as time and money allowed, seeing not only the Russian classics, but also foreign pieces such as *Hamlet* in Russian translation. In his early teens, he even created his own theatrical company with his school friends to act out the Russian classics.

Adversity   In 1875 Anton was severely ill with peritonitis. The high-school doctor tended him with great care, and he resolved to join the medical profession one day. That same year, his brothers Alexander and Nikolai, fed up with the beatings they received at home, decided to move to Moscow to work and study, ignoring their father's admonitions and threats. Anton now bore the entire brunt of Pavel's brutality. To complicate things further, the family shop ran into severe financial difficulties, and was eventually declared bankrupt. The children were withdrawn from school, and Pavel fled to Moscow, leaving his wife and family to face the creditors. In the end, everybody abandoned the old residence, with the exception of Anton, who remained behind with the new owner.

Although he was now free of his father's bullying and the hardship of having to go to church and work in the shop, Anton had to find other employment in order to pay his rent and bills, and to resume his school studies. Accordingly, at the age of fifteen, he took up tutoring, continuing voraciously to read books of Russian and foreign literature, philosophy and science, in the town library.

In 1877, during a summer holiday, he undertook the seven-hundred-mile journey to Moscow to see his family, and found them all living in one room and sleeping on a single mattress on the floor. His father was not at all abashed by his failures: he continued to be dogmatically religious and to beat the younger children regularly. On his return to Taganrog, Anton attempted to earn a little additional income by sending sketches and anecdotes to several of Moscow's humorous magazines, but they were all turned down.

The young Chekhov unabatedly pursued his studies, and in June 1879 he passed the Taganrog High School exams with distinction, and in the autumn he moved to Moscow to study medicine. The family still lived in one room, and Alexander and Nikolai were well on the way to becoming alcoholics. Anton, instead of finding his own lodgings, decided to support not only himself, but his entire family, and try to re-educate them. After a hard day spent in lectures, tutorials and in the laboratories, he would write more sketches for humorous and satirical magazines, and an increasing number of these were now accepted: by the early 1880s, over a hundred had been printed. Anton used a series of pseudonyms (the most usual being "Antosha Chekhonte") for these productions, which he later called "rubbish". He also visited the Moscow theatres and concert halls on numerous occasions, and in 1880 sent the renowned Maly Theatre a play he had recently written. Only a rough draft of the piece – which was rejected by the Maly and published for the first time in 1920, under the title *Platonov* – has survived. Unless Chekhov had polished and pruned his lost final version considerably, the play would have lasted around seven hours. Despite its poor construction and verbosity, *Platonov* already shows some of the themes and characters present in Chekhov's mature works, such as rural boredom and weak-willed, supine intellectuals dreaming of a better future while not doing anything to bring it about.

Studies in Moscow and Early Publications

As well as humorous sketches and stories, Chekhov wrote brief résumés of legal court proceedings and gossip from the artistic world for various Moscow journals. With the money made from these pieces he moved his family into a larger flat, and regularly invited friends to visit and talk and drink till late at night.

In 1882, encouraged by his success with the Moscow papers, he started contributing to the journals of the capital St Petersburg, since payment there was better than in Moscow. He was eventually commissioned to contribute a regular column to the best-selling journal *Oskolki* ("Splinters"), providing a highly coloured picture of Moscow life with its court cases and bohemian atmosphere. He was now making over 150 roubles a month from his writing – about three times as much as his student stipend – although he managed to save very little because of the needs of his family. In 1884 Chekhov published, at his own expense, a booklet of six of his short stories, entitled *Tales of Melpomene*, which sold quite poorly.

Start of Medical Career and First Signs of Illness There was compensation for this relative literary failure: in June of that year Anton passed all his final exams in medicine and became a medical practitioner. That summer, he began to receive patients at a village outside Moscow, and even stepped in for the director of a local hospital when the latter went on his summer vacation. He was soon receiving thirty to forty patients a day, and was struck by the peasants' ill health, filth and drunkenness. He planned a major treatise entitled *A History of Medicine in Russia* but, after reading and annotating over a hundred works on the subject, he gave the subject up and returned to Moscow to set up his own medical practice.

First Signs of Tuberculosis Suddenly, in December 1884, when he was approaching the achievement of all his ambitions, Chekhov developed a dry cough and began to spit blood. He tried to pretend that these were not early symptoms of tuberculosis but, as a doctor, he must have had an inkling of the truth. He made no attempt to cut down his commitments in the light of his illness, but kept up the same punishing schedule of activity. By this time, Chekhov had published over three hundred items, including some of his first recognized mature works, such as 'The Daughter of Albion' and 'The Death of an Official'. Most of the stories were already, in a very understated way, depicting life's "losers" – such as the idle gentry, shopkeepers striving unsuccessfully to make a living and ignorant peasants. Now that his income had increased, Chekhov rented a summer house a few miles outside Moscow. However, although he intended to use his holiday exclusively for writing, he was inundated all day with locals who had heard he was a doctor and required medical attention.

Chekhov made a crucial step in his literary career, when in *Trip to St Petersburg and* December 1885 he visited the imperial capital St Petersburg *Meeting with Suvorin* for the first time, as a guest of the editor of the renowned *St Petersburg Journal*. His stories were beginning to gain him a reputation, and he was introduced at numerous soirées to famous members of the St Petersburg literary world. He was agreeably surprised to find they knew his work and valued it highly. Here for the first time he met Alexei Suvorin, the press mogul and editor of the most influential daily of the period, *Novoye Vremya* (*New Times*). Suvorin asked Chekhov to contribute stories regularly to his paper at a far higher rate of pay than he had been receiving from other journals. Now Chekhov, while busy treating numerous patients in Moscow and helping to stem the constant typhus epidemics that broke out in the city, also began to churn out for Suvorin such embryonic masterpieces as 'The Requiem' and 'Grief' – although all were still published pseudonymously. Distinguished writers advised him to start publishing under his own name and, although his current collection *Motley Stories* had already gone to press under the Chekhonte pseudonym, Anton resolved from now on to shed his anonymity. The collection received tepid reviews, but Chekhov now had sufficient income to rent a whole house on Sadova-Kudrinskaya Street (now maintained as a museum of this early period of Chekhov's life), in an elegant district of Moscow.

Chekhov's reputation as a writer was further enhanced *Literary Recognition* when Suvorin published a collection of sixteen of Chekhov's short stories in 1887 – under the title *In the Twilight* – to great critical acclaim. However, Chekhov's health was deteriorating and his blood-spitting was growing worse by the day. Anton appears more and more by now to have come to regard life as a parade of "the vanity of human wishes". He channelled some of this ennui and his previous life experiences into a slightly melodramatic and overlong play, *Ivanov*, in which the eponymous hero – a typical "superfluous man" who indulges in pointless speculation while his estate goes to ruin and his capital dwindles – ends up shooting himself. *Ivanov* was premiered in November 1887 by the respected Korsh Private Theatre under Chekhov's real name – a sign of Anton's growing confidence as a writer – although it received very mixed reviews.

However, in the spring of 1888, Chekhov's story 'The Steppe' – an impressionistic, poetical recounting of the experiences of a young boy travelling through the steppe on a cart – was published in *The Northern Messenger*, again under his real name, enabling him to reach another milestone in his literary career, and prompting reviewers for the first time to talk of his genius. Although Chekhov began to travel to the Crimea for vacations, in the hope that the warm climate might aid his health, the symptoms of tuberculosis simply reappeared whenever he returned to Moscow. In October of the same year, Chekhov was awarded the prestigious Pushkin Prize for Literature for *In the Twilight*. He was now recognized as a major Russian writer, and began to state his belief to reporters that a writer's job is not to peddle any political or philosophical point of view, but to depict human life with its associated problems as objectively as possible.

Death of his Brother A few months later, in January 1889, a revised version of *Ivanov* was staged at the Alexandrinsky Theatre in St Petersburg, arguably the most important drama theatre in Russia at the time. The new production was a huge success and received excellent reviews. However, around that time it also emerged that Anton's alcoholic brother, Nikolai, was suffering from advanced tuberculosis. When Nikolai died in June of that year, at the age of thirty, Anton must have seen this as a harbinger of his own early demise.

Chekhov was now working on a new play, *The Wood Demon*, in which, for the first time, psychological nuance replaced stage action, and the effect on the audience was achieved by atmosphere rather than by drama or the portrayal of events. However, precisely for these reasons, it was rejected by the Alexandrinsky Theatre in October of that year. Undeterred, Chekhov decided to revise it, and a new version of *The Wood Demon* was put on in Moscow in December 1889. Lambasted by the critics, it was swiftly withdrawn from the scene, to make its appearance again many years later, thoroughly rewritten, as *Uncle Vanya*.

Journey to It was around this time that Anton Chekhov began con-
Sakhalin Island templating his journey to the prison island of Sakhalin. At the end of 1889, unexpectedly, and for no apparent reason, the twenty-nine year-old author announced his intention to leave European Russia, and to travel across Siberia to Sakhalin, the large island separating Siberia and the Pacific Ocean, following which he would write a full-scale examination of the penal colony maintained there by the Tsarist authorities. Explanations put forward by commentators both then and since include a

search by the author for fresh material for his works, a desire to escape from the constant carping of his liberally minded colleagues on his lack of a political line; desire to escape from an unhappy love affair; and disappointment at the recent failure of *The Wood Demon*. A further explanation may well be that, as early as 1884, he had been spitting blood, and recently, just before his journey, several friends and relations had died of tuberculosis. Chekhov, as a doctor, must have been aware that he too was in the early stages of the disease, and that his lifespan would be considerably curtailed. Possibly he wished to distance himself for several months from everything he had known, and give himself time to think over his illness and mortality by immersing himself in a totally alien world. Chekhov hurled himself into a study of the geography, history, nature and ethnography of the island, as background material to his study of the penal settlement. The Trans-Siberian Railway had not yet been constructed, and the journey across Siberia, begun in April 1890, required two and a half months of travel in sledges and carriages on abominable roads in freezing temperatures and appalling weather. This certainly hastened the progress of his tuberculosis and almost certainly deprived him of a few extra years of life. He spent three months in frantic work on the island, conducting his census of the prison population, rummaging in archives, collecting material and organizing book collections for the children of exiles, before leaving in October 1890 and returning to Moscow, via Hong Kong, Ceylon and Odessa, in December of that year.

The completion of his report on his trip to Sakhalin was *Travels in Europe* to be hindered for almost five years by his phenomenally busy life, as he attempted, as before, to continue his medical practice and write at the same time. In early 1891 Chekhov, in the company of Suvorin, travelled for the first time to western Europe, visiting Vienna, Venice, Bologna, Florence, Rome, Naples and finally Monaco and Paris.

Trying to cut down on the expenses he was paying out for *Move to Melikhovo* his family in Moscow, he bought a small estate at Melikhovo, a few miles outside Moscow, and the entire family moved there. His father did some gardening, his mother cooked, while Anton planted hundreds of fruit trees, shrubs and flowers. Chekhov's concerns for nature have a surprisingly modern ecological ring: he once said that if he had not been a writer he would have become a gardener.

Although his brothers had their own lives in Moscow and only spent holidays at Melikhovo, Anton's sister Marya – who never married – lived there permanently, acting as his confidante and as his housekeeper when he had his friends and famous literary figures to stay, as he often did in large parties. Chekhov also continued to write, but was distracted, as before, by the scores of locals who came every day to receive medical treatment from him. There was no such thing as free medical assistance in those days and, if anybody seemed unable to pay, Chekhov often treated them for nothing. In 1892, there was a severe local outbreak of cholera, and Chekhov was placed in charge of relief operations. He supervised the building of emergency isolation wards in all the surrounding villages and travelled around the entire area directing the medical operations.

Ill Health　Chekhov's health was deteriorating more and more rapidly, and his relentless activity certainly did not help. He began to experience almost constant pain and, although still hosting gatherings, he gave the appearance of withdrawing increasingly into himself and growing easily tired. By the mid-1890s, his sleep was disturbed on most nights by bouts of violent coughing. Besides continuing his medical activities, looking after his estate and writing, Chekhov undertook to supervise – often with large subsidies from his own pocket – the building of schools in the local villages, where there had been none before.

Controversy around　By late 1895, Chekhov was thinking of writing for the theatre
The Seagull　again. The result was *The Seagull*, which was premiered at the Alexandrinsky Theatre in October 1896. Unfortunately the acting was so bad that the premiere was met by jeering and laughter, and received vicious reviews. Chekhov himself commented that the director did not understand the play, the actors didn't know their lines and nobody could grasp the understated style. He fled from the theatre and roamed the streets of St Petersburg until two in the morning, resolving never to write for the theatre again. Despite this initial fiasco, subsequent performances went from strength to strength, with the actors called out on stage after every performance.

Olga Knipper　By this time, it seems that Chekhov had accepted the fact that he had a mortal illness. In 1897, he returned to Italy to see whether the warmer climate would not afford his condition some respite, but as soon as he came back to Russia the coughing and blood-spitting resumed as violently as before. It was around this time that the two founders of the

Moscow Arts Theatre, Vladimir Nemirovich-Danchenko and Konstantin Stanislavsky, asked Chekhov whether they could stage *The Seagull*. Their aims were to replace the stylized and unnatural devices of the classical theatre with more natural events and dialogue, and Chekhov's play seemed ideal for this purpose. He gave his permission, and in September 1898 went to Moscow to attend the preliminary rehearsals. It was there that he first met the twenty-eight-year-old actress Olga Knipper, who was going to take the leading role of Arkadina. However, the Russian winter was making him cough blood violently, and so he decided to follow the local doctors' advice and travel south to the Crimea, in order to spend the winter in a warmer climate. Accordingly, he rented a villa with a large garden in Yalta.

When his father died in October of the same year, Chekhov *Move to the Crimea* decided to put Melikhovo up for sale and move his mother and Marya to the Crimea. They temporarily stayed in a large villa near the Tatar village of Kuchukoy, but Chekhov had in the meantime bought a plot of land at Autka, some twenty minutes by carriage from Yalta, and he drew up a project to have a house built there. Construction began in December.

Also in December 1898, the first performance of *The Seagull* at the Moscow Arts Theatre took place. It was a re-sounding success, and there were now all-night queues for tickets. Despite his extremely poor health, Chekhov was still busy raising money for relief of the severe famine then scourging the Russian heartlands, overseeing the building of his new house and aiding the local branch of the Red Cross. In addition to this, local people and aspiring writers would turn up in droves at his villa in Yalta to receive medical treatment or advice on their manuscripts.

In early January 1899, Chekhov signed an agreement with *Collected Works Project* the publisher Adolf Marx to supervise the publication of a multi-volume edition of his collected works in return for a flat fee of 75,000 roubles and no royalties. This proved to be an error of judgement from a financial point of view, because by the time Chekhov had put some money towards building his new house, ensured all the members of his family were provided for and made various other donations, the advance had almost disappeared.

Chekhov finally moved to Autka – where he was to spend *Romance* the last few years of his life – in June 1899, and immediately *with Olga* 199 began to plant vegetables, flowers and fruit trees. During a short period spent in Moscow to facilitate his work for Adolf Marx, he re-established contact with the Moscow Arts Theatre and Olga Knipper. Chekhov invited the actress to Yalta on several occasions and, although her visits were brief and at first she stayed in a hotel, it was obvious that she and Chekhov were becoming very close. Apart from occasional short visits to Moscow, which cost him a great expenditure of energy and were extremely harmful to his medical condition, Chekhov now had to spend all of his time in the south. He forced himself to continue writing short stories and plays, but felt increasingly lonely and isolated and, aware that he had only a short time left to live, became even more withdrawn. It was around this time that he worked again at his early play *The Wood Demon*, reducing the dramatis personae to only nine characters, radically altering the most significant scenes and renaming it *Uncle Vanya*. This was premiered in October 1899, and it was another gigantic success. In July of the following year, Olga Knipper took time off from her busy schedule of rehearsals and performances in Moscow to visit Chekhov in Yalta. There was no longer any attempt at pretence: she stayed in his house and, although he was by now extremely ill, they became romantically involved, exchanging love letters almost every day.

By now Chekhov had drafted another new play, *Three Sisters*, and he travelled to Moscow to supervise the first few rehearsals. Olga came to his hotel every day bringing food and flowers. However, Anton felt that the play needed revision, so he returned to Yalta to work on a comprehensive rewrite. *Three Sisters* opened on 31st January 1901 and – though at first well-received, especially by the critics – it gradually grew in the public's estimation, becoming another great success.

Wedding and Honeymoon But Chekhov was feeling lonely in Yalta without Olga, and in May of that year proposed to her by letter. Olga accepted, and Chekhov immediately set off for Moscow, despite his doctors' advice to the contrary. He arranged a dinner for his friends and relatives and, while they were waiting there, he and Olga got married secretly in a small church on the outskirts of Moscow. As the participants at the dinner received a telegram with the news, the couple had already left for their honeymoon. Olga and Anton sailed down the Volga, up the Kama River and along the Belaya River to the village of Aksyonovo, where they checked into a sanatorium. At this establishment Chekhov drank four large bottles of fermented mare's milk every day, put on weight, and his condition seemed to improve somewhat. However, on their return to Yalta, Chekhov's health deteriorated again. He made his will, leaving his house in Yalta to Marya, all income from his dramatic works to Olga and large sums to his mother and his surviving brothers, to the municipality of Taganrog and to the peasant body of Melikhovo.

After a while, Olga returned to her busy schedule of rehearsals and performances in Moscow, and the couple continued their relationship at a distance, as they had done before their marriage, with long and frequent love letters. Chekhov managed to visit her in Moscow occasionally, but by now he was so ill that he had to return to Yalta immediately, often remaining confined to bed for long periods. Olga was tortured as to whether she should give up her acting career and nurse Anton for the time left to him. Almost unable to write, Anton now embarked laboriously on his last dramatic masterpiece, *The Cherry Orchard*. Around that time, in the spring of 1902, Olga visited Anton in Yalta after suffering a spontaneous miscarriage during a Moscow Art Theatre tour, leaving her husband with the unpleasant suspicion that she might have been unfaithful to him. In the following months, Anton nursed his wife devotedly, travelling to Moscow whenever he could to be near her. Olga's flat was on the third floor, and there was no lift. It took Anton half an hour to get up the stairs, so he practically never went out. *Difficult Relationship*

When *The Cherry Orchard* was finally completed in October 1903, Chekhov once again travelled to Moscow to attend rehearsals, despite the advice of his doctors that it would be tantamount to suicide. The play was premiered on 17th January 1904, Chekhov's forty-fourth birthday, and at the end of the performance the author was dragged on stage. There was no chair for him, and he was forced to stand listening to the interminable speeches, trying not to cough and pretending to look interested. Although the performance was a success, press reviews, as usual, were mixed, and Chekhov thought that Nemirovich-Danchenko and Stanislavsky had misunderstood the play. *Final Play*

Chekhov returned to Yalta knowing he would not live long enough to write another work. His health deteriorated even *Death*

201

further, and the doctors put him on morphine, advising him to go to a sanatorium in Germany. Accordingly, in June 1904, he and Olga set off for Badenweiler, a spa in the Black Forest. The German specialists examined him and reported that they could do nothing. Soon oxygen had to be administered to him, and he became feverish and delirious. At 12.30 a.m. on 15th July 1904, he regained his mental clarity sufficiently to tell Olga to summon a doctor urgently. On the doctor's arrival, Chekhov told him, "*Ich sterbe*" ("I'm dying"). The doctor gave him a strong stimulant, and was on the point of sending for other medicines when Chekhov, knowing it was all pointless, simply asked for a bottle of champagne to be sent to the room. He poured everybody a glass, drank his off, commenting that he hadn't had champagne for ages, lay down, and died in the early hours of the morning.

Funeral   The coffin was transported back to Moscow in a filthy green carriage marked "FOR OYSTERS", and although it was met at the station by bands and a large ceremonial gathering, it turned out that this was for an eminent Russian General who had just been killed in action in Manchuria. Only a handful of people had assembled to greet Chekhov's coffin. However, as word got round Moscow that his body was being transported to the graveyard at the Novodevichy Monastery, people poured out of their homes and workplaces, forming a vast crowd both inside and outside the cemetery and causing a large amount of damage to buildings, pathways and other graves in the process. The entire tragicomic episode of Chekhov's death, transportation back to Moscow and burial could almost have featured in one of his own short stories. Chekhov was buried next to his father Pavel. His mother outlived him by fifteen years, and his sister Marya died in 1957 at the age of ninety-four. Olga Knipper survived two more years, dying in 1959 at the age of eighty-nine.

Anton Chekhov's Works

Early Writings   When Chekhov studied medicine in Moscow from 1879 to 1884, he financed his studies by writing reports of law-court proceedings for the newspapers and contributing, under a whole series of pseudonyms, hundreds of jokes, comic sketches and short stories to the numerous Russian humorous magazines and more serious journals of the time. From 1885, when he began to practise as a doctor, he concentrated far more on serious literary works, and between then and the end of his life he produced over 200 short stories, plus a score or so of dramatic pieces, ranging from monologues through one-act to full-length plays. In 1884 he also wrote his only novel, *The Hunting Party*, which was a rather wooden attempt at a detective novel.

A number of his stories between the mid-Eighties and his journey to Sakhalin were vitiated by his attempt to propagate the Tolstoyan moral principles he had espoused at the time. *Invention of a New, "Objective" Style of Writing* But even before his journey to the prison island he was realizing that laying down the law to his readers, and trying to dictate how they should read his stories, was not his job: it should be the goal of an artist to describe persons and events non-judgementally, and let the reader draw his or her own conclusions. This is attested by his letter to Suvorin in April 1890: "You reproach me for 'objectivity', calling it indifference to good and evil, and absence of ideals and ideas and so forth. You wish me, when depicting horse thieves, to state: stealing horses is bad. But surely people have known that for ages already, without me telling them so? Let them be judged by jurymen – my business is to show them as they really are. When I write, I rely totally on the reader, supposing that he himself will supply the subjective factors absent in the story." After Chekhov's return from Sakhalin, this objectivity dominated everything he wrote.

A further feature of Chekhov's storytelling, which developed throughout his career, is that he does not so much describe events taking place, but rather depicts the way that characters react to those – frequently quite insignificant – events, and the way people's lives are often transformed for better or worse by them. His dramatic works from that time also showed a development from fully displayed events and action – sometimes, in the early plays, quite melodramatic – to, in the major plays written in the last decade or so of his life, depicting the effects on people's lives of off-stage events, and the way the characters react to those events.

His style in all his later writing – especially from 1890 onwards – is lucid and economical, and there is a total absence of purple passages. The works of his final years display an increasing awareness of the need for conservation of the natural world in the face of the creeping industrialization of Russia. The breakdown of the old social order in the face of the new rising entrepreneurial class is also depicted non-judgementally; in Chekhov's last play, *The Cherry Orchard*, an old estate belonging to a long-established family of gentry is sold to a businessman, and the final scenes of the play give way to the offstage sounds of wood-chopping, as the old cherry orchard – one of the major beauties of the estate – is cut down by its new owner to be sold for timber.

Major Short Stories   It is generally accepted that Chekhov's mature story-writing may be said to date from the mid-1880s, when he began to contribute to the "thick journals". Descriptions of a small representative selection of some of the major short stories – giving an idea of Chekhov's predominant themes – can be found below.

On the Road   In 'On the Road' (1886), set in a seedy wayside inn on Christmas Eve, a man, apparently from the privileged classes, and his eight-year-old daughter are attempting to sleep in the "travellers' lounge", having been forced to take refuge from a violent storm. The little girl wakes up, and tells him how unhappy she is and that he is a wicked man. A noblewoman, also sheltering from the storm, enters and comforts the girl. The man and the woman both tell each other of the unhappiness of their lives: he is a widowed nobleman who has squandered all his money and is now on his way to a tedious job in the middle of nowhere; she is from a wealthy family, but her father and her brothers are wastrels, and she is the only one who takes care of the estate. They both part in the morning, on Christmas Day, profoundly unhappy, and without succeeding in establishing that deep inner contact with another human being which both of them obviously crave.

Enemies   Chekhov's 1887 tale 'Enemies' touches on similar themes of misery and incomprehension: a country doctor's six-year-old son has just died of diphtheria, leaving him and his wife devastated; at precisely this moment, a local landowner comes to his house to call him out to attend to his wife, who is apparently dangerously ill. Though sympathetic to the doctor's state, he is understandably full of anxiety for his wife, and insists that the doctor come. After an uncomfortable carriage journey, they arrive at the landowner's mansion to discover that the wife was never ill at all, but was simply getting rid of her husband so that she could run off with her lover. The landowner is now in a state of anger and despair, and the doctor unreasonably blames him for having dragged him out under false pretences. When the man offers him his fee, the doctor throws it in his face and storms out. The landowner also furiously drives off somewhere to assuage his anger. Neither man can even begin to penetrate the other's mental state because of their own problems. The doctor remains full of contempt and cynicism for the human race for the rest of his life.

In 1888, Chekhov's first indubitably great narrative, the *The Steppe* novella-length 'The Steppe', was published to rapturous reviews. There is almost no plot: in blazing midsummer, a nine-year-old boy sets out on a long wagon ride, lasting several days, from his home in a small provincial town through the steppe, to stay with relatives and attend high school in a large city. The entire story consists of his impressions of the journey – of his travelling companions, the people they meet en route, the inns at which they stay, the scenery and wildlife. He finally reaches his destination, bids farewell to his travelling companions, and the story ends with him full of tears of regret at his lost home life, and foreboding at what the future in this strange new world holds for him.

Another major short story by Chekhov, 'The Name-Day *The Name-Day Party* Party' (also translated as 'The Party'), was published in the same year as 'The Steppe'. The title refers to the fact that Russians celebrate not only their birthdays, but the day of the saint after whom they are named. It is the name day of a selfish lawyer and magistrate; his young wife, who is seven-months pregnant, has spent all day organizing a banquet in his honour and entertaining guests. Utterly exhausted, she occasionally asks him to help her, but he does very little. Finally, when all the guests have gone home, she, in extreme agony, gives birth prematurely to a still-born baby. She slips in and out of consciousness, believes she too is dying, and, despite his behaviour, she feels sorry for her husband, who will be lost without her. However, when she regains consciousness he seems to blame her for the loss of the child, and not his own selfishness leading to her utter exhaustion at such a time.

'A Dreary Story' (also known as 'A Tedious Story') is one *A Dreary Story* of Chekhov's longer stories, originally published in 1889. In a tour de force, the twenty-nine-year-old Chekhov penetrates into the mind of a famous sixty-two-year-old professor – his interior monologue constituting the entire tale. The professor is a world expert in his subject, fêted throughout Russia, yet has a terminal disease which means he will be dead in a few months. He has told nobody, not even his family. This professor muses over his life, and how his body is falling apart, and he wonders what the point of it all was. He would gladly give all his fame for just a few more years of warm, vibrant life. Chekhov wrote this story the year before he travelled to Sakhalin, when he was beginning to display the first symptoms of the tuberculosis which was to kill him at the age of forty-four.

The Duel   In Chekhov's 1891 story 'The Duel', a bored young Civil Servant has lost interest in everything in life, including his lover. When the latter's husband dies, she expects him to marry her, but he decides to borrow money and leave the town permanently instead. However, the acquaintance from whom he tries to borrow the money refuses to advance him the sum for such purposes. After a heated exchange, the Civil Servant challenges the acquaintance to a duel – a challenge which is taken up by a friend of the person who has refused to lend the money, disgusted at the Civil Servant's selfish behaviour. Both miss their shot, and the Civil Servant, realizing how near he has been to death, regains interest in life, marries his mistress, and all are reconciled.

Ward No. 6   In 'Ward No. 6' (1892), a well-meaning but apathetic and weak rural hospital director has a ward for the mentally disturbed as one of his responsibilities. He knows that the thuggish peasant warden regularly beats the lunatics up, but makes all kinds of excuses not to get involved. He ends up being incarcerated in his own mental ward by the ruse of an ambitious rival, and is promptly beaten by the same warden who used to call him "Your Honour", and dies soon afterwards. This is perhaps Chekhov's most transparent attack on the supine intelligentsia of his own time, whom he saw as lacking determination in the fight against social evils.

Three Years   In 1895, Chekhov published his famous story 'Three Years', in which Laptev, a young Muscovite, is nursing his seriously ill sister in a small provincial town, and feels restricted and bored. He falls in love with the daughter of her doctor and, perhaps from loneliness and the need for companionship, proposes marriage. Although she is not in love with him, she accepts, after a good deal of hesitation, because she is afraid this might be her only offer in this dull town. For the first three years this marriage – forged through a sense of isolation on one side and fear of spinsterhood on the other – is passionless and somewhat unhappy. However, after this period, they manage to achieve an equable and fulfilling relationship based on companionship.

In the 'The House with a Mansard' (1896), a talented but *The House with a* lazy young artist visits a rich landowning friend in the country. *Mansard* They go to visit the wealthy family at the title's "house with a mansard", which consists of a mother and two unmarried daughters. The artist falls in love with the younger daughter, but her tyrannical older sister sends both her and her mother abroad. The story ends some years later with the artist still wistfully wondering what has become of the younger sister.

In 'Peasants' (1897), Nikolai, who has lived and worked *Peasants* in Moscow since adolescence, and now works as a highly respected waiter at a prestigious Moscow hotel, is taken very ill and can no longer work, so he decides to return to the country village of his childhood, taking with him his wife and young daughter, who were both born in Moscow. He has warm recollections of the village, but finds that memory has deceived him. The place is filthy and squalid, and the local inhabitants all seem to be permanently blind drunk. Since anybody with any intelligence – like Nikolai himself – is sent to the city as young as possible to work and send money back to the family, the level of ignorance and stupidity is appalling. Nikolai dies, and the story ends with his wife and daughter having to become tramps and beg for a living.

In 1898, Chekhov published 'The Man in a Case', in which *The Man in a Case* the narrator, a schoolmaster, recounts the life of a recently deceased colleague of his, Byelikov, who taught classical Greek. A figure of ridicule for his pupils and colleagues, Byelikov is described as being terrified of the modern world, walking around, even in the warmest weather, in high boots, a heavy overcoat, dark spectacles and a hat with a large brim concealing his face. The blinds are always drawn on all the windows in his house, and these are permanently shut. He threatens to report to the headmaster a young colleague who engages in the appallingly immoral and progressive activity of going for bicycle rides in the countryside. The young man pushes him, Byelikov falls down and, although not hurt, takes to his bed and dies, apparently of humiliation and oversensitivity.

The Lady with the Lapdog 'The Lady with the Lapdog' (1899) tells the story of a bored and cynical forty-year-old senior bank official who, trapped in a tedious marriage in Moscow, takes a holiday by himself in Yalta. There he meets the thirty-year-old Anna, who is also unhappily married. They have an affair, then go back to their respective homes. In love for possibly the first time in his life, he travels to the provincial town where she lives, and tracks her down. They meet in a theatre, and before her husband returns to his seat, she promises to visit him in Moscow. The story ends with them both realizing that their problems are only just beginning.

Sakhalin Island As well as being a prolific writer of short fiction, Chekhov also wrote countless articles as a journalist, and the volume-length *Sakhalin Island* ranks as one of the most notable examples of his investigative non-fiction. As mentioned above, Chekhov's decision to travel to Sakhalin Island in easternmost Siberia for three months in 1890 was motivated by several factors, one of them being to write a comprehensive study of the penal colonies on the island.

Chekhov toured round the entire island, visiting all the prisons and most of the settlements, and generally spending up to nineteen hours a day gathering material and writing up his findings. Chekhov returned from Sakhalin at the end of 1890, but it took him three years to write up and start publishing the material he had collected. The first chapter was published in the journal *Russian Thought* (*Russkaya Mysl*) in late 1893, and subsequent material appeared regularly in this magazine until July 1894, with no objection from the censor, until finally the chapters from number twenty onwards were banned from publication. Chekhov took the decision to "publish and be damned" – accordingly the whole thing appeared in book form, including the banned chapters, in May 1895.

The book caused enormous interest and discussion in the press, and over the next decade a number of substantial ameliorations were brought about in the criminals' lives.

Major Plays Chekhov first made his name in the theatre with a series of one-act farces, most notably *The Bear* and *Swan Song* (both 1888). However, his first attempts at full-length plays, *Platonov* (1880), *Ivanov* (1887) and *The Wood Demon* (1889) were not entirely successful. The four plays which are now considered to be Chekhov's masterpieces, and outstanding works of world theatre, are *The Seagull* (1896), *Uncle Vanya* (1899), *Three Sisters* (1901) and *The Cherry Orchard* (1904).

The central character in *The Seagull* is an unsuccessful
playwright, Trevlev, who is in love with the actress Nina. However,
she falls in love with the far more successful writer Trigorin. Out
of spite and as an anti-idealist gesture, Trevlev shoots a seagull
and places it in front of her. Nina becomes Trigorin's mistress,
and subsequently marries him. Unfortunately their baby dies,
Nina's career collapses, and Trigorin leaves her. However, on
Trevlev renewing his overtures to Nina, she tells him that she
still loves Trigorin. The play ends with news being brought in
that Trevlev has committed suicide offstage.

The second of Chekhov's four dramatic masterpieces,
Uncle Vanya, a comprehensive reworking of the previously unsuccessful *Wood Demon*, centres on Vanya, who has for many
years tirelessly managed the estate of a professor in Moscow.
However, the professor finally retires back to his estate with
his bored and idle young wife, with whom Vanya falls in love.
Vanya now realizes that the professor is a thoroughly selfish
and mediocre man and becomes jealous and embittered at his
own fate, believing he has sacrificed his own brilliant future.
When the professor tells him that he is going to sell the estate,
Vanya, incensed, fires a pistol at him at point-blank range and
misses – which only serves to compound his sense of failure
and frustration. The professor and his wife agree not to sell up
for the time being and leave to live elsewhere. Vanya sinks back
into his boring loveless life, probably for ever.

In *Three Sisters*, Olga, Masha and Irina live a boring
provincial life in their brother's rural country house, remote
from Moscow and Petersburg. All three remember their happy
childhood in Moscow and dream of one day returning. A
military unit arrives nearby, and Irina and Masha start up
relationships with officers, which might offer a way out of
their tedious lives. However, Irina's fiancé is killed in a duel,
Masha's relationship ends when the regiment moves on, and
Olga, a schoolteacher, is promoted to the post of headmistress
at her school, thus forcing her to give up any hope of leaving
the area. They all relapse into what they perceive to be their
meaningless lives.

The Cherry Orchard, Chekhov's final masterpiece for the
theatre, is a lament for the passing of old traditional Russia
and the encroachment of the modern world. The Ranevsky
family estate, with its wonderful and famous cherry orchard,
is no longer a viable concern. Various suggestions are made to

stave off financial disaster, all of which involve cutting down the ancient orchard. Finally the estate is auctioned off, and in the final scene, the orchard is chopped down offstage. The old landowning family move out, and in a final tragicomic scene, they forget to take an ancient manservant with them, accidentally locking him in the house and leaving him feeling abandoned.

Select Bibliography

Standard Edition:
The most authoritative Russian edition of the stories in this volume can be found in Chekhov's *Полное собрание сочинении и писем* (*Polnoye sobraniye sochinenii i pisem*; *Complete Works and Letters*) produced in Moscow in 1978 by the Nauka publishing company.

Biographies:
Hingley, Ronald, *A New Life of Anton Chekhov* (Oxford: Oxford University Press, 1976)

Pritchett, V.S., *Chekhov: A Spirit Set Free* (London: Hodder & Stoughton, 1988)

Rayfield, Donald, *Anton Chekhov* (London: HarperCollins, 1997)

Simmons, Ernest, *Chekhov: A Biography* (London: Jonathan Cape, 1963)

Troyat, Henri, *Chekhov*, tr. Michael Henry Heim (New York: Dutton, 1986)

Additional Recommended Background Material:
Helman, Lillian, ed., *Selected Letters of Anton Chekhov* (1984)

Magarshack, David, *Chekhov the Dramatist*, 2nd ed. (London: Eyre Methuen,1980)

Malcolm, Janet, *Reading Chekhov: A Critical Journey* (London: Granta, 2001)

Pennington, Michael, *Are You There, Crocodile?: Inventing Anton Chekhov* (London: Oberon, 2003)